Tales of the Protectors

TALES of the PROTECTORS
ALMOST HEAVEN

a novel

LISA PENCE

NEW YORK

LONDON • NASHVILLE • MELBOURNE • VANCOUVER

Tales of the Protectors

Almost Heaven

A Novel

Published in New York, New York, by Morgan James Publishing. Morgan James is a trademark of Morgan James, LLC. www.MorganJamesPublishing.com

ISBN 9781642797848 paperback
ISBN 9781642797855 eBook
Library of Congress Control Number: 2019913235

Cover Design by:
Rachel Lopez
www.r2cdesign.com

Interior Design by:
Christopher Kirk
www.GFSstudio.com

Ilustrations by:
Rachel Stengele

Morgan James is a proud partner of Habitat for Humanity Peninsula and Greater Williamsburg. Partners in building since 2006.

Get involved today! Visit
MorganJamesPublishing.com/giving-back

To Randy,
Always laughing because of you.

Contents

A Note from the Author

The Tales of the Protectors seeks
only those who possess
the ability to believe.
If you were not one of those few,
this book would not have found its way
to your hands.

1

The Turnstile

Maxwell O'Malley, twelve years old and the youngest son of Reginald and Margaret O'Malley, has blond hair, brown eyes, and is somewhat thin but not scrawny. He is quite ordinary looking except for a freckle in the middle of his right earlobe, which can give the unwanted appearance of an earring. This small blip of a freckle has been the cause of more than one unprovoked fight in his short-lived life, but it also ensured Maxwell could stand up for himself at a younger age than most. Maxwell's grandfather has told him to wear it proudly, due to the fact that he has one in the exact same spot.

Maxwell lives with his family on Mackinac Island, Michigan, a unique island because no automobiles are allowed except for a fire truck, a police car, and an ambulance. The weather is cool on most breezy summer days and bitterly cold in winter, but with a quaint, Christmassy charm. Depending on the season, people in the community can be seen riding their bikes or snowmobiles while on their daily errands downtown. Mornings are busy times with horses pulling drays full of shipments, making deliveries of needed supplies for the shelves of the mercantile and food for the numerous restaurants.

Maxwell has lived on Mackinac Island his entire life; even his mother grew up on the island. His grandfather owns a livery stable here, and in the summer, he rents out the horses for trail rides and to pull buggies for the tourists. It was August, so his grandfather's stables were extremely busy with vacationers ferrying over from the mainland to buy fudge and explore the island. Maxwell spent most tourist seasons helping his grandfather with the horses and setting up trail rides for the visitors. He was hoping this summer to save enough money for some sorely needed new ice skates and a replacement hockey stick for the one he had accidently broken last winter.

Maxwell's stable responsibilities included cleaning the stalls, adding shavings, sweeping, and making sure the horses had clean water and plenty of food. His favorite time with the horses was in the evening after they had eaten and had time to relax. He would brush them and spend time talking with each one. A special horse named Ole Henry had been with the stable since before Maxwell was born. Henry was especially gentle with all the customers and would bellow a *neighhhh* every time he saw Maxwell. This could be because, each evening, Maxwell would slip him an apple before bedtime. Henry and Maxwell had a special connection, which is hard to understand unless you have an extraordinary animal yourself. Those of you with this type of relationship know exactly what I mean.

Maxwell loved living on Mackinac. He loved the cool summers when he could ride his bike between sugar maples and the sweet-smelling lilacs, and the long winters when he could skate and play endless hockey with the guys. His grandparents had always told him Mackinac was a magical place, and Maxwell knew, deep down, it was true.

Before we continue, I must share a very unhappy, nonmagical, and devastating event from Maxwell's past. It happened several years ago when Maxwell was eight, his younger sister, Sophia, was six, and his older brother, Benjamin, was thirteen. Every winter, after at least a week of sub-zero temperatures, an ice bridge will form across Lake Huron. After the Christmas holiday, local residents place their Christmas trees on the ice to mark the ice bridge route across the lake. The trees are spaced at intervals to allow individuals to see the safe path along which to travel, whether by snowmobile or on foot. It is four miles from the island to the mainland, which is quite a distance, especially when you're traveling on ice. This specific winter had been especially long and frigid.

Benjamin decided to go to town across the lake on one of his father's snowmobiles to meet friends at a local arcade, which he had done many times before.

"Be home an hour before dark," said his mother as he sped out the door. Benjamin made it across the ice bridge in thirty minutes, which was a new record for him, due to the weather being especially nice that day with little wind. While he was playing games, he glanced several times at the neon clock hanging on the wall. The time had not changed since he checked twenty minutes ago. He worried it might be later than he thought.

After getting the correct time from the owner of the arcade, Benjamin scrambled to collect his things. It would be dark in half an hour. He saw the dim glow of dusk as he ran out of the arcade. He had a brief thought of maybe calling his parents first, but by this time, he was already on his snowmobile. He knew staying all night with his friends on the mainland was another possibility. He weighed his options quickly as his eyes scanned the ice. He knew he had made the journey here in the required amount of time to arrive back before dark. It had been a clear day. On the return trip, he might even have some luck with the wind at his back. He made the fateful decision to head home.

Benjamin made excellent time crossing the ice. He was nearing the halfway point across the lake, and he could see the island ahead but just barely. All of a sudden, a thick fog appeared, bearing in on him from his right. He pulled back on the accelerator for more speed.

Within minutes, circumstances went very wrong. The fog engulfed him. His progress began to slow as the markers on the ice got more and more difficult to locate. Panic set in after it had been several minutes since he had seen a tree marker and could locate nothing in the mix of fog and blackness before him. Benjamin stopped the snowmobile. He wanted to try to get his bearing and check his position against any figures in the horizon. Only the sound of the engine purring softly while idling could be heard. Suddenly, a crack as loud as thunder echoed in his ears, and he felt the ice beneath him move. His heart beat rapidly as he felt the sharp, stinging pain of freezing water.

"Where is Benjamin?" Maxwell's worried mother kept asking as she looked out the front window for the third time this evening. Maxwell's father and Alexander Justice, his grandfather on his mother's side, had already gone to the lake to search for the missing teen. They had been gone for more than two hours. Margaret wanted to be at the lake with them, but she was afraid Benjamin, or someone else who may be involved, would try to call. She wanted to be home to answer the phone. She would have to stay at the house and wait.

Maxwell watched his mother pace back and forth. He wished his dad and grandpa had let him go along. He knew his older brother would be searching for him if the tables were turned.

Another tortuous two hours passed before the doorknob turned and in walked Maxwell's father with Jess, the local police chief. Margaret knew from the grim look on their faces, it was bad. She could tell her husband had been crying. Reginald looked at his wife and shook his head. "He didn't make it, Maggie."

She began sobbing and fell into her husband's arms. Jess gently told her how Benjamin must have lost his way in the fog and found himself off the safe path of the ice bridge. During the search, they had found Benjamin's body caught between several floating pieces of ice. They had arrived too late. Alexander stayed with his grandson's body at the dock. Maxwell stood up while Jess was still talking. He went to his room and shut the door. He didn't want to hear any more. He was only eight years old, but he knew enough. He knew he would never see his brother again.

It had been nearly four years ago, and Maxwell still remembered that tragic day like it was yesterday. It was a devastating memory that would not fade. Out of nowhere, he would flash back to those events, and his heart would cringe. Even now, once a week, Maxwell would ride his bike up Fort Hill to visit his brother's gravesite.

Today was perfect for his weekly cemetery trip because it was a cool summer afternoon. When the lilacs were in bloom, he always picked a handful to put on his brother's gravestone. The location of the cemetery, in the middle of the island, and surrounded by trees, kept Maxwell busy each trip clearing debris off his brother's grave. This was a job he wanted to do. It was his way of staying connected to him. If no one was around, Maxwell would talk to Benjamin while he worked. It made him feel as though he was still with him. This was their time together each week.

A narrow, paved road ran parallel to the cemetery. Along the sides, a canopy of leaf-filled tree limbs cast shade over him and his bicycle. The cemetery was surrounded by a white, wooden picket fence with a matching white turnstile centered in the front where a gate would normally be found.

Maxwell sat on his bike as he studied his surroundings. The oddity of walking through a turnstile to enter a cemetery suddenly struck him. This cemetery dated back to the 1800s, and the turnstile had been here as long as he could remember. Who came up with this idea, and what was the purpose of the turnstile? Did the fence builder want people coming and going in an orderly fashion? *Single file visitors only!* thought Maxwell as he chuckled to himself. Whatever the reason, it seemed out of place.

Maxwell swung his leg over and slid off his bike. He leaned the bike next to a bench close to the entrance. Today was not his normal day of the week to visit his brother's grave, but the perfect weather, along with the feeling that he needed to be here, was a compelling combination.

Suddenly, he noticed a slight chill in the air; the sky had turned gray and cloudy. A faint breeze rustled the leaves in the trees around him. He was unusually aware of nature's movement, and this sensitivity made him cautious.

Pausing in front of the turnstile, he felt a bit ridiculous. *I'm glad no one is here to see me*, he thought as he glanced over his shoulder. Maxwell hesitated a moment more, then made himself move ahead through the turnstile. It creaked from his forward motion. The next moment, all images before him swirled and slowly faded from his view. He struggled to catch himself before he fell as his world went black.

2

Into the Light

Maxwell opened his eyes, but he could see nothing. It was so dark, he kept opening and closing his eyes to be sure they were open. Maxwell knew he was not alone, but what was occupying the area with him, he was unsure. He felt the flutter of wings lightly brushing against him, but not the sort to be claustrophobic or scary. It was understood the feathers were there to protect him, not to do harm. There were moments when he recognized the smell of a forest, but he could feel no trees, only the sensation of lightly packed cotton, which continually moved around him.

Maxwell quickly reviewed his situation: *I was walking into the cemetery; the wind blew; I arrived here in darkness. Am I dead? Did a tree branch break and knock me in the head? If it did, where am I now? This doesn't feel like death—not that I know what death feels like.*

One thing he knew for sure, the feathers were definitely moving in a specific direction. When Maxwell attempted to alter course, the softness would gently move him back toward the original route. The journey continued for several more minutes; then he suddenly stopped moving, having apparently arrived at his intended destination.

The soft silkiness that had surrounded them moved away. The lights in the room slowly lit as the softness disappeared. Maxwell could now see three other children. The four of them were standing in the middle of the room facing each other, about two feet apart. No one spoke as they were all still adjusting to the light.

A movement behind the children caused them to turn around to see more clearly the softness that had enveloped them. What they saw is difficult to imagine, especially to those who struggle to believe, so remember this if you retell the story to others at a later time. They may dismiss it entirely.

Maxwell and the other three children were surrounded by several large, handsomely beautiful, strong, and agile winged beings. *Could they be angels?* All the beings were faced outward, with their backs to the children, which had allowed their wings to envelop them. As the beings expanded their circle around the children, they turned to face them. Their mannerisms were that of soldiers. The children immediately turned back around and looked at each other. They were still standing in the middle of a room. All was quiet. *What are we waiting on?* wondered the children. *What will happen next?*

Slowly, out of the darkness, from behind the winged creatures, another winged man-like being appeared. His presence overwhelmed the children to the degree their nerves caused them to shake. He wasn't frightening in a fearful way, but it was like nothing they had ever encountered or imagined. Their young minds had trouble processing what they were seeing. Upon his arrival, the winged beings surrounding the children left the room in a single file. The astonishing newcomer walked to the middle of the room where the children were standing. They immediately backed up so as not to be too close.

"Welcome, young ones!" proclaimed the being. "My name is Raphael, and I am your host, your protector and commanding officer while you are here." Hearing his soft-spoken voice, the children immediately relaxed, but they did wonder at his words: *commanding officer?*

"Please introduce yourselves to the others. Tell your Earth age and where you are from, beginning with you." Raphael pointed to Maxwell.

After a brief, contained panic, Maxwell blurted out, "My name is Maxwell O'Malley. I'm twelve years old and from Mackinac Island, Michigan." Short and sweet. The other children flashed him a puzzled look but said nothing. Maxwell could tell they didn't know there was an island in Michigan but he did not clarify. He looked over to the girl on his right and raised his eyebrows, giving her a silent prompt that it was her turn to go next and remove the unwanted attention from him. The young lady took her cue and spoke up.

"My name is Gem Lovell," she immediately interjected. "It is spelled G-E-M not J-I-M." The other three children nodded with approval. "I am eleven years old and from Charleston, West Virginia." She, in turn, did as Maxwell had done and looked to the young man on her right.

"My name is Jack Lewis. I am thirteen Earth years old," he added "Earth" to his age to be his amusing self. He glanced over to Raphael to see if he noticed. Raphael appeared not to be paying attention and did not look up or change his expression, but Maxwell quietly chuckled. The girls just smiled. Jack thought he should continue but stick to the facts for now. "I am from Jackson Hole, Wyoming." He, following the pattern of the others, glanced to his right to the last remaining child.

"I am Eden Shepherd. I am twelve years old and from New York City." She did not say her state because she knew everyone knew New York City was in New York. She immediately looked away from the other children over to Raphael, and the other children did as well.

Raphael looked up from a small parchment, which had held his concentration during introductions. He spoke with authority, "Based on qualities you possess, the four of you have been chosen to be trained as Protectors. The locality in which you find yourself is not heaven, and you are not dead. This is Everwell, your headquarters and training facility.

Raphael continued, "Protectors are a group of humans selected to assist angels in the care of those on your planet during perilous times. Most Protectors are chosen at a young age due to their still-remaining connection with the spiritual realm from before their birth. Some are chosen as young as ten Earth years, and may remain a Protector through-out adulthood as long as they are needed. You may cease being a Protector at any time you choose. Once you end your service, you do not start again. Another will be chosen to replace you. There have been exceptions to this rule in the past, but they are rare.

"Your job will be to monitor adults or children who require constant coverage. While you are here, you will undergo extensive preparation for future assignments. The training will be difficult and exhausting. If you do not master each aspect of your training, you will be released. Your assignments last approximately three months each Earth year or until your assignment is complete, whichever is shorter.

"You will train here for approximately one month before your first assignment. That may seem a brief amount of time, but your abilities here are different than those on Earth. You eat the best food, breathe the freshest air, drink the purest water, and have the best trainers. We believe within you are the qualities to become a highly effective Protector, or you would not have been chosen. Each time you return here for your rotation, your skills will continue to improve. Eventually, when you return for your assignments in the future, you will need no new training, just briefings, which will also take place here at Everwell. If the assignment is long and extends past your three-month service, the next four Protectors on rotation will pick up where your group left off. This will continue until the assignment is finished."

"What about our families?" questioned Gem. "Won't we be missed?"

"When each of you passed into this dimension through our portals, your soul, spirit, and body were split, with half returning back into your world. This other half, which is really you as well, will be filling in while you are away. When you return and cross back into your dimension, you will reconnect with your other half and assume all their memories of events that happened while you were away. You will simply have memories of both dimensions. Even though these events occurred at the same time but in two different dimensions, your brain will simply read it as two locations. The time element will cause no confusion for your memory," explained Raphael. The children listened intently.

"If you choose to accept this assignment, your training will begin early tomorrow. If you decline, you will be swiftly returned to your earthly dimension with no memory of this place or this conversation. You will be returned to the moment before you entered our portal, but the door here will be closed. You all entered our portals through turnstiles this time, so you will simply pass through the turnstile normally. We have identified backup children from your country who will be offered the same opportunities if any of you do not accept.

"Under different circumstances, I would normally give you a few moments to make your decision, but from my past experience with young Protectors, I find they know immediately if they are in or not. I want to warn you; this is extremely dangerous. We will train you to the best of our abilities, but the enemy is strong. We have had several deaths in our ranks. I am asking all of you to rise above your fear but I will not judge if any of you turn down this assignment. Sometimes you just want to be a kid with no worries, and I completely understand. I need an answer from each of you," stated Raphael.

The four children stared at each other, wide-eyed and with no expression, wondering who would speak first.

"I'm in," said Gem, as she burst into a smile.

"Me, too," said Eden.

"Absolutely," chimed Jack. Raphael turned to look at Maxwell, who didn't seem as enthusiastic as the other three children.

"And you, Mr. O'Malley? Will you be joining us?" asked Raphael.

Maxwell, having made his decision but wanting a little fun, stared back at Raphael solemnly while the other three children watched, motionless. They were all fooled by his act. He paused and said, "Well, I think I will say . . .Yes!" They all cheered exuberantly.

"Excellent," replied Raphael, "you're all in." Another angel, who was just as large but, for some reason, less intimidating, walked up to Raphael.

Raphael explained, "This is my assistant, Josiah. He will take you to see Deborah, our training coordinator. She will go over your schedules, which structure the short time you are with us. Josiah will answer any questions you may have and will also show you to your resting quarters. I will check in on you daily, either through Josiah or with you personally to see how you are progressing. Be on your way. Much training is ahead, and your assistance in the field is greatly needed."

Josiah motioned for the children to follow him. Raphael remained in the empty room, still studying his parchment. The children followed Josiah out of the room and down a long corridor with large marble overhead arches. Eden noticed it was well lit but not bright. She could see no light fixture, but light was everywhere, with not so much as one dark corner.

"How is there light without a source?" asked Eden. "I don't see any light mounts or even sunlight coming in through a window."

"We have no darkness or night here," replied Josiah, very matter-of-factly.

"Then how do we sleep?" questioned Jack.

"You have a switch in your room to turn on the dark," answered Josiah. The children tossed puzzled looks at each other while they followed the assistant to two empty shafts. The shafts resembled an earthly elevator but with no door, no compartment to stand in, and no cables to lift and lower those who stepped inside. Beings were entering and exiting very casually while conversing.

"I'm not getting in that thing!" announced Gem. "I don't like fast drops." She assumed she would plummet like the stones she had dropped from the bridge over Elk River at home. At that very moment, another angel hurriedly stepped out of the left shaft and exchanged greetings with Josiah.

Josiah ignored Gem's comment and explained the system, "We call this form of internal transportation a GUST. It stands for Gravity Utilizing Speedy Transport. You step into the GUST with nothing above or below. A constant, strong wind blowing up on the GUST to the right lifts you to higher levels. A slower wind blowing up on the GUST to the left allows you to drop down to lower levels at an appropriate speed. The greatest advantage of the GUST is that you never wait more than a few seconds, if that. You need only remember to do a quick check before you step in. If no one is there, the GUST will immediately whisk you up or down. It will assist you by making room as you step in. If you step before looking, however, you may bump into someone on his or her way up or down, so do be careful. Each exit level is clearly marked inside. Shall we go?"

"I'll go first!" exclaimed Maxwell and Jack simultaneously. The girls stood silently, observing beings stepping in and out of the GUST. They both seemed content to let the guys go first.

"It seems the young gentlemen will lead us this time, and the young ladies will follow," instructed Josiah. "I will be behind the four of you to make sure there are no mishaps. Exit on Level Alpha." The boys ran toward the GUST and jumped at a speed much faster than Josiah had instructed. Their jump was so swift they actually dropped a few feet before rising. Both boys yelled with excitement as the force of the wind blew them upward.

"It works better if you *step* into the GUST," critiqued Josiah to the girls. He shook his head. Gem walked up to the GUST next. Knowing Josiah had complete faith they could all do this helped her confidence. She believed she could do it as well but still stopped for one more look before stepping in.

"We'll step in together," said Eden as she grabbed Gem's hand. Gem smiled and nodded she was ready. They both stepped and vanished in an instant.

They had expected their hair to blow straight up and to feel a strong pressure against them, as if on a roller coaster, but it was nothing like that. They felt the air blowing as they stepped in, but now that they were inside the GUST, it was as if they were floating up by their own power. They felt no outside force.

They looked up and saw the boys exiting the GUST. They looked below, and Josiah was only a few feet from them. They were approaching the Alpha level, so the girls squeezed their hands tightly together before jumping. They felt a small burst of air, and suddenly, outside the GUST they jogged to a stop. The boys were still laughing with excitement as the girls joined in.

"It was really easy. Josiah was right all along," said Gem enthusiastically as Josiah stepped off the GUST and smiled at the children's enjoyment.

"Off we go, Protectors. Deborah is waiting on us," said Josiah, leading the way.

"He called us Protectors," whispered Maxwell proudly to the others. They all smiled in agreement.

The children followed behind Josiah and turned to face another long corridor with vaulted ceilings that looked as though it came out of a book on Roman architecture. Before them on both sides were what appeared to be meeting rooms with large windows. Individuals walking in the hall could see what was happening in the rooms; however, you could not hear what was being said unless the door was open. Josiah slowed his walk as he came to one of the open doors. The woman inside gestured for Josiah to enter.

"Come, Protectors, she's ready for you," said Josiah to the children. Maxwell leaned over to brag about being called a Protector again, but everyone shushed him.

Deborah, the training coordinator, smiled as she welcomed the Protectors. "We feel very fortunate to have the four of you join our team," said Deborah. "It is my job to oversee new recruit training and ensure you have all the items you need to accomplish your assignments successfully. You will see me checking in on you from time to time. Feel free to let me know if you are having any problems adjusting. Josiah will check in with you periodically as well." The Protectors were listening to her every word.

"You will need to get settled into your resting quarters first," continued Deborah. Your accommodations are side by side on Level Sigma. "You will be fitted later for your weaponry before your assignment."

"Weaponry?" asked Eden. "Why do we need weaponry? I thought we were protecting kids and adults from accidents and mishaps."

"You will not only be protecting against accidents but also from purposeful harm," corrected Deborah. "I know you have many questions about your assignments and what is expected from you, which will be answered at the applicable time during your training. Now, you need to become familiar with your resting quarters, where you will spend much of your time when not training. Following this tour, you may take your nourishment on Level Alpha," instructed Deborah.

"Take nourishment? You mean eat?" cracked Jack, smiling.

"Yes, Jack. I mean eat," answered Deborah. "You will not need as much food during your stay with us, so we will only dine twice daily. Every meal is truly a heavenly delight as well as complete nourishment. The meals are so in tune with your biological needs, it is impossible to experience negative digestive issues as a result of eating. So, enjoy; it will be one of your fondest memories of us when you have returned to Earth. Toward the end of your training, you will find you need less food and less sleep the longer you are here."

"Here is a training schedule for each of you." Deborah handed each child a rolled-up piece of tan linen secured by a worn, satin ribbon.

Each child unrolled their linen to reveal the training schedules. Maxwell showed Jack his schedule. They were identical.

TRAINING SCHEDULE

0900 LEVEL GAMMA - RESCUE
1100 LEVEL BETA - MESSENGER
1300 LEVEL DELTA - PROTECTION
1500 LEVEL ZETA - FLIGHT

"Each training is for one Earth hour in duration, except for Flight, which can run longer," Deborah explained. "That is why it is the last session of the day. You may have a break between sessions. Use your extra time to practice what you have learned or familiarize yourself with your surroundings.

"We use the Greek alphabet to identify our floor levels. I understand this alphabet is rarely used in your world today. We have considered updating our level descriptions, but it has worked so well for centuries, no one wants to change. I'm sure you will have no difficulty adjusting to it. All your training instruction and manuals will be in your modern alphabet, so no need to panic."

Deborah smiled as she instructed the children, "We protect and care for the inhabitants of Earth, who operate on a twenty-four-hour day. For this reason, we likewise run our operations on a twenty-four-hour schedule. Our first meal each day is from six o'clock until eight. After breakfast, you will begin your training, which will end approximately one hour before your evening meal. You may spend the remainder of your day practicing what you have learned, visiting with friends, or exploring your new surroundings. New Protectors are allowed on every level, except Omega.

"Some of our Protectors prefer to rest after their strenuous training days. It will take time for your body to adjust to the diminished sleep and nourishment needs. Your bodies operate here at their full potential. We take complete advantage of this during your training. Does anyone have any training or schedule questions?" asked Deborah. All the children began raising their hands and speaking at once.

"One at a time, and we only have time for one question each. Maxwell, I saw your hand raise first," she instructed.

"What's on Level Omega?" he smiled as he asked his question.

"That is not a training or scheduling question, and you will find out when you are no longer a new Protector," said Deborah as she returned his smile. "Eden, you're next."

"How long will we be in training before our first assignment?" Eden asked. "Raphael said we would most likely spend a month here at training."

"Most of our new Protectors take four to six weeks for the first training session and fewer weeks on each subsequent visit," replied Deborah. "Eventually, no training will be required, and you will be given an assignment upon your arrival."

"Your mind is like a sponge while you are here," continued Deborah. "You will not be able to get enough information. The information you do get will be processed immediately, and you will have greater understanding, like never before. You will be more creative, a greater problem solver, and your physical abilities will be at an optimum level, all at supernatural speed. Next question, Jack?"

"What is Flight training about?" asked Jack. "Will we be flying a vehicle, or will each of us have a set of wings like the angels in our pictures back home?"

"You will have wings for flying, but it will not be flight as you know it on Earth," answered Deborah. "You will not use your wings while you are at training except during Flight training. Gem, you're next."

"Are there other children here?" asked Gem.

"Most definitely," said Deborah reassuringly. "You will see them before, during, and after training each day. We keep approximately four Protectors from each country on Earth here at one time. All of you are under eighteen Earth years of age. We call you Zone Minors. We also have a group of adult Protectors called Zone Majors who assist us on some assignments. We do not allow adults to be Protectors unless they have first served as a child. The adult mind is not as flexible and open to new ideas as a child's. We wouldn't want to bring an adult here and cause them to be harmed mentally from exposure to this place. Some adults would have no problem acclimating, but we can never be sure who will succeed. Thus, the ratio of children is much higher. We can't take the chance on adults. We have far fewer Zone Majors because most Protectors resign as they get older. They become too busy or can't assume the risk. The adult Protectors who do not resign work our toughest cases or assist us during training.

"You will enjoy the friendships you form here," added Deborah. "Most of the children are similar to the four of you. They all have qualities which set them apart. You will have much in common, and many of your friendships will last your lifetime and beyond."

"May I ask one more question?" said Maxwell. "Especially since you really didn't answer my earlier question?" He had a pleading look on his face.

"Last one for all of you," answered Deborah.

"I know you said we would find out in Protection training, but from whom exactly are we protecting humans? Is it from other humans who are evil and want to hurt people, or is there something else out there we may need to deal with?" Maxwell asked, somewhat concerned. Deborah's smile disappeared from her face and a solemn look appeared.

"Maxwell, another place in this universe serves to organize evil, just as good is organized here," said Deborah grimly. "Everyone on Earth has choices they make every day of their lives. We do our best to help the human race decide on the right choice, but the other side makes the wrong choice look very appealing. In the end, humans have free will and they must decide. As a Protector, you will fight many battles against the other side every day. In addition, you will also protect humans from their own kind who want to do evil against them. You have much to learn about the forces of good and evil. We will make sure you are ready before your first assignment."

The four children stared without blinking at Deborah. *Maybe this wasn't going to be as much fun as I imagined,* thought Gem.

"Protectors, it's time to see your resting quarters," said Deborah. "Josiah, can you show them?"

"Certainly," he replied. "This way, children."

The children quietly filed into a double line behind Josiah and followed him back to the GUST. Not a word was spoken, as the four Protectors were lost in their thoughts of what possible adventure awaited them in this place.

3

A Place of Rest

J osiah walked the four Protectors to the GUST and instructed them, "We will be dropping down three levels, so be sure and enter the GUST on the left. We do have the same gravity pull here as on Earth, so you will feel a slight drop as you step off. It feels a little different than going up but you will soon get used to both of them."

Gem glanced at Eden and scrunched her eyebrows in a worried fashion. Josiah saw the look. "The GUST will be blowing from beneath you. You cannot fall, even if you wanted to," reassured Josiah. "Off we go. Same formation. I will follow."

Gem seemed to quickly forget her fears. Josiah's words had produced their intended effect. Not waiting on the others, the boys immediately ran for the left side GUST and leaped without slowing down. They jumped with so much speed, they free-fell for ten feet before crashing into Raphael, who was already riding the GUST on his way down to a meeting. They had plummeted almost an entire level before the air was able to correct their forceful drop.

Josiah closed his eyes, not wanting to witness the result of the collision. Slowly, he peeked over the edge. He saw Raphael with a hold on the back of both boys' shirts and was exiting the GUST on the level below. Within five seconds, Raphael had returned back up to the level with Josiah and the girls after exiting the right side GUST with both boys in tow.

"These boys may prove to be an interesting challenge for you to oversee," said Raphael sternly to Josiah while releasing his hold on the back of their shirts. "Maybe they will be too much of a chore to train. You may want to send them back and choose two others." Raphael eyed both boys as he spoke. They both lowered their eyes and apologized in unison, talking over one another, as Raphael reentered the GUST, ignoring them and continuing on to his meeting.

Josiah looked at Maxwell and Jack but said nothing. Eden and Gem ran over to Josiah and each grabbed one arm.

"Please don't send them back, Josiah," pleaded Gem.

"They were just testing the limits on the GUST," added Eden.

"Talk to Raphael and explain this is all new and exciting," added Gem again. The girls had barely spoken to the boys, but they already felt a bond they didn't want broken. They were in this together. They were a team, a team of Protectors.

"No more goof-ups," said Josiah briskly, while pointing his finger at the boys. "We can tolerate mistakes in the beginning but not purposeful irresponsibility. This was uncalled for and unnecessary." The boys once more apologized and agreed to never again mess up, although we all know this is impossible. "You are about to find yourself in serious situations," reiterated Josiah. "Foolishness that results in consequences for others will not be permitted."

Once again, they entered the GUST but this time slowly. The four-some followed Josiah on the way to their resting quarters. They exited on Level Sigma.

"This entire floor houses all the Protectors from every country," said Josiah while pointing to a variety of flags, one on each door. "Everyone in training, during one of our rotations, will have a temporary home in these quarters where they can relax. We have four rotations a year, which last about three months. You may pick up in the middle of an assignment where another Protector left off, depending on the circumstances. Some assignments will last longer than three months. Likewise, you may need to return home before your assignment is completed. We do this because we do not want to keep you away from your earthly life, with both halves split, for an extended period of time. It is not fair to you or your family to have you away too long. Even though you are not fully away, you are not fully present either." Josiah mumbled the last sentence as though he were talking to himself.

He then continued, "As you were told when you arrived here at Everwell, part of you returned to resume your role on Earth. When you return from your assignment here to Earth, you will reconnect with your other half and regain memories from both halves. I'm sure Deborah has probably covered most of this with you already, so I will change topics." The children were listening with spotty attention while they took in their surroundings. As he spoke, Josiah walked down a similar corridor with alcoves containing two doors on both sides.

Josiah turned the corner and kept talking. "Each rotation of three months has a name. We name them after the seasons on Earth to keep it simple with the order of progression. It was near the end of summer when you left Earth, so you are in the fall rotation. We may call you in for one rotation per year, or it may be once every three or five years. It depends on how much you are needed. It could also be twice a year. On very rare occasions, we have used Protectors for the entire year, as in

WWI and WWII. You never know when your presence will be required. When you do get called back, it will always be with the other three of you, unless one of you resigns . . . Here we are. Boys on the right, girls on the left."

Josiah had stopped at an alcove with two doors. The doors were made of aged wood, ornately carved and attached by metal hinges. In the upper center of each door was an American flag with a sign beneath: "United States." Gem reached up and touched the flag on the girls' door. It was made of heavy cotton with stars and stripes sewn into the cloth. She could see the attention to detail that went into its making.

"Feel free to explore your quarters and if you wish, have a look around this entire level. Please respect others' privacy. Maxwell, Jack, try not to get kicked out for at least twenty-four hours." Josiah smiled to ease the blow of his last statement but not so much as to dismiss it.

"It will be time for dinner at the never-ending table on Level Alpha in an hour. Just follow the crowd as you exit the GUST. We always have room for more, so don't worry about finding a seat. It never fills up."

The Protectors looked at each other, trying to process a never-ending table. *It is impossible,* they all thought. *Everything starts and stops.* But no one voiced their objection. They had learned in their short time here, it was of little advantage to question. They would just wait and check things out when they were there.

"You will taste food like none other at the never-ending table," continued Josiah. "Food here is in its purest form. Nothing at this table is unhealthy, and all of the food has healing properties. We do not eat animals like you do on Earth. You can rest easy that no living animal is harmed here for your nourishment."

"Is it organic?" asked Eden.

"Our food is purer than organic," replied Josiah. "Your planet has not had the ability to cultivate food of this quality for many ages."

"I don't like healthy food," added Jack, smiling. "Where can a guy go to get a plain hotdog?" Maxwell couldn't help smiling, too. He also wondered where he could get a burger.

"You will like our nourishment," answered Josiah. "Talk to me after you have tasted the food."

"Oh, we will. Don't you worry about that," said Jack, trying to talk like a grown-up. Jack smiled at the other Protectors. They knew he was only kidding Josiah, but the Protectors did wonder if Josiah knew as well. He did.

"I'm going to leave you on your own now," said Josiah. "Hopefully, I will see all of you at dinner." He returned back down the corridor from whence they came.

The young men slowly opened the door to their room as the young ladies did the same. Both pairs stood in their doorways and just stared for a minute. It was a lot to take in. The walls were smooth, a white pearl from top to bottom. Two bed frames made of stone stood on either side of the room. Upon the stone frames were mattresses at least a foot thick, with soft pillows piled to the top. The sheets were heavy-weight, pure cotton with matching pillows, topped by quilts, which looked new but not uncomfortable or stiff (more like your favorite blanket at home).

The corners of the beds had stone spears on all sides, and a shield adorned the headboard and footboard. The shield had two swords crossed with images of two beings facing each other, angels or Protectors (they were unsure as to which), behind the swords. On the wall between the two beds stood an oversized bookcase filled with very old books. A desk and a dresser, which were made of the same wood as the bookcase, were on each side. The timber was unrecognizable to either boy. You could tell it had been carved and decorated by a craftsman. Maxwell thought to himself, *Furniture like this should be in a museum, not my room.* He ran his hand over the dresser and gave a small push. It didn't budge.

"It's extremely heavy," commented Maxwell. Jack shoved on the desk. No movement. The boys continued to examine every inch of the room. Jack noticed how well the room was lit but again, could find no light source. He saw switches and small shelves hanging on the wall on each side of their room. Upon one of these shelves sat a remote control.

"Maybe one of those has something to do with the lights," said Jack. Maxwell flipped one of his switches first as he was the closest. The entire wall beside his bed lit up like a movie screen. It reminded him of a nature film from Earth. He saw birds flying and the tops of cedar, spruce, and balsam fir trees. He could even see a lake in the distance. When Maxwell looked more closely, he realized it was very similar to his lake, Lake Huron, in Michigan.

Jack waited no longer and flipped on his corresponding switch. A completely different view of Earth moved across his wall. He saw the Teton Mountains in the background and Snake River carving its path through the terrain. Eagles were flying; elk and bison were grazing. He realized he was looking at his home in Wyoming, just as Maxwell's wall showed him a view of his home in Michigan.

"What's this?" said Jack as he grabbed the remote on the shelf beside his switch.

"It looks like a game controller from home," replied Maxwell, picking his up as well. Jack noticed he could change his view of home by pushing buttons. He quickly ran through all the different location options. When he moved the lever on the remote, the view would go left or right and could zoom in or out. Maxwell could tell it was running in current time because he noticed the touring horses were being exchanged out for rested ones, which took place every day at this time. Jack turned the dial beside the buttons, which obviously controlled the volume as he could now hear birds or the roar of the river.

By this time, Maxwell had maneuvered his controller until he had a wide-angle view of the entire downtown area of Mackinac Island on his wall. He saw the tourists on bicycles going up and down the street, the shops selling fudge and ice cream, and the fort up at the top of the hill in the distance. Likewise, Jack had zoomed in on the Snake River, noticing a family slowly drifting down the waterway in a large float. He scanned the dock and saw his friends, gathered in a circle, talking, on their skateboards. He wondered why his other half wasn't with them.

"I guess it's okay if we use these," said Maxwell holding up the remote, looking over his shoulder at Jack.

"I don't think they would have put them in our rooms if there was some kind of restriction," replied Jack, not bothering to stop scanning his hometown.

Maxwell pushed the directional controller on the remote forward, and the scene downtown moved forward as well. Maxwell lowered his view to make it seem as if he were riding a bicycle down Main Street, zipping in and out between the tourists. He could speed up or slow down with the push of his thumb. "This is so cool!" exclaimed Maxwell. He turned to see if Jack was flying over a mountain or doing something exciting. Jack was staring at a house, not moving his controller.

"What's wrong?" asked Maxwell, walking over to Jack.

"Nothing," answered Jack, coming out of his daze. "This is where I live. I was just wondering if my mom was home. The controller won't let me look inside. I can only view the outside." Jack paused and moved the controller over to their garage. The garage door was open so he could access that building but when he moved the controller back to the house, he still could not open the door. "Evidently if the door is closed, you can't go in the building. I like to check in regularly on my mom. I'm all she has, so I try to look after her since my dad left."

Jack seemed embarrassed after his admission and flipped off his switch. His wall returned to its previous pearly white. He shoved Maxwell back on his side of the room, as boys do when conversations get awkward, then ran and jumped on his bed, headfirst into the pillows. He came up smiling. Maxwell knew Jack's lighthearted mood had returned, so he followed his example and did a side leap into his bed with a shout. Maxwell no more than sat up in his bed when they heard a gentle knock on the door. They immediately quieted and looked at each other. *Were they in trouble? Had they made too much noise?*

"Come in," Jack's voice cracked with nervousness. It was the girls.

"Thank goodness it's you," said Maxwell, falling back in his bed. The girls, having no idea what was happening, assumed the boys were extremely glad to see them. The girls looked at each other, puzzled but smiling.

"We wanted to see your room," said Gem. "It's very similar to ours. Your furniture is a little different, more suited for guys."

"I want to look at your books!" exclaimed Eden, dashing over to their bookcase and running her hands over the spines. She read titles such as *Techniques of Advanced Swordplay* and *When You Fear One of Your Family is a Manip* and *Steps to Avoid the Pits of Peril.* "They are different from ours. How will I read them all?" she squealed with delight. The boys rolled their eyes.

"I say it's time we begin our adventure and have a look around this training ground," said Maxwell. Everyone's face lit up, except Eden's.

"This floor only. You heard Josiah. He doesn't want you guys horsing around on the GUST. Agreed?" cautioned Eden.

"Agreed," said the boys in unison. Eden smiled and strolled out of the room like a newly appointed supervisor. Gem trailed along behind. As Eden walked past them, the boys noticed her satisfied expression. Jack leaned over to Maxwell and whispered, "Who made her the boss?" He jabbed Maxwell and laughed.

The boys took a quick peek in the girls' room. They saw deer running through a mountain forest on Gem's wall and joggers running through Central Park on Eden's. The girls' furniture was made of a lighter color wood and did present a more feminine touch in the way of flowers and birds in the carvings.

When the Protectors had left their rooms and were on their way down the hall, they met another group of kids coming out of their rooms. The sign on the door read "Japan," and above it, the Japanese flag was displayed, just like the American flag on their doors.

"Hello," said Eden and Gem with a wave. "Hello," was returned with smiles from all. "Oh, you speak English?" said Gem.

"No, we don't," replied one of the Japanese boys. "I am glad to hear you speak Japanese."

"We don't," replied Gem. "We only speak English."

"We are hearing you in our native Japanese language," said one of the Japanese girls. Everyone shook their heads with disbelief as they tried to comprehend how this was happening.

"I'm sure it's because we're here in this place. I can't imagine what we will discover next. By the way, my name is Su." She gestured to the other Japanese girl and said, "This is Norio." Then she pointed to the Japanese boys. "This is Ming and Kato. We are on our way to dinner if you would like to walk with us."

Maxwell introduced all the members of his party, and they followed the Protectors from Japan down the hallway. They passed several groups of four from Africa, Australia, Germany, China, and the United Kingdom. Introductions were made. Everyone could understand everyone else. The written signs located on each Protector's door, likewise, could be read by all.

What the Protectors didn't know at this time, but I will share with you, is that when they were in this dimension, no differences were apparent. They were one group of Protectors, all from the planet Earth. It was that simple. The different countries only signified which geography they were from. Any grievances from Earth, past or present, were not transported to Everwell.

After much discussion amongst the children, Maxwell voiced his opinion that the translation occurred in each Protector's brain, and this was not incorrect. He knew it had to do with being here and thought it may even be possible when the individuals arrived at the training grounds from different countries that they at once had a unified language. Maxwell always liked to know the why so he decided he would ask Josiah when the time was right. Perhaps he would see him at dinner. He had begun to wonder what type of meal would be waiting on them.

The Protectors arrived at the dinner hall on Level Alpha. They found the room lit in soft light but again with no source, just like the other rooms they'd seen so far. In the center of the room was the largest, most beautiful table the children had ever seen, made of wood that was almost black, with slivers of brown woven throughout. It was quite massive and the first thing you noticed upon entering the room.

The Protectors straightaway looked up to see if they could see the other end of the table. After much straining and squinting, then standing on their tippy toes, they realized it was useless, but they could see the wall on the other end of the room, which made no sense. (But what here did?) Greenery, in the form of trees, plants, and flowers, some like on Earth, others not, surrounded the space with the feel of late summertime in this room. Bees were buzzing from flower to flower with the smell of the honeysuckles, lilacs, and roses permeating the air. The aroma of the flowers seemed stronger than those on Earth and some were unrecognizable but delightful. The girls walked over to be closer to the flowers. Right away, they noticed the roses had no thorns. The girls had never seen a garden with such beauty in all their lives. After a few moments, the boys were motioning the girls back over to the table.

"I don't believe this table is never-ending," said Jack. "I can see the wall right over there." He pointed to the far side of the room. "It's not even that far away. After we eat, let's go have a look." The other three Protectors agreed.

Several door openings were positioned on both sides of the room. More and more children were filing in, grabbing open chairs as the four discussed the size of the table. "I'm not sure if this room is large enough to hold everyone," said Jack. The four Protectors watched in amazement at how many children were entering the room and instantaneously were seated. In no time at all, Maxwell and the others realized no more open seats were visible in their area. They would need to walk down the length of the table to find an unoccupied spot.

As soon as they began their stroll, the four were grabbed by an invisible force and moved quite rapidly down the length of the table into an open chair. For a moment, they didn't even know what had occurred.

They found themselves sitting in sturdy chairs covered in velvet with padding in the seat and against their backs. The velvet was covered in flowers the same color as the plants in the room. Emma, one of the Norwegian Protectors sitting across from the Americans, told Eden the chairs changed color with the flowers in the room. When winter or autumn flowers were featured, the chairs reflected this as well. She told Eden it was always exceptionally beautiful. This was the Norwegians' third assignment. Maxwell and the others watched them as they interacted with one another. They behaved very contentedly, as if their time here was completely ordinary.

"Look!" exclaimed Gem, pointing toward the wall with the end of the table you couldn't quite see. The wall was expanding lengthwise and the table with it. The room was growing to accommodate more children. "So, that's what they mean by never-ending," said Eden. "It adjusts itself to fit those dining, always providing enough room. How magnificent."

The children suddenly noticed the food on trays being lowered from above. No one held the trays as they were floating down. The children looked above the food to see where it came from, but a thick cloud obstructed their view.

As the food was lowered, Jack couldn't help wondering what would be on the trays. He was a picky eater and couldn't hide the worried look on his face. If it was all leafy greens, he was going to protest. The trays touched down ever so gently and were perfectly placed right in the middle, stretching over the entire length of the table. The foursome took a moment to inspect their choices.

The first tray, which lay before them, contained all fruit. Twenty or more different varieties were on display, all sliced, deseeded, peeled, and ready to eat: pineapple, watermelon, apples, oranges, kiwi, mango, and some options they had never before seen but were just as delicious. All were picked at the peak of ripeness to produce more sweetness than their taste buds could savor. The Protectors dug in.

While they were still eating fruit, another tray softly landed. This one was piled with salad, featuring a large assortment of dark and light green leaf lettuces, tomatoes, radishes, and cucumbers adorned with a dressing of sweet honey and dew. Maxwell and the girls filled their plate with sample bites of everything. Jack scrunched up his face and wanted no part of the salad tray, but he was tempted when Gem pushed a forkful of salad covered in the honey dew dressing under his nose. It didn't smell green like salad from Earth. (I can't describe to you the smell of green. I can only tell you, if you don't like salad, you already know.) He decided he would try to sneak a bite when the others weren't watching.

Next, to whet their appetite, trays of nuts and cheeses were lowered before them. Pitchers of the purest water and the richest milk arrived to fill their glasses. There were baskets of warm assorted breads so rich in flavor they made the Protector's mouth water for more. They feasted on trays of vegetables: ears of corn dripping in butter; mashed, baked, and sweet potatoes; green, lima, and pinto beans; fried okra; and carrots.

The Protectors could eat no more—until the dessert trays arrived. Sticky buns covered in gooey sweetness, decorated with sprinkles and nuts, and topped with whipped cream were too much to resist. Some desserts were puddings and gelatins; others were cookies and cakes. Most were dusted with sugar and delicious.

When the Protectors had eaten their fill and believed they possibly would burst, they laid down their silverware and leaned back in their chairs. The remaining trays on their table began floating upward, along with any morsel of food or drink that had been spilled on the table. A spotless table resulted in seconds. The foursome smiled at each other in wonder during the spectacle.

"What an unbelievable meal," said Jack, putting his hands behind his head and stretching to make more room in his middle.

"My grandmother is the greatest cook in the world, but this food tops everything I've ever tasted," added Eden.

"I feel like it's time for bed," said Gem. "It has to be late. I know we have been here for hours."

Maxwell gave Jack a look that indicated, "Not us."

"We are going to have a little look around," said Jack smiling. "You both are welcome to join us if you'd like."

"Jack, you two should call it a day as well. We've already had this discussion," snapped Eden in her sternest voice yet. "The two of you have been in enough trouble for the four of us." Jack could tell Eden was genuinely concerned.

"Relax, Eden," said Jack. "We'll stay on this floor and just walk around. Nothing will happen. You have my word."

"We haven't had a chance to explore any of the training grounds. We'll be back in our room in an hour," Maxwell reassured her.

Gem raised an eyebrow as she bit the side of her lip and looked at Eden for consensus. Eden shook her head and said, "Very well."

"Maxwell, don't you and Jack ruin this for all of us," said Gem. "We don't want to start over with new partners."

"We promise," said the boys in unison, as if they were in kindergarten.

"Good night," grunted the girls as they turned and walked down the hallway, admiring the ornate carvings of plants and animals placed now and then on the wall.

When the girls were out of sight, the guys scanned the room looking for Josiah. He was nowhere to be seen. Now was as good a time as ever to have a look around. They surveyed all the doors, which ran along the entire length of the never-ending table on both sides of the banquet room. The boys took notice of how the wall at the far side of the room was shrinking back toward them as most of the children were finished eating and making their way out of the room.

"Let's try this door," suggested Maxwell. He had chosen the door beside the hallway from which they had first arrived. He figured this would make it easier to not get turned around when they returned. It also concerned him that one of the farther away doors could disappear if the room shrank much more. They opened the heavy door at a normal speed as if they knew exactly where they were going, not slowly as one who didn't know what waited on the other side.

The boys found themselves in a dark hallway, which was, in itself, out of the ordinary for this place. Ahead were winding corners with doors and windows to rooms on one side of the corridor. Activities in these rooms could never be hidden by anyone in the hall because the windows were so large and took up most of the upper portion of the wall. The rooms they had passed thus far, at the beginning of the hall, had the lights on and the doors open with only a few occupants.

They strolled past two very large rooms toward the middle of the hall; one was marked Defense and one marked Offense. Both were empty of people but filled with physical training equipment and sparring weapons. Next, they passed a room marked Scheduling and another marked Portal. Both doors were closed, but through the windows, the boys could see a great deal of activity going on. To prevent being seen, and possibly being sent back to their rooms, their reaction was to lean toward the far wall as they walked by. It was dark in the hallway and they assumed it would be more difficult for the occupants in the rooms to see them—not impossible but not easy either.

They continued around more corners and more empty rooms until they were almost to the end of the hallway. They saw no lights farther ahead, except in the last room, and it was a faint light, not bright like the other rooms. They debated whether to even walk to the end to check it out as this had been a disappointing first attempt at exploration. The rooms that looked exciting were unoccupied, and the occupied rooms resembled those terrible offices on Earth where you sit for long periods of time waiting for your name to be called. But they decided they had come this far and would walk on ahead to see what was happening in the last room.

As they approached the lit room, they could hear heated conversation. Maxwell and Jack both bent down to stay below the windows. They raised themselves ever so slowly to glimpse inside. The boys hit the ground quickly when they saw a room full of winged beings with Josiah in their midst.

"Great! Just our luck," said Jack excitedly. Both were stooped below the windows with their backs pressed against the wall.

"Just sit still and don't move," whispered Maxwell. "I'm fairly sure we haven't been seen." Since the room wasn't as bright as the other rooms, it would be easier for the occupants inside to see anyone standing in the hallway looking in. Only the speaker, standing in the front of the room, was illuminated. No one came out in the hall to investigate even with the door ajar. Everyone was too preoccupied with what was happening in the room to be concerned with a slight movement in the hallway. After their heartbeats calmed, the boys could hear the speaker in the room.

"We should not be putting the Protectors' lives in jeopardy!" exclaimed a tall, studious-looking angel. The room erupted with, "Hear, Hear," from those in agreement and, "Whoo, Whoo," from those in opposition. The angel continued, "Recco is very dangerous and not a being to be approached by a novice."

A stockier, tougher-looking angel jumped up to defend his position. "Tillie, the new Protectors will be nowhere near Recco or any of his Manips," he argued.

"Hampton, these children are entrusted to us. We cannot risk another Protector death," replied Tillie in a faint voice. The group of angels again mumbled approval and disapprovals. Maxwell looked at Jack and mouthed the words, "Another death?"

"Steps have been taken to protect our new trainees from harm," insisted Hampton defensively. "They will all receive less hazardous assignments but we cannot be as effective in our guardianship without the Protectors. They possess the insight how their kind will likely react in different situations. They are most valuable."

"Settle down, both of you!" exclaimed an older angel, with his hands outstretched like a referee at a boxing match. He was clearly one of the leaders of the group. "Nothing will be resolved this day. I suggest all of us observe the new Protectors over the next couple of days. We will have finished two full days of training by that time and should then have some idea of the new Protectors' abilities in combat and flying. We will discuss the subject in a more informed manner at this same time, the day after tomorrow. Good day, everyone."

"Run!" said Maxwell as quietly as a person in extreme panic can manage. The boys scrambled to their feet but remained in a bent-over position. They ran while taking care not to rise up above the window line. When they had turned the first corner, they straightened up and kept a fast pace but not so fast to resemble a run. They didn't want to arouse suspicions as they passed the other occupied rooms.

If this hallway had not been full of turns, this story would be short, indeed, for our Protectors would have been caught by Josiah and sent home for sure. As luck would have it, there were several corners, and they were able to clear each stretch of the hallway just in time. They frantically exited the doorway back into the dining room as several late-dining Protectors glanced in Maxwell and Jack's direction.

"Act natural," whispered Jack. "Nothing is unusual. We were supposed to be in that corridor."

The boys casually strolled toward the hall that led back to their rooms. Seconds later, the angels from the meeting room at the end of the hallway filed into the dining room. The boys quickened their exit as they glanced behind. As Hampton, Tillie, and the other angels entered the room, Maxwell and Jack ducked into the adjoining hallway.

Jack stopped when they entered the hall and peeked back through the window in the door to get one more look at the group from the meeting room. He saw Josiah, a worried look on his face, mumbling something to Raphael. Raphael's expression displayed the same concern. Jack didn't remember seeing Raphael in the previous meeting. He thought perhaps Josiah was catching him up with the events of the assembly.

"We've got to tell Eden and Gem," said Jack as they hurried back to their room. When they arrived at their room, it was 10:20, Earth time, and the girls' door was shut. They knew tomorrow was a big day for all of them. Their training would begin, and they needed to be rested and ready to go.

"They could be sleeping. We'll have to wait until tomorrow to tell the girls," said Maxwell disappointedly as he turned the knob to enter their room. Jack quietly knocked on the girls' door anyway. Maxwell shot Jack a look and said, "I'm so glad you listen to me."

"I can't wait until tomorrow. I won't get any sleep," answered Jack as he knocked again. It took several minutes for Gem to answer the door. She looked befuddled, like she had awakened from a deep sleep. Several seconds had passed before she made sense of Jack and Maxwell's ramblings.

"We need to talk to both of you now!" insisted Jack. Gem walked away from the opened door and woke up Eden. The boys followed her in. Eden slowly awoke during the confusion and propped herself up in the bed, leaning on her elbows.

"What happened now?" asked Eden in a calm but serious tone. She thought Maxwell and Jack were in trouble again. When they started talking, it didn't take her long to wake up as the guys poured out the details of the last hour. They told the girls about Recco, the mysterious death of a Protector, and how trouble seemed to be brewing again. When the boys stopped talking, everyone continued to sit silently on the bed, not knowing what to say.

Eden spoke first, "We will try to find out more tomorrow. Our training starts early, so you guys really should go and try to relax for a few hours."

"You'll love the sleep here," added Gem. The boys looked puzzled, so she clarified, "No bad dreams."

"How do you know?" asked Maxwell, not buying it. "You've only been asleep once and for an hour or less."

"I don't know how I know; I just know," replied Gem. "You'll see once you've tried it."

Eden patted Jack on the shoulder. "Try not to worry. I'm sure the angels won't intentionally put us in harm's way," she reassured him.

"Not *intentionally*," repeated Gem, concerned. Everyone noticed her tone. The boys stood up to leave and said they would see them in the morning.

After settling into their room, the boys put on their pajamas, which were way too loose at first but adjusted themselves to fit. "Let's try to get some sleep," said Maxwell, ignoring his self-adjusting pajamas as if it were normal. Jack agreed as he jumped into his bed to get comfortable. He realized the light was still on.

"How do we get the light off?" asked Jack, looking up at the ceiling. "I still don't know where it's coming from."

Maxwell looked around the room and noticed a button on the wall labeled "rest." He walked over to the button and slowly pushed it in. He looked up in anticipation of the lights clicking off. Instead, a soft dusk settled over the room until it was quite dark.

"How do they do that?" pondered Jack, amazed.

"They probably turn on the dark the same way we turn the light on," answered Maxwell.

"With a black bulb?" replied Jack, trying to be funny.

"Maybe," said Maxwell. "Something tells me we have enough to bother about here to where turning on the dark will be the least of our questions." Maxwell retired to his bed, and neither spoke. It had been a long day for everyone. Within minutes, both boys had temporarily forgotten the mystery and were engulfed in the most peaceful sleep either had ever experienced.

4

The Beginning of the First Day

The next morning, at ten minutes until six, the darkness in the room began gradually lifting. By six, their room gleamed as if they were outside on a sunny day but standing in shade.

"Do you think they're trying to tell us to get up?" cracked Jack. Maxwell sat up, hung his legs over the side of the bed and onto the floor. Jack took his covers and pulled them up over his head.

"This place can be a little overwhelming if you think about it too long," said Maxwell, staring at the floor. Jack pulled his cover down from around his head and sat up. Maxwell looked up at Jack. "There's so much to take in, and we haven't even started training. From the freaky way we arrived here, to beginning our training today, to becoming a Protector responsible for another person's life, it's a lot to take on—not to mention the conversation we overheard last night. What have we walked into, Jack?" rambled Maxwell.

"I'm sure everything will be fine," replied Jack, jumping out of his bed and sitting on Maxwell's. "I'm telling you, they wouldn't risk our lives with a protection assignment that was overly dangerous. Like the guy said last night, they will assess our abilities in training. It makes no sense to kill us to save someone else. We'll be ready, or I'm sure they won't send us out."

The boys' conversation was interrupted by a knock. Jack jumped up to answer the door and playfully shoved Maxwell's head as he did so. Maxwell began to feel more assured. Most likely Jack was right; everything would be fine.

When Jack answered the door, the girls were both standing there smiling. "We don't want to be late on our first day. You'd better get dressed," said Gem cheerfully as she walked into the room.

"What are you wearing?" asked Maxwell with a raised eyebrow.

"It was in our closet," answered Eden. "Check yours." The girls were dressed in a white linen shirt and navy blue pants. Eden's shirt buttoned up the front and had some red flowered embroidery on the front, while Gem's had ocean surf embroidered, also in red. The pants were tapered at the legs but with plenty of room for movement. "It's quite comfortable."

"I'm not wearing anything with red flowers!" announced Jack as he stepped toward his closet. "Now, this is more like it." He pulled out his attire: blue pants and a white shirt similar to the girls. But instead of red flowers, his shirt had a red lion embroidered on the front. Maxwell's displayed a red eagle. The boys' and girls' uniforms had a small American flag on the upper left sleeve. Eden mentioned she didn't think it was a coincidence that the colors of their uniform matched the colors of the flag on their sleeve.

"We'll wait outside; hurry and get dressed," said the girls. They went back out into the hallway. When the boys pulled on their clothes, once again, they were way too loose. Within seconds, the clothing adjusted to the boys' sizes, just as the pajamas had done. The clothes sensed the wearer's size, then expanded or shrunk to fit perfectly. The boys checked out their uniforms in the mirror to make sure nothing was backwards or inside out. That would be embarrassing on the first day.

"I'm ready if you are," said Maxwell.

"Let's be off then," said Jack in a Shakespearean-style voice as he marched toward the door. Both boys laughed and joined the girls waiting in the alcove.

"Looking good, guys," said Gem as both girls burst out giggling. The boys looked down at their uniforms to double-check if something was out of place. They quickly realized the girls were only messing with them and then laughed themselves as they headed for breakfast, chattering like chipmunks with excitement.

When they arrived at breakfast, many of the Protectors from other countries were already seated and eating their morning meal. Others, like the American Protectors, were just arriving and filing into the dining hall now. Eden brought it to her group's attention that the Protectors from each country were, indeed, dressed in their flag's colors, just as she said they would be.

"I think wearing your flag colors is a great idea," said Eden. "You know just by looking at someone, where they are from, plus, I bet it helps to keep everyone organized," added Eden as if she were privy to this information.

"I imagine they do it to help us," said Maxwell. "I don't think they have any trouble keeping the Protectors grouped. I would say they thoroughly know each one of us." The other three nodded in agreement.

Today, their first meal was already on the table. They helped themselves with whatever selection suited them, as if at home. Everything was hot and fresh as if it had just been served. There were oats, scrambled eggs, and fresh fruit. The biscuits reminded Gem of Biscuit World back home.

They had a Southern touch, with apple butter and blueberry jam. Eden found bagels she felt sure would never top those in New York, but she was pleasantly surprised. The soon-to-be Protectors devoured their morning meal, anxious to get started on their day. When they had eaten as much as they possibly could without getting sick, Eden hurried everyone along.

The Protectors rushed off with anticipation toward the GUST. They watched and waited for an opening with no one traveling up, but the flow was constant. Obviously, the GUST was quite crowded at this time of day, which caused Eden to make a mental note to leave earlier tomorrow.

"We'll have to look for an opening and make a jump for it," said Maxwell. "Eden, you choose when, and the rest of us will follow right behind you." Eden was quite pleased she was chosen to lead. She accepted the challenge, confident she would succeed.

"Everyone ready?" Eden said with a smile. "Follow me."

"If it doesn't work, she can't yell at us," whispered Maxwell to Jack. Now Jack understood Maxwell asking Eden to go first. He thought, *Who knows? Maybe she can find an opening.*

The four Protectors readied themselves for the jump. With no notice at all, Eden shouted, "Now!" Eden bounded first, with Maxwell, Gem, and Jack very close behind. Amazingly, when they landed in the GUST, they were alone. They could see vague figures above them as well as below but could make out no specifics about any passengers except for each other. They wondered if, perhaps, you could only see clearly those who entered the GUST together.

They clutched each other in laughter and gave pats of praise to Eden who had certainly chosen a perfect moment to jump into the GUST.

Josiah had hinted to the girls how the GUST worked better if you simply step in but they didn't pick up on the clue. The GUST was created to place the traveler in the next opening to prevent any unnecessary conges-tion. It isn't common knowledge that you must have faith it will carry and deliver you to your desired level. When your faith wavers, your ride will be like a wave on the ocean, blown and tossed in every direction. The leaders stopped telling this to the Protectors because they found it caused more doubt. Maxwell and Jack had their difficulties earlier due to running and jumping while entering the GUST. They didn't realize fast motion isn't necessary and causes more problems in which the GUST has to compensate.

The Protectors waited for Level Gamma to arrive and jumped with eagerness out of the GUST. Again, speed wasn't necessary, so the four came tumbling out, catching their breath and stumbling to their feet. They were greeted by many stares, faint mumblings, and a few chuckles.

Gem noticed a small group of angels and Protectors entering the GUST on Level Gamma—with no running or jumping. They weren't even watching inside the GUST for an opening. They simply stepped in. After an instance, they were gone. The youngest of the group began to figure it out.

"Guys, we're doing this GUST thing all wrong," suggested Gem. "We're making this harder than it has to be. No one else is running and jumping." The other three observed different individuals using the GUST and Gem was right. "Next time, we just step in like everyone else," Gem declared.

They straightened their crumpled clothes and messed-up hair and headed for their first training session in Rescue.

When the Protectors arrived in the Rescue room, they saw high stools positioned in a circle, with lower stools in front of those and a large open space in the center of the room resembling a performance ring in the circus. In this open space stood two muscular angels who introduced themselves as Weatherly and Collin and told the Protectors to choose any seat. Weatherly was tall with dark skin and black hair. Collin was shorter and stockier, with lighter skin and short, thinning brown hair.

When all the stools were filled, the two angels stood in the center of the ring and presented a scenario. They first described an individual hiking on a path near a steep drop. Instantly the center area surrounding them transformed into a faint hologram of a wooded region. One angel acted as if he were a hiker and the other the rescuer. The hiker purposely fell off the cliff while the other angel showed different scenarios for rescuing him. For example, he positioned a branch for the hiker to grab on to. Another time, he used the force of air from his moving wings to keep the hiker close to the cliff facing. Lastly, he cushioned the hiker's fall with debris. While the angels were in the ring, they were able to interact in any scenario they would describe. The scenario would instantly appear around them and disappear when they were finished.

After the two angels had demonstrated several scenarios, they explained to the trainees how this was a learn-by-watching-and-doing process. Even though the Protectors didn't yet have use of their wings, they were confident everyone would be able to pick up this rescue skill and advised them not to worry if they struggled in the beginning. It was time for the Protectors to take a turn. The angels had made it look easy. The Protectors diverted their eyes, each hoping to not be selected first.

The Rescue trainers chose two Protectors from Australia to go first in their own randomly selected Rescue scenario. The Aussie Protectors introduced themselves as Thomas Horne and Nicholas Bonner. After the introductions, they promptly found themselves in an outback scenario, but still in the center of the room for all to witness. Weatherly informed them they would be attempting a bicycle rescue.

Thomas thought he had been handed good fortune until he found himself on a bicycle with no brakes; he was speeding out of control down a steep, rocky hill with intermittent patches of grass. Nicholas was expected to rescue Thomas from this disastrous situation and to do it quickly. The Protectors in the room could see Thomas speeding down the hill, but oddly enough, he was almost motionless as his surroundings sped past him. The situation didn't feel motionless to Australian boys for they couldn't see out of the hologram to get their bearing.

Nicholas quickly tried to think of some action to save his friend. He pushed a tree branch in front of Thomas, hoping he would grab on. Instead of grabbing hold, which was impossible at the speed objects were flying past him, Thomas slammed directly into the branch. He hit his head, flipped off the bicycle, and landed with a thud on the training room floor. They found themselves back in the room with no hologram of the outback surrounding them, only Protectors muffling their laughter. Thomas and Nicholas returned to their seats, red faced with their heads lowered.

Weatherly and Collin stood up before the trainees. "What could Nicholas have done differently, Protectors?" asked Collin.

"He could have not hit Thomas with the tree branch," answered a Protector from New Zealand. Everyone laughed except Thomas and Nicholas.

"He could have grabbed the back of Thomas's bike and steadily slowed the forward motion—not an urgent or dramatic stop but a smooth, slowing pull until Thomas had control," suggested Collin.

The next moment, the two angels were back in the outback in front of the room, just as Thomas and Nicholas had been. Weatherly was on the bike, out of control, with Collin trying to slow him with a steady pull. Weatherly came to a stop on the bike with no spill.

"As all of you can see, it is not easy to pick up these skills. It will take much practice before we can send you out on your first mission!" exclaimed Weatherly.

The trainers then went through several scenarios with all the Protectors in the room. They did see improvements in their performance with each attempt. The Protectors who observed picked up skills from watching the others.

"Keep vigilant, Protectors," added Weatherly. "I have a feeling this group will be my most spectacular rescuers to date. We will see all of you, same time tomorrow."

With that farewell, the Protectors rose from their seats to leave. Everyone gathered around Nicholas and Thomas on the way out to make sure Thomas was okay. He had cuts and bruises from the ordeal, but they had already begun to heal.

"This is going to be tough," said Maxwell, with conviction, to his three companions. "When I saw Thomas with blood on his arm from falling off the bike, it became more real. People will depend on us to keep them safe."

"You heard them, Maxwell," said Jack. "They're not going to send us out until we're ready. Stop worrying. You're worse than my mother." Jack rolled his eyes.

"I agree with Maxwell," Eden added. "I hope I'm up for this. This is more responsibility than most adults have on Earth. Here we are, young people, being put in charge of saving one, ten, hundreds of people. We just don't know. Talk about pressure."

Silence fell as the four lost themselves in thought. Maxwell unrolled the linen containing his training schedule. He broke the quiet with a suggestion: "We have almost an hour before Messenger training. Let's go to Level Zeta and watch some of the Flight training. I want to be better prepared and know what's expected from me before I get to try out my wings."

"What wings?" replied Jack, pulling up Maxwell's shirt like he was looking for something not there. Everyone laughed but thought this was a wonderful idea and began walking toward the GUST.

"Let's try to do a better job this time on the GUST," reminded Gem. The GUST was just as busy as it had been before, due to children switching levels. Gem walked up to the GUST with no hesitation and stepped in. The remaining three hurried to be close to her but slowed to a walk as they entered the opening. In an instant, all four were standing together and rising to Level Zeta. The GUST had rapidly positioned the remaining three with Gem, even though she had stepped in several seconds earlier.

As they exited the GUST on Level Zeta, it appeared as though they had walked outside with a large, green expanse of soft, blowing grass before them. Overhead, a wide-open, baby-blue sky with cotton-candy-looking white clouds scattered haphazardly in every direction lit up their surroundings. Large live oaks and maple trees grew on both sides of the meadow outlining the field. The children could've sworn they were back on Earth had it not been for the group of angels and their current trainees in the center of the bowl-shaped landscape. Gem immediately took notice of her earthly surroundings and decided this was her favorite location at Everwell. It felt like home.

A soft, cool breeze was steadily blowing as they watched a group of trainees practice their flights down below in the center of the arena. They couldn't overhear the instruction from their observation position on the upper edge of the meadow, but they could see the attempts. Some were successful, but most were not.

"Ah-ha. Getting a sneak preview?" The Protectors thoughts were interrupted by a familiar voice. It was Josiah.

The Protectors jumped to attention as if they had been caught in some wrongdoing. All four were a bit skittish with Josiah since the earlier GUST incident. Josiah's smile relieved their anxiety. "We refer to this area as the flight deck."

"The Flight training looks amazing," said Maxwell, looking over to Josiah. A crash, mixed with some screams and yelling, grabbed everyone's attention and focused it back on the meadow. The current trainee had sped out of control into some spectators, and the instructor appeared to be delivering a scolding.

Josiah took advantage of the opportunity to reinforce the seriousness of the task before the children. "It's imperative that you pay careful attention in Flight training," he said. "Flight training and Protection are the two departments where it is possible to fail and be sent back to Earth. There are worse fates that could await you if you pass the training and then fail during your assignment," Josiah warned mysteriously. Four pairs of eyes darted back and forth between themselves, then landed on Josiah's expression, which was solemn and distant.

"What do you mean by that last part?" asked Jack carefully. "Is there something more we should know, Josiah?"

Josiah stared at the four, looking each one in the eyes. "Yes, there are many things you will need to know before your first assignment." Jack knew he had dodged the question. "Every day, you will battle with great evil," continued Josiah. "You will learn more about dealing with this evil in Protection training, but I do feel there are other circumstances you should be aware of, especially you, Maxwell." Josiah concentrated his gaze on Maxwell, which caught him off guard at the mention of his name. "But those above me want to handle things differently," he continued.

"Me? Why me?" asked Maxwell.

"Your family has a history here," answered Josiah. "I didn't even want you brought here due to the danger. I mustn't say any more without proper permission, but I do want you to be aware." As quickly as Josiah appeared, he was gone. A blanket of mystery fell over the Protectors.

"My family has a history here? What is he talking about? I think I would know if someone from my family had ever been here!" exclaimed Maxwell.

"Maybe not," added Eden. "And what was all the talk about danger? I don't want to get Josiah in trouble, but we need to do more snooping around and find out all we can. We need some answers."

"Look who wants to snoop around. It's Miss Follow All the Rules," said Jack looking sternly at Eden.

"It's getting late, and we need to go to Messenger training," interrupted Gem, wanting to change the direction in which this conversation was heading. It worked; Eden didn't even reply. She didn't want to be tardy for their next training. They returned to the GUST for a refreshingly uneventful ride.

They exited on Level Beta to a hallway cluttered with odds and ends. As they walked, the Protectors couldn't help but stare at the items, the next one more interesting than the one before. The children knew the objects were from Earth but from different time periods. Eden thought it resembled a movie studio storage room she had once seen on television, with old vehicles, bicycles, lamps, tools, chains, ropes, suits of armor, and several old, worn pictures in frames. The children thought there must be one of everything here from decades back. The older items from WWII really interested the boys: old uniforms, weapons, dog tags, radios. Everything you could imagine.

"My grandfather fought in WWII," said Maxwell. "He has some stuff similar to these." He pointed to the flashlight and boots sitting close to his own feet. The Protectors continued walking. The corridor led on for several yards where one hallway forked to the right and one to the left. A small group of Protectors had already gathered ahead, and all their eyes were on the foursome as they neared.

"I believe the arrival of these Protectors completes our group, so let me introduce myself." A chubbier, older angel stood before them with a warm smile and a kind face. He didn't appear physically old, but he did have an air of maturity about him.

"My name is Nathan. I have been the trainer of Messaging for millenniums. I am fortunate enough to have been around since before your planet was created. What a glorious time that was." He paused for a moment, reflecting on times past. The trainees looked at one another, not knowing if someone should cough or say something to break the silence.

One of the Protectors moved in their chair, which snapped Nathan back to the present. He chuckled, "I apologize for my absentmindedness. I remember everything, and if you had seen the things I have seen, you would get lost in your thoughts, too." He continued to chuckle. "Let us begin. Everyone place your chairs round here in front of me."

The Protectors set up their chairs in several rows, positioned in a half-moon shape, with Nathan standing before them. It was difficult for them to remain focused with so many interesting items surrounding them. Nathan took notice of the children's lack of attention, and then went over to the wall to dim the lights around the edge of the room before he began. The lights stayed bright on Nathan and the Protectors, but now you could only faintly make out the surrounding items in the room.

Nathan explained, "Messaging is a method of communication between the spiritual world and the physical world," he began. "Many humans pray for guidance and protection, either for themselves or a loved one. This training is to prepare you in that guidance.

"The items you see around you are used every day in messaging. Old, tattered signs guide the way on roads with no markings. The vehicles in this room have also been used many times in rescue. There have been instances when humans have been stranded in snowstorms with no hope, when along comes a stranger traveling in their direction, who then transports them to safety. Sometimes we physically show ourselves as those disguised strangers; other times, we just place a helpful item where it will be found to help resolve the situation.

"We use many different means of messaging, from manipulating dreams to placement of articles. Sometimes an idea will come to the humans from nowhere, when in reality, it was triggered from an object we put before them. If they act on that idea, circumstances will improve. You, the Protector, will be the ones creating these messages. Throughout the messaging process, it is always best if you are quick, unseen, and most importantly, successful.

"This rotation we will be concentrating on using objects in messaging," said Nathan. "We will deal with dream communication next time after you have gained more experience with the general idea of messaging. Using objects to express your message will help you gain that experience.

"Now, let us begin learning the technique of how to send a message by practicing with some of the items around us," continued Nathan. He gave the Protectors a scenario; then he would pick up a random item out of the room and ask them how to send a message using the item. Just like in Rescue training, when Nathan described a scenario, it would appear in the front of the class as a hologram. He chose two girls from France, Camila and Ivy, to demonstrate first.

Their scenario took place at a fairly large pond covered in frozen ice located in the middle of the woods. Two hologram children were sitting around the edge of the frozen water, putting on their ice skates, unaware of the danger of thin ice toward the middle of the pond. Nathan looked around the outskirts of the room to select an item to send the children a warning message. He found a stone the size of softball and tossed it over to the French Protector girls. When Camila caught the stone in her right hand, they instantly found themselves in the hologram with the children, who were now standing up after putting on their skates. The French Protectors had moments to decide how to use the stone.

Ivy noticed the thicker ice around the edge of the pond where the children were standing. She whispered something to Camila, and both Protectors flew to the center of the pond where the ice was thin. Camila took the stone and struck the thin ice with force directed toward the children. The result was a crack that sounded like thunder splitting the ice.

The children standing near the edge of the pond were so frightened that they jumped off the ice and back onto the grass.

Camila and Ivy smiled, gave each other a high five, and cheered. They knew they had succeeded. Seconds later, the scenario disappeared, and they were standing beside Nathan in front of the others.

"Excellent, excellent," said Nathan as he clapped his hands. "Not only did the young ladies warn the children, they quickly came up with the idea and were undetectable to the humans given that the stone sunk to the bottom of the pond. Great job, girls."

Involving different Protectors, Nathan demonstrated an assortment of techniques with several items in the room. Some did better than others, but all were successful at sending a message. The Protectors watching the scenarios would make suggestions afterward for different uses of the items, which is what Nathan hoped to accomplish during this first session. He wanted his Protectors engaged and excited about sending messages. Nathan told the children how pleased he was with their progress as he dismissed the training and told them he would see them tomorrow. The Protectors were talking enthusiastically as they exited the hallway, looking at the different items and discussing new messaging ideas on the way out.

5

Protection

When the Protectors arrived on Level Delta, they noticed a sign upon exiting the GUST that indicated Protection training was to the right and the Communication Department was to the left.

"Why do they have a Communication Department?" asked Gem.

"I'm sure they need a way to contact one another when they aren't here," suggested Maxwell.

"Whatever it is, it doesn't concern us. Let's get to training," added Eden. They darted for Protection training through a herd of mingling Protectors.

When they arrived, they found themselves in a large room, one similar to the Flight training room but not nearly as expansive. Instructors were standing at various stations in the room with an assortment of weaponry drill equipment at each station. A crowd of Protectors surrounded an angel who stood at the far end of the room.

"Attention, young Protectors," said the angel, very matter-of-factly. "My name is Joshua. I am your head instructor for Protection training. You will be divided into six groups and will spend ten minutes at each station. This is not much time, so you will need to pay attention. The station instructors will spend several minutes demonstrating the moves. You will spend several more minutes correctly learning the moves and then the remaining minutes practicing with a partner while being critiqued by your station instructor.

"I cannot emphasize enough how important mastering this class is to the success of your training. While you are protecting your humans, you will fight many battles. Rest assured; those who battle against you will be well trained," said Joshua with conviction.

"For some of you, these skills will come easily; for others, it will require you to work harder. Remember, this assignment is not about you; it's about whom you are protecting. So, work diligently."

The children exchanged glances, but not nearly as many as in earlier trainings. The Protectors were realizing the seriousness of their training, and everyone wanted to be prepared.

"Get in your groups of four and find a station so we can begin," stated Joshua. "It does not matter which station you pick as you will have a turn at each one."

The Protectors stepped out of the crowd and assembled in groups by their countries. Every group located a station and waited to begin.

"When you hear a chime at the end of fifteen minutes, you will set down your weapons and move clockwise to the next station," Joshua explained.

At their station, the Protectors noticed long wooden sticks leaning against a metal support and a younger-looking angel standing, wide stance, with his arms folded in front of him. "Good day," said the angel, "I am Anthony. What are your names?"

Maxwell replied back for the group. "Hello, Anthony. I am Maxwell. This is Jack, Gem, and Eden. We are from—"

"Grab your staffs. Ready?" interrupted Anthony, who had already picked up a staff from the metal support and was in starting position. Maxwell and Jack, standing in the front, scrambled toward the leaning staffs and knocked them over with a loud crash, causing them to fall into each other and topple out of the metal support. Eden and Gem and the other Protector groups in their section watched as the two boys tried to catch some of the falling sticks, only to domino into one another, creating more noise and confusion. Anthony stood observing with no reaction. Maxwell and Jack quickly picked up the extra staffs and placed them gently back on the support so they would not fall again. They lined back up in front of Anthony, staffs ready as the rest of the Protectors grabbed a stick.

"Watch me without moving," instructed Anthony. "All of our beginning moves are defensive." He held the staff out in front of him, parallel to the floor, with both hands. He moved in a slow, graceful flow, making it look easy. He repeated the move several times, each time picking up a little speed, until finally he was at a normal pace.

"Now it is your turn," said Anthony.

The children eagerly held out their staffs parallel to the floor. Looks of anticipation showed on their faces. "Ready? Begin," Anthony instructed.

Staffs turned every which way, heads were knocked, elbows smacked, and knees cracked. Groans, moans, and, "Watch it," came from every mouth.

"Halt!" yelled Anthony. "Back to the starting position. Let's begin again but more slowly. Watch me." He turned his back to them and instructed, "Move your staff at the same speed as mine. Mimic my moves."

With looks of agitation, they followed orders and held out their staffs once more. The second go-around was much improved. No heads were knocked nor elbows smacked.

"Again!" commanded Anthony. The third time was even better. "Again!"

Anthony was speeding things up. "Again!" He pushed them, ordering, "One last time!"

The Protectors stopped the final exercise in unison.

"Perfect!" their instructor proclaimed. Smiles spread over their faces. They knew they had improved. Anthony was even smiling.

The Protectors took the next several minutes sparring with one another using the skills they had just learned. Anthony made some minor adjustments to techniques and staff positioning in each group, then he called for everyone's attention.

"It's almost time to switch stations. I want you to practice this maneuver tonight after dinner," he reminded them. "The Protection room is open at all times. You are welcome to come here at any time to practice. You will need to review the moves each evening to increase your muscle memory and not fall behind. It is better if you don't have to think and your body just knows how to react.

"At the end of your training, you will receive your assignments according to your skill level, so master this move with the staff and be ready to impress me tomorrow."

With this last instruction, the chime rang, and they switched stations. The Protectors believed Anthony's precision at ending his training showed his ability to sense the ringing of the chime. It was timed too perfectly.

When they switched stations, a different instructor stood waiting. This one was a bit older than Anthony and more easygoing. He introduced himself as Aaron and described the skill they would be learning at his station would be discus throwing. "At this time, each Protector will be throwing a discus toward a stationary target and they will progress to moving targets," said Aaron. "Remember, throwing distance is not as important to us as accuracy. Everyone can increase their strength but not everyone can hit a target." He spent several minutes demonstrating and showing them the proper way to throw and how to aim when releasing the discus. When each took a turn, no one hit the mark.

This is embarrassing, thought Maxwell. *How are we supposed to protect anyone when we can't even hit a still target, not to mention a moving enemy?* Disgust at their performance showed on every face by the time the chime rang. Aaron showed no disappointment in their performance, but he did tell them to practice tonight and it would take time.

By the time the Protectors had moved through all six stations, their spirits were about as low as they could go. They were at their last station when Maxwell glanced at the group beside them. He wondered if other countries were having as much difficulty as they were. One boy who was sparring with swords at his station caught his attention. It took him about eight seconds to disarm everyone's weapon in the group. With his teammates' weapons on the ground, he turned to face his instructor.

"How about you?" said the boy to his instructor. "Would you like to take a turn?"

Maxwell took a deep breath in. He couldn't believe the boy had the nerve to say that to an instructor, especially an instructor here. Before Maxwell could see what happened next, everything went black. When he awoke with a throbbing headache, all three Protectors were standing around him. He was told Gem had hit him in the head with a dense, weighted club while his attention was elsewhere.

"Sorry, Maxwell," apologized Gem. "That one got away from me. By the time I used my strength to heave it in the air, I noticed you weren't holding up your shield. I couldn't stop the forward motion."

They had been practicing deflecting blows using a shield. After the club incident, their instructor decided to dismiss them early. The four left the Protection room with their shoulders drooped and their self-esteems deflated. Jack was the most discouraged.

"We looked like a troupe of clowns!" exclaimed Jack. "I feel sorry for the person who gets us as Protectors."

"Don't be so dramatic," scolded Eden. "This is our first day. They don't expect us to be perfect. We shouldn't expect to be either."

"You should've seen the guy beside us," said Maxwell, taking Jack's side.

"I saw him, too," added Jack. "Who is that kid, and how is he that skilled with a sword at his age?"

"I didn't see him spar, but I noticed he behaves differently," added Gem. "He acts more grown up. Even the way he speaks. It's not like someone our age."

"I'm pretty sure that group was from Egypt," said Eden, disappointed she had missed everything.

"Maybe he's a prince or some kind of royalty," whispered Maxwell.

"I'm sure he wasn't *that* much better than us. I know how you boys exaggerate," interrupted Eden. "I did see the instructor reprimanding him for something."

"Wait until tomorrow; we'll show you how good he is then," said Jack. The girls rolled their eyes at precisely the same time, as only girls can do.

"We have just under an hour to spare before Flight training. I thought maybe we could visit the Hall of Records and see if we could find something interesting to look at," suggested Gem.

"I'm not doing any reading!" exclaimed Jack. "My brain needs a break."

"I think I'm with Jack," replied Maxwell. "Not to mention, my head still hurts. You girls go ahead, and we'll meet you on the flight deck in an hour."

"Maxwell, I'm so sorry I hit you," said Gem. "It was a total accident."

"I'll be fine," answered Maxwell. "Eventually." Jack snickered.

Gem grabbed hold of Eden. "Come on, Eden. Let's see what interesting things are waiting for us in the Hall of Records." The girls darted off while the boys took their time heading back to their room.

"Where is the Hall of Records?" asked Eden, walking down a corridor toward the GUST.

"I saw it listed on our schedule as a good place to spend free time. Let me check again for the location." Gem took her schedule out of her pocket. "It says Level Pi. We've never been on that floor." The girls hurried off toward the GUST.

6

Hall of Records

When the girls exited the GUST, they saw a sign pointing the way to the Hall of Records. They made their way down a long, wide hallway that smelled musty, like the basement in Gem's public library back home. They knew they were getting close. At the end of the corridor was a large, wooden door with beveled, smoky glass that couldn't be seen through. The girls opened the door.

When they walked into the room, they were standing in one of the largest enclosed rooms they had ever been in. Many workers behind an elongated desk were rushing this way and that, with what appeared to be too much work to do. Some were carrying very old scrolls, parchments, and Egyptian papyrus. Others had ancient writings on clay tablets and stones. Even more were shuffling books and thin metal panels in and out of shelves for their readers.

Standing at the desk, many Protectors and angels were asking for assistance finding material, but with so many workers, no one had long to wait. Someone waiting would ask a worker a question. The next moment, the worker's wings would whisk himself away to retrieve the requested information and then back again.

The girls walked slowly as they stared wide-eyed at all the coming and goings. After a few steps, it felt as if they had gone through some sort of vacuum. It was invisible to the eye, but they felt a brief suction as they passed through. They turned to examine the force. It looked like a translucent rolling wave stretching across the entire entrance. It reminded the girls of a distorted view of the desert on a hot day. There was definitely something there.

They overheard one inquirer, who spoke way too fast, requesting information on the galaxy Andromeda, specifically detailed pictures and specific dimensions of each planet. The worker didn't ask any questions to clarify; he just disappeared and returned so quickly it was difficult to comprehend if he ever left. The worker was holding one of the metal writing panels and handed it to the requestor. It didn't look as though it originated from Earth.

"Next!" shouted the same worker from behind the desk. A female Protector stepped forward.

"I'm looking for the coordinates of the Ark of the Covenant on Earth and how it came to arrive there," responded the Protector. The worker didn't disappear quite as quickly. He flew up to an area behind the desk and made his way down an aisle marked, "Heavenly Beings Only. No Protectors Allowed." The worker returned with two volumes tied in gold string.

"These volumes must remain in this Hall. They are not allowed past the force field. When you are through, return them to me," commanded the worker without glancing up.

"I've got to get back there and look at those books," whispered Eden as she grabbed Gem.

"Another time, Eden," replied Gem, pulling her away. "Plus, it says *No Protectors*. You're around the boys one day, and you start acting like them," scolded Gem. "Let's check out these other rooms in the Hall, and then we need to head on to Flight training."

The girls walked the area with looks of amazement, taking in the beauty of the Hall of Records. The ceiling, like all the other levels, had no light source, yet light abounded. Unlike other levels, it sparkled. Upon closer examination, which amounted to the girls just staring for a really long time, they noticed thousands of diamond clusters lit up and spread out sporadically on the ceilings. The girls had no way of knowing, but this ceiling was an exact replica of the nighttime view of the stars from one designated point on Earth. The point on Earth would change daily, so the observer's view of the ceiling would change as well.

"Is it possible this hall could have a ceiling filled with diamonds?" wondered Eden aloud. Gem thought anything was possible here but changed the subject when she saw what was on the wall in the next room.

"Look at all of these portraits," said Gem in amazement. Eden turned around to see life-size pictures of Protectors about their daily task of defending the human race.

"I'm glad I didn't have to fight this one!" exclaimed Eden as she pulled Gem up to the next portrait of a Protector battling some sort of being in the background. The being still had some human characteristics, but it was different, more distorted. Two soldiers dressed in WWII uniforms from opposing sides were fighting in the foreground. It was obvious it was a battle from long ago. The gold plate at the bottom titled the portrait, *The Defeat of Norris*.

"Who's Norris?" asked Gem.

"Beats me, but he looks like a bad fellow and someone I don't want to meet. I'm glad he was defeated," replied Eden. "The caption under *The*

Defeat of Norris reads, 'By Protector Alexander Justice.' That's amazing! One of us defeated this thing."

"Do you notice anything particular about Alexander Justice, Eden?" asked Gem. Gem studied the picture for a few more seconds and then fixed her gaze on Eden.

"He looks just like Maxwell," said Eden as quietly as possible. "Same eyes, same chin, almost the same face—even the same determined look. This is too long ago to be his dad; plus, the last name is different."

"Maybe it's his grandfather on his mother's side or a great uncle," suggested Gem. "This could be the 'history' Josiah referenced. This is more than chance. We have to show the guys."

"I wonder if any Protector portraits look like us," said Eden. The girls continued through the hall, looking at the many portraits and landscapes lining the walls.

"Wouldn't it be wonderful if we could visit some of these places and meet interesting people like this on our adventures?" asked Gem. "Can you imagine the stories the Protectors in these portraits could tell?"

"I know one place we'd better visit right away, and we'd better not be late," said Eden, pulling her partner away from the portraits.

7

Up in the Air

The boys ran into the girls at the entrance of flight instruction and all of them together, made their way into the training grounds. "How was the Hall of Records?" asked Maxwell sarcastically as he and Jack laughed at the thought.

"For your information, it was great," snapped Eden.

"Oh, yes, I'm sure it was marvelous," joked Jack, flipping his fingers forward like a proper lady waiting for her hand to be kissed. "Sir Maxwell, do let us work the Hall of Records into our schedule of free time."

"Yes, let's," replied Maxwell in the same tone of voice. The girls were so angry that they stomped off without ever mentioning the likeness of the portrait of Alexander to Maxwell. They had full intentions of dragging the boys to the Hall after class. Truth be told, the girls didn't even think of it again for some time.

A loud chime caught everyone's attention. By now, they realized this as the signal some classes used for the beginning of training. The Protectors formed a half circle around two individuals in the middle of the field.

"Good day, Protectors. Welcome to Flight training," said one of the leaders. "My name is Matthew. This is Michaela. We will be your instructors for this first level of flying."

"Flying is a crucial skill in your ability to protect your human," added Michaela. "Some of you will be natural-born flyers. Others will need to work a little harder and practice a little longer just to keep up." She looked at Gem when she said this. Gem made no reaction to the look, but she did wonder why Michaela cast her stare in her direction.

"It is imperative that you keep up with the other Protectors," continued Matthew. "This is one training that if you cannot maintain minimum abilities, you will be sent home. If you are an adequate flyer but not quite up to our standards, you will be assigned to a nonflying assignment, usually located here at Everwell. These assignments are just as important as the flying assignments, just less exciting . . . and you can continue to work on your flying skills to reach the minimum requirements and then be reassigned."

"So, pay careful attention, Protectors," continued Michaela. "On average, we usually send 10 percent of you home and assign 20 percent to nonflying details. Keep practicing, work hard, and I'm sure you will succeed. Any questions?"

One of the British girls raised her hand. Michaela already knew her name. "Yes, Katie?" said Michaela, pointing to her location in the crowd.

"How can we fly if we have no wings or power source?" asked Katie.

"Are you sure you have no wings, child?" queried Matthew, smiling.

"I'm pretty sure!" exclaimed Katie, taking a quick glance over her shoulder.

"I think each of you has more abilities than you ever dreamed possible," said Michaela.

Maxwell thought she might be talking about something other than wings. Puzzled looks flashed across every face in the group. They were all looking at each other's backs. No one had wings but the two instructors.

"We need to get everyone in four rows with arms stretched out horizontal to the ground for spacing. No hands should be touching," instructed Michaela. Each Protector hurried to get in rows with their friends. After a moment, the rows were complete and everyone's arms outstretched.

"Arms down!" commanded Michaela. Everyone's arms slapped against their sides.

"Today we will be learning the takeoff and landing," said Matthew. Excited voices began buzzing with this announcement. Matthew turned to face the same direction as the Protectors. Michaela continued to face the Protectors so they would have a front view as well as Matthew's back view.

"Elbows bent and tucked, hands not clenched but not flopping. Your hands must be ready to block, grab, and punch," instructed Michaela as she assumed the position she described in front of the group.

"Now the legs," said Matthew, turning his head around but with his back to the children. "Feet shoulder-length apart, knees slightly bent. Bend down into a half-crouching position and vault for the clouds with all your might."

A few Protectors jumped in the air before the instructors said to begin, but they barely cleared six inches. Most of the remaining Protectors snickered under their breath. It looked like they were playing Simon Says back on Earth, and several had just been eliminated.

"Before we begin practicing the takeoff, let's learn the correct form of landing," said Michaela, ignoring the slight distraction. "Assume the same shoulder-length stance as takeoff," she demonstrated. "You will touch down in this position with your legs slightly bent to absorb the shock of the landing. When you land in a wide stance, it is easier to take off in a run, as is sometimes necessary. This will also help keep your feet from tripping, which would be a problem if you were being chased or were doing the chasing."

"Let's try an actual jump where your feet leave the ground," instructed Matthew. "Watch me and do as I do but most of all . . . is everyone listening . . . go slow." Matthew walked them through the crouching takeoff position. He began counting down. "Three . . . two . . . one . . . jump!" he yelled.

Protectors were jumping like fleas all over the field. A couple inches here, four inches there, several were in the six-to-ten-inch range. Over and over, the Protectors jumped, only to come right back to where they began. It didn't take long for the complaining to begin: "All we're doing is jumping"; "I thought we were going to fly"; I saw flying in an earlier class." The instructors smiled at each other because this same grumbling happened each year with every new training group.

"Okay, land lovers, let's try this in the air," said Matthew, still smiling. "Everyone get back in your rows." Immediate silence fell on the group. The Protectors scrambled back to their original positions.

"First, we must uncover our wings," said Michaela.

About half the class glanced over their shoulders again to see if anything had suddenly appeared since their last look. Nothing. Puzzled faces returned to Michaela. She turned around, with her back facing the Protectors. Her wings were now gone.

"Watch and listen carefully," she instructed. She hunched her shoulders forward then crossed her arms in front of her body as if making a "X." While in this position, she kneeled down on one knee and a set of wings burst out. When the excitement in the room calmed down, Michaela continued, "Expand your shoulder blades out by pulling your shoulders forward. When you kneel down in this position, your wings will extend."

"Are you telling us we've had wings all along?" blurted our Ivy Dubois, one of the French Protectors who had raised her hand to be recognized but didn't wait to be called on.

"No," answered Michaela, "you have had your wings since you arrived here, but that doesn't mean you get to keep them. Flying is not as easy as it looks. If you cannot control your flight, you cannot keep your wings. Just to reiterate the previous warning, if you cannot keep up, you could be sent home or assigned to a stationary post. Difficulty with flight is an extreme disadvantage in battle, so Protectors, please pay attention."

"We will try to expand our wings together," instructed Matthew, who still had his wings within. "On the count of three, everyone pull your shoulders forward and kneel on one knee."

Eden glanced at Gem with a concerned expression. "Relax, you'll be fine," whispered Gem. She wished she could be certain all would be fine. The boys were all smiles. They could barely hold still; they were so excited.

"One, two, three!" said Matthew steadily. It sounded like a flock of birds had entered the room. Wings were protruding from nearly every back. Some had one wing in, one wing out. Other Protectors had half a wing out, caught somewhere in between.

Maxwell, Jack, and Gem had fully extended their wings. Eden had hers totally out, but one was folded under like it was broken. She was tremendously distressed over her condition. Gem ran over to Eden and unfolded the wing. It sprang upward as if there had never been a glitch.

"See, no worries," said Gem as she straightened the wing and gave a caring smile. Eden mouthed a thank you. Matthew and Michaela walked around the group, fixing the many wing issues the Protectors presented. The instructors walked back to the front of the group.

"Our first exercise will be a simple vertical lift about fifteen feet off the ground," instructed Michaela as she turned her back to the crowd to demonstrate. "A simple vertical flap, up and down, is all that is needed to produce lift. Not too fast. We do not want anyone to get too high on his or her first flight. When you reach the desired height, slow the up and down motion, and you will slow up. Then, start to descend. If you stop the motion altogether, you will fall. Protectors, pay attention to your wing movements. Again, go slowly and do not go too high in case you have problems navigating. Once again, we will count down to one. Ready? Three . . . two . . . one . . . jump!"

The next instant, approximately half the group actually left the ground. Of the half that did leave the ground, some looked like bottle rockets flying out of control in a fireworks warehouse. Protectors were flying up, then down. Some went up, then immediately turned and crashed headfirst in the ground. Others went up, then landed bottom first; some belly flopped the landing; a few tipped sideways. A couple of children even flapped their wings horizontally instead of vertically. They flew across the room, spinning sideways like a cartwheel, and crashed into other Protectors, knocking all to the ground.

Of the half that left the ground, three had shot so high they were now out of sight. About ten had succeeded in attaining the correct height, but coming down proved to be more difficult than going up.

Maxwell and Jack came down too quickly and toppled when they landed. Gem somehow managed to tip forward on her way down and landed on her belly. Eden was the only one of her group who did a perfect ascent and descent. When she landed, Eden bent over and helped Gem to her feet.

"How'd you do that?" said Gem laughing.

"I was just lucky," replied Eden with a smile. Both of the guys scrambled to their feet. They congratulated Eden on a great flight and also asked her how she did it.

"Let's try it again, trainees!" announced Michaela before Eden could answer. "Those of you who left the ground but had trouble landing, move to the right of the room so Matthew can work with you on takeoff and landing. Meanwhile, I will work on takeoff and stability

with the second group. The four of you who were able to take off and land with no problems will assist me with the second group. Please come forward."

Eden wondered if she was one of the four. She looked up at Michaela and noticed her motioning her forward with the other three. Eden slowly made her way to the front.

As Michaela was grouping the Protectors in lines, the three trainees who had shot out of sight came plummeting to the ground and landed in heaps. They had been forgotten in all the confusion. None of them moved, but groans of pain could be heard.

"Call the healers," instructed Matthew to his assistants as he pointed to the adjoining room at the edge of the field with a yellow halo on the door. Two of his assistants immediately flew to the room and returned with three healers.

They were dressed in light blue scrubs with yellow halos over the left side of their chest. The healers were followed by what looked like white-water rafts from back home, but they were flatter and smaller, more like a soft surfboard with raised edging. The boards were self-floating, air-inflated body transports and the same color as the healer's scrubs and had the same yellow halo on the top; one had arrived for each patient. The transports responded to the healer's instructions. When the transports were told to pick up a patient, they would float over to the body's location, dissolve around it, and materialize underneath. The transport would then rise in the air with the patient in tow. The healers quickly returned to the room at the edge of the field with the transports, now carrying the patients, following behind.

"Let this be a lesson to you all," lectured Matthew. "We are not here to play. When in the air, always err on the side of caution and fly carefully. Your life and the lives of those you protect depend on your being qualified to do your duty. Now, let's get back in our groups."

Maxwell, Jack, and Gem made their way to the right side of the room with half the class. Eden returned to the front with Michaela and the other three assistants.

"Let's try the same takeoff and landings again," instructed Matthew. They finished the two hours of Flight training going over and over this same exercise. By the end of class, all four were comfortable in their starting and stopping abilities.

The four Protectors made their way back to their living quarters at a much slower pace than they kept at the beginning of their day.

"I thought we weren't supposed to get tired," complained Maxwell.

"Or hurt," added Jack.

"We never said it would be painless." The children jumped, startled by the voice coming from behind them. "First day is always a struggle," encouraged Deborah, the training coordinator. "It's an adjustment your body will make soon enough." She smiled as she surveyed the children's condition.

"I hope the adjustment is over soon," replied Maxwell. "I'm starving and exhausted."

"Grab some dinner and take it easy tonight. You will wake in the morning refreshed and renewed. I promise," said Deborah as she walked past the four down the corridor.

The four decided to go on to dinner without going to their rooms. Eating was a blur. The food was delicious, and they did feel better after eating, but all anyone could concentrate on was getting back to their rooms to sleep.

The four returned to their rooms, exchanged good nights, and closed their doors. Maxwell collapsed into his bed without even changing his clothes. "Turn on the darkness, will you, Jack?" mumbled Maxwell. After no response, Maxwell looked over toward Jack's bed. He was already out cold lying on his belly on top of his covers. Maxwell smiled. "Don't bother, I've got it." Maxwell crawled out of bed and flipped on the switch.

8

The Other Side

itch-black darkness wrapped around Norris like a blanket—just the way he liked it. *Where are Dover and Zantos?* They had left over an hour ago to confirm the rumors another Justice had shown up in the Protector ranks. Norris heard someone creepily approaching.

"It's true," spoke a raspy voice from a face Norris could not see. It is perpetually dark in the Manip's world, just as it is forever light in the Protector's world. Norris recognized the voice as one of his reasonably loyal minions, Dover. Norris snapped a shadow stick so he could see the expression of his underling. (A shadow stick is similar to our glow stick on Earth, but it illuminates with a red glimmering that is invisible to Protectors' eyes.) The red glow is so dark, there are days when even Norris struggles to see while using one. Today was not one of those days.

"Another Justice is among them," interjected Zantos while eagerly watching his chief for any sign of anguish upon the delivery of this news.

"They obviously have not learned their lesson," replied Norris with no emotion. Dover and Zantos laughed in their sinister way. Both of Norris's underlings had been working with him since his demotion from second in command to a simple chief-Manip. Every being working on this side is in a League of Manips (short for Manipulators). They all have characteristics and personalities that take delight in causing discomfort in any form—both physical and mental—to human beings. They are the complete opposite of the Protectors, who are, in every way, good. The Protectors try to prevent harm to humans; the Manips try to cause harm. You get the idea. It made Norris nauseous to even think about the offspring of Alexander Justice in Everwell learning to protect and help others, thereby ruining his life further than his/her relative had already done.

Norris had been a golden child for the other side. None had been more wicked—except for Recco himself—who was the controller of all the Manips. He wasn't the manager or the leader. No, he was the controller because that is exactly what he did. He controlled them.

Norris's parents had died when he was three. Since he had no extended family, he was raised by an uncle named Gastoff (who was really not an uncle). Gastoff was a next-door neighbor who took Norris, merely for the monthly payout from the state, and raised him to be his servant. Uncle Gastoff, as he liked to be called, never showed young Norris any love or kindness. Any time Norris was at home, Gastoff tore him down, telling him how worthless he was. Hate grew in young Norris's heart like a weed that would not die.

Recco had been secretly observing Norris since he started school. He showed all the signs of an unhappy child: not many friends, poor concentration at school, the desire to stay away from home as much as possible, and often feeling sick. Recco knew he had potential as a future Manip.

With limited positive influences in his life to steer him toward a brighter future, Norris was nearly a sure thing.

The one positive aspect to Norris's life was his dear friend, Samuel Miller, who had been there for him since kindergarten. Sam's parents had five children, and Sam was the youngest. His parents were barely making ends meet; even with the mother staying home to manage the kids and his dad working two jobs, they were living week to week. Growing up, Norris and Sam were in the same limited situation where money was concerned but there was a significant difference. Uncle Gastoff spent all the money the state gave him to raise Norris on gambling at the racetrack every weekend, whereas Sam's parents' money went towards the basic needs and education of their children.

Neither child had anything extra. Sam would half his lunch with Norris while in elementary school, which is probably what kept Norris alive. But then Norris's thinking became twisted, and he started resenting Sam for helping, reasoning he provided the food that kept him alive to endure Gastoff's abuse.

Norris also felt resentment for Sam's parents for not taking him in. As a child, Norris would dream about being part of Sam's family. He didn't care that they had few material possessions. They loved their children, which was all Norris wanted. Sam's parents didn't know Gastoff was not Norris's real uncle when the two met in grade school. If they had realized the abuse, they would have taken Norris in, no matter how dire their own circumstance.

Whatever the defining reason, Norris began hanging out with the wrong crowd in middle school. He didn't need half of Sam's lunch anymore because he stole anyone's lunch he wanted. He cared not about the consequences of his actions. When he was with his new friends, he began teasing Sam over the worn-out hand-me-down clothes and sneakers he wore to school. It didn't matter that his clothes were no better.

By the time Norris was in high school, a deep bitterness had taken hold of his heart. He was in charge of the bullies, and without even realizing it, he was getting closer and closer to something dreadful. Norris stole anything left unattended, picked on anyone smaller or more unfortunate, and was repeatedly suspended from school. The principal knew his home life was not ideal, but Norris's second chances were running low. The end of his trickery came when Norris was caught trying to steal from his teacher's purse while she was at lunch. She had left her purse in her desk, and the vice-principal walked in on him in the act. Norris was caught red-handed, so he was called into the principal's office and expelled for good. Recco decided this was the time to make his move.

Recco sent Nyr, one of his henchmen, out of the underworld to fetch Norris. Nyr appeared in the middle of the night on the street outside Norris's house. Gastoff wasn't home from drinking and gambling yet, so Norris was alone in the house. He knew he had a beating coming when Gastoff returned home and discovered his expulsion from school. Norris heard noises outside and presumed Gastoff had returned early. He looked out the window and panicked, trying to decide if he should hide or quickly run away, but Gastoff's car wasn't in the driveway. He crouched down and hid his face as the front door blasted off its hinges. There stood the scariest looking creature Norris could ever have imagined.

When Norris arrived in the underworld, he was terrified. Recco gave him a choice. He could return immediately to the life he was living, or he could accept the gift of power, control, and dominance over others. Recco explained how they would entice and manipulate both the prideful put-ons and the predatory humans into carrying out their wishes.

"It's really quite easy to recruit them," said Recco. "It's the ones who don't label their actions as good who are the toughest. They aren't kind to one another because it gets them praise and attention; they do it because they think it's the right thing to do." Recco shivered at the thought of them. He quickly changed the subject back to Norris. "I can assure you, once you have honed your skills of deception over others, the power and control will be exhilarating."

Norris knew there was no decision to make. His mind was easily made up. Of course he would accept. What fool wouldn't? *Well . . . Sam probably wouldn't*, thought Norris. Norris quickly shook this thought from his head and enthusiastically accepted Recco's proposal. As he cut his hand to seal the deal in blood, he couldn't shake the thought, *Like I said, what fool wouldn't? . . . Only a fool like Sam.*

9

The Advancement of Norris

The Manips normally weren't rotated back and forth from their earthly life to the underworld like the Protectors who moved between assignments and Earth. Transitioning back to Earth was too difficult for Manipulators. They couldn't let go of the power and control they wielded over others and return to normal life. It wasn't part of a Protector's demeanor to care about controlling others, so going back to their homes was something they looked forward to each rotation.

Norris thought he had no one to go back to, so he never wanted to return. He trained relentlessly and then trained even harder. Pride shown on his face, as he knew he was excelling. Recco would smirk as he watched Norris strike down other Manips. Norris knew he was special because he was handpicked by Recco, the "Overlord" himself, which no other Manip could boast. His quick movement up the ranks of the underworld supported his belief.

By Norris's third year, he was in charge of all new recruits and many of the experienced Manips as he got promoted to lieutenant general. Jealousy flared through the ranks as Manips congregated together to tittle-tattle: "Who does this Norris think he is? He's no more evil than the rest of us. What's so special about him?"

The veteran Manips plotted Norris's demise, but they faced one major problem. Norris was under the watchful eye of Recco, and no one dare lay a finger on him. Recco ruled the underworld with a type of fear and pain that would course through every nerve ending of your body if he was not pleased. The older Manips stood down—for now.

Norris never saw Recco's wrath when he first joined the League of Manips because Recco and his underlings, during their first assemblies, only showed Norris the intoxicating power and control available to him. Norris found out later this is how all new recruits are treated. They are misled to believe they will be all-powerful, but in reality, they are only carrying out Recco's bidding, not their own plans. To put it simply, they are Recco's slaves. When an assignment fails due to a disruption caused by the Protectors, all Manips involved feel Recco's wrath. Slowly, the pain of the Overlord's anger began to creep in—even on Norris.

Norris had lived with pain for most of his childhood, so he adjusted to his new role rather quickly. While growing up, his hurt had been more emotional, but given the choice, he would have chosen physical pain because then he would have been removed from Gastoff's house by the state. Mentally, Norris was beaten down throughout his childhood, and Recco capitalized on this weakness. He would throw tantrums that reminded Norris of Gastoff. The worst part of Recco's tantrums was the quakes of fear he caused you to feel. After one of his worst episodes, Norris's body would convulse, out of control. Norris only had to withstand a light dose of Recco's rage to know it was almost more than he could bear.

Norris would sometimes wonder if he had made the wrong choice in becoming a Manip. He would think about Sam on Earth and wonder what path his life was taking. They would've both been out of school by now and perhaps roommates in a college somewhere. Norris had tried to check in on Sam a few times, but he could never locate him. This was very odd because normally Manips can find anyone. Perhaps he was hiding from Norris, or more likely, someone was hiding him. Either way, it was strange. Norris scolded himself for this ridiculous daydreaming. He didn't want to fall into "what if "scenarios again. He knew he had made the only choice available to himself, and he would have to make the best of it.

Norris continued his reign as the golden Manip for another ten years, but his preferred status fell apart in Recco's view after one very important assignment. It happened during the Second World War while Hitler was in power over Germany. His armies were toppling countries one after another with many innocent lives being lost, either in battle or by extermination because of their nationality. Norris's task was simple but vital. He was to oversee the success of Hitler's grand evil plan and disrupt any counterattacks of the Allies. The only end result Recco would accept was Hitler's world domination. Norris's prime objective was to thwart any attempt by the Protectors to aid the Allies.

Norris and his underlings were effective in their battles as numerous Protectors lost their lives as well as the lives of those they were protecting during the beginning of the war. Norris was having quite a string of victories and continued his steady climb up the Manip chain of command until everything changed when the war reached Britain.

Norris had incredible ideas on how to crush this small island country. He knew their citizens would surely crumble like all the others. Norris made sure he was in on every meeting of Hitler's high command and he would be the little voice in their heads giving them strategic ideas on how to proceed. All his extra effort was going according to his plan—until it wasn't.

Norris paid attention when the defeat of this country was taking longer than it should have. His plans were becoming less and less effective. The Nazis would come up with a strategic maneuver, and Britain would counter with a better move. If the Nazis attacked a beach, the British were waiting on them. When they would fly a bombing raid at night, they would miss their intended targets. It was as if the Allies knew the Axis plans before they were executed.

Battle followed battle with always the same result: no victory and no surrender. The British would lose soldiers and planes, but the Nazis lost more. It was taking a toll. Hitler stopped listening to the voice inside him, which was Norris. He began listening to one advisor, then another, then another. Nothing was working. He began getting conflicting information: "Attack the weak area on the western side"; or "An air invasion is the only feasible plan"; and "Keep up the night bombing; wear them down."

Hitler grew weary of the tiresome battle with this little country. He decided to open a second front, attacking the eastern side of Europe and Russia. Norris knew this was a mistake, but he could not get Hitler to heed his inner voice. Eventually, Hitler split his army, which weakened both of his front lines. By December of 1941, the Russians had chased the Axis fighters out of Moscow, and America had entered the war. *What else can go wrong? Something out of the ordinary is happening to make such a dramatic turnaround in the war—but what?* Norris had no idea, but he knew something beneath the surface had caused a shift.

Battles were fought. New offensives were launched. Ground was gained; ground was lost. As months went by, the war was looking grim for Hitler and the Axis powers. By March of 1945, US troops had crossed the Rhine River, and by April, the Soviets had Berlin surrounded. Hitler took his own life later that month, and Germany surrendered to the Western Allies and the Soviets in May of 1945. Fury tore through Recco at the loss of the war. And most of his rage fell on Norris.

10

The Reason for Victory

Norris found out several weeks after the initial turnaround in the war that a new Protector had entered the ranks of his enemies. He had also discovered his identity: Alexander Justice. Norris had his underlings gather information on this new Protector. He was a skinny teenager who was tall for his age, and the only weakness that could be found was his affinity for chocolate—especially Hershey bars, plain with no almonds. (The almonds just took up space where more chocolate could be.) But even Norris couldn't find a viable plan to exploit chocolate as a weakness. He decided his only choice was to be more cunning and devious. Norris knew he was capable of victory.

Alexander was assigned to Britain during WWII. His protection assignment was a young German scientist by the name of Alfred Mauser who had lived in Britain most of his adult life. Mauser's older brother, Thomas, who still lived in Germany, was assigned to the Axis powers intelligence squad, but he had grown disheartened from witnessing the senseless killings of the innocent.

Thomas began smuggling secrets to his brother, who in turn sent them to British intelligence by leaving anonymous packages. The packages contained diagrams for new Nazi weaponry, an outline of areas most likely to be bombed next, and the locations of fuel and supply storages. The British never found out where the information came from, only that it was very reliable and accurate.

British intelligence had a code name for the mysterious man whom they could never identify who dropped off packages filled with valuable information. They called him "Cousin Alfie." When Mauser would send the information to a secure place, British intelligence would contact Prime Minister Churchill and tell him, "Cousin Alfie left you another package."

Alexander watched for any members of the Axis military who seemed to be turning away from their barbaric behavior. He made opportunities available for them to work as double agents and help the Allies. Many Germans were against the Nazis and contributed to Hitler's ultimate defeat. Alexander located dissenters early and presented opportunities for them to help.

This one Protector was driving Norris insane. As each day went by, his plans for victory crumbled. His inferior Manips were no equal to Justice's sword skill or his ability to expose the war's atrocities committed by the Axis powers to concerned observers who could change their loyalties. Norris once heard a member of his crew refer to Justice as "Alexander the Great." *How dare they bring glory to any Protector!* Needless to say, Recco had that Manip for supper the next day, and I don't mean as a guest.

Recco pressured Norris to put an end to this Protector who was single-handedly winning the war for the Allies. "This will fall on you if the war is lost. He should've been eliminated months ago," bellowed Recco in Norris's face. It was obvious to Norris that if he wanted to salvage this war, he must get more personally involved in Justice's capture. His opportunity came sooner rather than later.

Alexander knew the war was coming to a close. If he could help the Allies land one more crushing blow, it would be over. He decided to pay another visit to Axis headquarters, which he had done undetected all along. He noticed more Manips than usual guarding the Axis leaders. They must be planning something big. He would need to be careful.

Without spending too much time on the details—which will be told later, and what a grand story it is, indeed—Alexander was caught off guard while at Axis headquarters and Norris captured him and his sword. Alexander was able to devise an escape but could not retrieve his weapon. Norris had laid claim on his sword but with a price. When Norris picked up the sword, it had seared both of his hands.

When Norris and the Manips were back in camp after letting Alexander slip from their grasp, Recco was furious. He nearly strangled Norris to death upon first receiving the news. After a few tense moments with Manips watching, wide-eyed and silent, Recco released his grip on Norris.

"I gave you two tasks to complete, Norris," growled Recco as he furrowed his brow in anger. "Assist the Nazi leader in winning the war and bring me the Justice Protector. You accomplished neither! You had the Protector and let him escape!" Recco circled Norris like a wolf before the kill as he spoke.

Norris's hands still throbbed with pain from the burn he received while picking up Alexander's sword, but the pain from the burn Norris could bear. The real agony was the mark that had been left on both his palms. It was the crest of the Protectors from the hilt of Alexander's sword and was forever engraved into the skin of a Manip. Norris knew if Recco found out he carried this mark on the inside of his hands, he would kill him immediately.

After Recco finished inflicting the highest level of pain a body could stand without dying, he demoted Norris to a chief Manip. This is the lowest entry level a Manip commander can be, but Norris didn't care. He was glad to be alive.

The only good outcome from the demotion was Norris's acquisition of two new assistants, Dover and Zantos. They looked up to Norris like he was a hero, who only had to speak a command and they would obey. They held nearly the same rank as Norris but were too dumb to question his commands. They followed him blindly.

Recco promoted Spear as the new lieutenant general of the Manips. He was a newcomer to the Manip commanding ranks who Norris had always suspected of maneuvering for his position. Norris's past assistants, Vince and Colden, were now assisting Spear, and he could have them. *They were as loyal as a black widow spider,* thought Norris. He knew they would betray Spear as soon as the opportunity presented itself. They were his problem now.

In the ranks of the Manipulators, it's an ongoing threat to be replaced by a subordinate. To Norris's knowledge, there had never been a demotion. Recco always eliminated the Manip, so the position could be easily filled. Norris had held the position of lieutenant general longer than anyone else since Recco had become boss. Perhaps this was the reason Recco spared his life. Deep down, Norris knew better. He knew that more likely they were saving him for a future assignment to be used as expendable bait in a snare.

Nevertheless, he can still call himself a Manip—a demoted Manip with a scar on each hand but still a Manip. Norris hung Alexander's sword above the mantle in his doldrum (living quarters and rendezvous point for each team of Manips while on assignment). Norris had to use metal grips to hang the sword since, obviously, Manips cannot touch Protectors' swords. He wanted the weapon to serve as a constant reminder that one day this Justice Protector would pay for his humiliation. When Norris had finished with him, he would wish he had never heard of the Protectors.

11

The Next Day

Maxwell awoke to find Jack already dressed and watching the wall of his home in Jackson Hole, Wyoming. "Did I over-sleep?" said Maxwell while stretching and rubbing his eyes. Without realizing it, he was watching Jack's wall, too.

"No, you're fine," replied Jack. "I was just hoping to catch a glimpse of Mom or the other me back home. It's kinda weird how life back home just rolls on, even though we are here."

"I don't really understand it all either, but I'm sure we will figure it out in time," reassured Maxwell as he got out of bed. "I need to check on my home in Michigan, too. My island is a bit small, so I should see someone I know." He picked up the controller and turned on his wall.

It was early in the morning on Mackinac Island, and not many people were on the streets. The ferry docks were busy in preparation for the day's passengers. "There's Brad Conley at work already," said Maxwell as he watched him sweeping the deck at Shepler's Ferry dock. "He was my brother's best friend before the accident."

"What accident?" questioned Jack as he left his side of the room and walked over to Maxwell's.

Maxwell didn't answer immediately. He never spoke about his brother to anyone. He mentally scolded himself for mentioning his brother out loud. He decided he had opened the door, and since it was Jack, he would go ahead and walk through.

"My older brother was killed in an accident when I was younger," said Maxwell. "One winter he fell through the ice on Lake Huron." Jack continued looking at Maxwell but said nothing. "Brad really took it hard, as hard as all of us. He blamed himself for not being with Benjamin when he started home. He was a good friend to my brother. He was even pretty nice to me, too, tagging along all the time."

On Maxwell's wall, the streets of Mackinac Island got busier. Both boys watched the scene, lost in their own thoughts. The drays being pulled by the teams of horses were being loaded with goods from the ferries to be delivered to Main Street's businesses.

"We'd better get moving," said Maxwell, breaking the silence and turning off his wall. "Don't forget about the meeting tonight. Maybe we can get answers to some of these questions that keep popping up all around us. We want to make sure we stay clear of that Recco or whoever is killing Protector trainees."

"We need to come up with a plan for tonight. I don't want to take any chances," replied Jack. "We need more cover than we had a couple nights ago, and we need to be able to hear better."

"Maybe we could check out the meeting room ahead of time," added Maxwell. "We might find somewhere inside the room to hide so we won't miss any of the details." Jack shook his head in agreement as they heard a knock at the door.

It was the girls. "Guys, you ready?" said Eden.

"In a minute," answered Maxwell. The boys jumped out of their pajamas and into their training clothes and went to open the door.

"We're ready to eat!" said Jack as he swung open the door so quickly that it startled the girls.

"You're always ready to eat," said Gem as she shoved Jack for scaring them. "Did you guys do any reading from your books last night?"

"We both read about an hour before bed," added Eden.

"Uhhhh . . . yeah . . . of course we read," stammered Maxwell as he glanced at Jack to play along. The girls chatted on about how they read this and the other read that and how it would help them during training. The boys nodded in agreement at the girls, then smiled at each other in silence. They decided it would be better to remain quiet and let the girls talk amongst themselves so they wouldn't be asked too many questions.

While at breakfast, Eden couldn't help but notice the beauty surrounding her. It had been too much for her to take in during the first couple of days, but now she saw how the walls of the dining hall were covered with small mosaic tiles. When you stood back and looked at the tiles, you saw, mixed in intermittently, scenes of Protectors in their day-to-day duties: saving children from dangers, delivering meals for the hungry, and providing companionship to the elderly. More scenes than you had time to count were depicted. Eden hoped that one day her picture would be up on that wall. Then she rethought, *Maybe that's something a Protector shouldn't want.*

She didn't want to forget a saying she had learned on the first day of training: "It's not about you; it's about whom you are protecting." Gradually, Eden realized her initial thought was okay. To her, it wasn't about the glory. She really hoped one day she would be on one of the tiles because that would mean she had helped make a difference and made things better. Jack broke her concentration.

"Eden, you've got to try this." He tore off a piece of bread and handed it to her. "It's Exodus bread. It tastes great!" Jack was mumbling because his mouth was stuffed with bread. Jack took another piece for himself as soon as Eden had taken the piece into her hand. The bread was a brown color, similar to wheat bread on Earth, but it had a sweet, sparkling coating over the top. Eden took a small bite. She wasn't a fan of wheat bread back home, but the Exodus bread was the sweetest, most satisfying bread she had ever eaten. The four Protectors enjoyed their meals more each time they ate. They would have to be careful and not overeat. With food this appetizing, it was difficult to control yourself.

The four were sitting beside the Australian Protectors at breakfast. They had enjoyed the Exodus bread as much as the Americans. Proper introductions were made. Everyone knew Thomas and Nicholas from Rescue training, and the girls were named Christina and Kelly. Maxwell and Jack took the opportunity to get in some ribbing on Thomas and Nicholas about their spills in Rescue training.

Maxwell noticed Kelly staring at him long enough to make him feel uncomfortable. He glanced away, then back. She was still staring. He returned the stare.

"Maxwell, what is your last name?" questioned Kelly.

"O'Malley," he answered.

She responded with a disappointed expression. "Oh, okay. You look so much like a portrait we saw of a famous Protector, we thought you might be related," said Kelly. "But I guess not. You have different last names." Before Maxwell could ask the Protector's name, the Australians excused themselves and left for training.

"We saw the same portrait, Maxwell," said Eden. "It was a picture in the Hall of Records. I don't remember his name, but he is the spitting image of you." As they left for Rescue, Maxwell decided he would make time today to check out that portrait.

12

To Maxwell's Surprise

"Welcome back to Rescue training, Protectors," said Collin with a smile on his face. His smile made the young Protectors wonder what he had planned for the day. "This week we are concentrating on rescuing during falls. Your training will include how to prevent falls and how to recover your human with as little damage as possible when prevention is not an option. This training will help you handle accidents of every variety. We will not be saving humans from other high-risk humans this rotation. That will be covered more in Protection training. Only accidents will be covered while you are here this time. We will start small and work up to major accidents. Weatherly, what lucky volunteers will be demonstrating and assisting us first?"

"Maxwell O'Malley and Jack Lewis," answered Weatherly while looking down his list. A snicker could be heard from the Australians. Maxwell and Jack looked over to see Thomas and Nicholas pointing at them while mouthing, "Your turn." Maxwell and Jack stood up and walked nervously to the front of the room.

"Relax, boys," said Weatherly, detecting their uneasiness. "Today is snow and ice. It'll almost be fun." With that, he sneaked them a wink. The center of the room immediately transformed into a slippery slope of ice and snow. Jack began sliding down the hill, out of control, legs wide apart on skis (and he was from Wyoming; he knew how to ski).

"Let's watch as Maxwell tries to save Jack. Then, as a group, we will critique his rescue," instructed Weatherly.

Jack lost sight of the group and of Maxwell. He thought there must be a coating of ice on the snow because he seemed to be picking up speed, even though he was trying hard to slow down. He noticed how quickly the tree line of the newly appearing forest was approaching. He hoped Maxwell wouldn't try the tree branch rescue the Australians attempted previously.

Maxwell saw Jack slipping down the slope as soon as their environment turned to snow. He assessed the situation quickly, then remembered his training. He grabbed the back of Jack's shirt to keep him on his feet, but they were moving too quickly down the hill.

He could only think of two options. He could pull back on Jack's clothes and try to reverse the momentum by using his wings, or he could try to turn Jack sideways and slowly dig his skis into the snow to stop him. Maxwell decided, without much debate, that his wing skills were too limited. He just didn't have confidence he would be able to fly in reverse. Option two seemed more doable. If only Maxwell had known there was way too much frozen ice on top of the snow to be able to ski successfully.

Maxwell tried to steer Jack's legs toward the side instead of straight forward, but he underestimated how slick the snow and ice were. When he grabbed Jack to turn him, he turned too far, making Jack face backwards, still sliding down the hill.

"*Maaaxxxwell*!" screamed Jack as he continued sliding out of control, backwards. He was only able to remain standing due to Maxwell's hold on his shirt, which Maxwell quickly lost hold of when he flipped him back around forward. As soon as Maxwell lost his hold, Jack fell face-first into the snow and slid another twenty feet on his belly due to the ice. By the time the two Protectors got their bearing and realized what had happened, they were back in front of the group with the snow nowhere to be seen. Jack was still lying facedown on his belly, and Maxwell was trying to pull him up by his shirt.

No snickers could be heard this time. The class had burst into outright laughter. Even Collin and Weatherly were trying to control the smiles on their faces. Collin gained his composure first.

"Trainees, attention!" said Collin. No one stopped laughing. "Protectors, I need your attention!" he repeated while pounding on his podium. The group quickly hushed, though many were still showing silent signs of amusement. "Who has suggestions for assisting in this type of snow and ice?" questioned Collin.

"Trip them," joked Jacob from the United Kingdom.

"That would certainly stop them," replied Collin. "Any other suggestions that don't involve falling on your face?"

"Fly in front, face the victim, and push against them?" ventured Norio, one of the Protectors from Japan.

"Quite a splendid example," said Collin. "All of you are more skilled at flying forward at this stage of your training, so use your strengths. What matters is that you are successful. Make the rescue yours. Every situation will be different. The more experience you have, the better Protector you will become."

"Now, Protectors, let's pair up and have everyone work on snow and ice spills," instructed Weatherly. "When you are finished with one rescue, switch places with your partner and do it again. Get in groups of eight; we will have four stations. Rotate turns within your group. Take chances in your attempts. Don't be afraid to fail. This is how we learn."

The Protectors got into their groups and took turns running through the rescues. Collin and Weatherly flew continuously around them, taking notes and offering constructive recommendations. With several minutes left in training, Collin and Weatherly turned off the ice slope and had everyone return to their seats.

"Before we dismiss today's training, we have one more topic to touch on," started Collin. "It is called the Last Resort Rescue. It is a fail-safe healing option available at all times, which will prevent the death of any Protector.

"You have, no doubt, already heard that if you are killed during your protection assignment, your human life on Earth will simultaneously perish. Many of the past Protectors who have sat in your seats have asked us, how your stand-in, who is still on Earth, would die. It would happen by some random accident; your earth-bound self would not just drop to the ground. Your work here is completely camouflaged to those on Earth.

"If you are critically injured while on assignment and have no time to return to Everwell, you have one life-saving technique that can heal a Protector of any injury, but it comes at a cost."

All the Protectors were dead silent. Weatherly paused so Collin could take his turn: "Another Protector can use a Protector sword to slice off the bottom tip of your wing," said Collin as the Protectors winced with the thought of cutting their wing. "A clear, gel-like fluid will drip from the wing. Apply this fluid to the injury, and you will be healed immediately and transported back to your earthly life. Since you cannot cut your own wing, due to the strength needed to perform this action, you will need your partner with you—or at least another Protector."

Collin paused and looked at the Protectors before he continued, "After your wing is cut and the gel extracted, you can never again return to being a Protector." The Protectors gasped.

"When each of you arrived at our training facility, you received your wings without even knowing it," added Weatherly. "Inside each of those wings is an extension of your life force, which allows you to survive here. You do not need much sleep, much to eat, or even oxygen to breathe. This life force even allows you to fly. It also has healing properties from within, but with a critical life-threatening wound, it must physically touch the injury. After this life force is gone from your wings, your capability to remain a Protector and the abilities that come with the role are gone for your lifetime. You will still have your earthly life to live, the preservation of which is the ultimate goal when using your wing's life force. We will cover this in more detail and demonstrate to everyone the technique of Last Resort Rescue after you have served for several rotations and your assignments get more dangerous. We hope you will never have to use it."

"Protectors, you have made much progress today," added Collin. "We are proud of your effort. We will see you tomorrow." With that, training was dismissed.

"I'm glad we have some time before Messaging," said Jack. "Do you want to go back to the room and see if we can locate our families on our wall? I never did find mine this morning."

"No, go ahead without me," answered Maxwell while leaning toward Jack so he could whisper the next part. "I'm going to check out the room where the meeting will be held tonight. I'll see if I can find us some better hiding places."

"I'll go with you," said Jack.

"No, go on back to the room," replied Maxwell. "It'll look more suspicious with both of us lurking around. Not to mention, it's easier to get caught if there's two. If I get caught, I can always say I'm lost."

"Okay," replied Jack, "but if you're not back in thirty minutes, I'm coming to look for you."

"Deal," said Maxwell. The girls, who had been in a conversation of their own, walked over to the guys.

"We'll meet you in Messaging," said Eden. "We have some reading we want to do before training." The boys agreed, and the girls went on their way. They decided to wait until the girls were out of sight before they left.

"Listen, Jack, let's make a change of plans," said Maxwell. "I can't get that portrait in the Hall of Records out of my head. Why don't we make a fast trip up there and check that out first? It's probably nothing. After we take a quick peek, I'll go check out the room, and you can check on your family."

"Let's go," said Jack, excited at the suggestion.

The boys stepped off the GUST and their first reaction to the Hall of Records was identical to the girls, mouths open in awe. They both walked through the force field, which only slightly blew their short hair. They, like the girls, looked up to find the origin of the breeze but saw nothing until they completely passed through and looked behind them. Puzzled, they kept walking forward while still staring back at the force field. They watched angels flying back and forth, retrieving volumes for the patrons standing at the counter. Maxwell and Jack stood behind some of these individuals, eavesdropping as they were requesting information.

Maxwell noticed the African Protectors, who had been beside him and Jack in Flight training, getting a volume at the front of the line. "Here is your publication on immediate level flying," said the angel behind the desk.

"Thank you for your assistance," replied one of the young Africans.

I need to introduce myself to them, thought Maxwell. *They were one of the groups who were exceptional at flight. Maybe they could help us with our technique.* Maxwell and Jack strolled past the desk but stopped, turned, and listened several times when subjects caught their attention.

"City of Atlantis will need to remain in the Hall of Records," said the worker angel to another Protector. "You will need to read it here, but take all the time you need."

"*Building of the Pyramids* will need to remain in the Hall of Records," said another worker angel as they handed over the volume. Again, the same instruction was given.

"Wow, both of those books sound really interesting, and I don't even like to read," said Jack as he passed through the first room. "And maybe there are pictures too. I wouldn't even need to read it." Maxwell laughed at Jack's efforts to avoid actually reading. The two boys entered a passageway with other halls branching off in both directions. They saw portraits hung throughout the halls as they glanced down a couple of passageways with endless rows of books, scrolls, and papers. *Where should they begin?* Maxwell glanced back down the main portrait hall and noticed a girl standing in front of one of the portraits. He jabbed at Jack to take a look.

"I thought you had reading to do before Messaging," said Maxwell to Eden, sneaking up behind her. She jumped as though she had been caught doing something dreadful.

"I do have reading to do, and I'm doing it!" said Eden. "I didn't say what kind of reading I would be doing."

Maxwell nodded his head as though he wasn't buying her reasoning.

Eden continued, "I'm trying to find out who this Protector is and if he's related to you. Josiah said you had 'history here.' I'm willing to bet it has to do with this Protector." Eden pointed up to the portrait before her. Maxwell glanced up at the portrait for the first time and reacted like he immediately recognized the person in the picture.

"It can't be!" exclaimed Maxwell as his eyes dropped down to the description plate at the bottom of the portrait.

"Who is it?" asked Eden. "You know him, don't you?"

Without answering her, Maxwell stared at the portrait, taking in all the detail, for what seemed like an eternity to Eden. He was trying to get some understanding. *It can't be . . . my . . . ? . . . And who is this . . . Norris?* He thought as his mind kept spinning.

"Tell me, Maxwell, who is in the portrait?" shouted Eden as she shook him and turned him to face her. With all her commotion, she noticed some of the surrounding Protectors looking in her direction, followed by multiple *shhhhs* by the angels in charge. Eden whispered, "Sorry," to everyone around her, and then immediately went back to her serious face, looking directly at Maxwell.

"It's my grandfather," said Maxwell with an expressionless look on his face.

"I knew it. I knew it," said Eden, again at a volume that was met by more *shhhhs*. In a calmer tone, she said, "I knew he had to be related to you; he looked too much like you. This is great, Maxwell. Your grandfather is a hero."

"It's just so hard to believe. He's so quiet and soft spoken at home," replied Maxwell. "When he was young, he started a horse livery business on our island. To my knowledge, he's never gone anywhere or done anything other than run the stable. My grandparents wouldn't even leave to go on a vacation. This is almost too much for me to believe, but I'm standing here looking at his picture."

"So, his name is Alexander Justice?" asked Eden. "And does he look like an older version of the Protector in the portrait?" Maxwell and Eden both looked back up at the portrait.

"Yes, to both questions," answered Maxwell without elaborating. They both just stood and stared for a moment. Then Eden broke the silence.

"It's him, then," she said, "whether you believe it or not." Jack had run into Gem, and they both walked over to join Maxwell and Eden looking at the portrait.

"He does look just like you," added Jack as both Protectors proceeded to fill them in on the conversation of the last five minutes.

"I've got to find out what happened back then," said Maxwell.

"*We've* got to find out what happened," corrected Eden. "It will take all of us to get to the bottom of this. Everyone here is so secretive."

"This is all intertwined somehow. I'm sure of it," added Maxwell. "From the little we heard at the meeting the other night, it seems this Norris is still around."

"The first thing we need to do is find out what happened concerning this battle and your grandfather," said Eden. "We can't ask anyone, or they might become suspicious and cut off any leads we could've found or, worse yet, send us home for knowing too much."

"I agree," added Gem. "We need to find out all we can on our own first."

"Then we can ask Josiah," added Maxwell. "He knows something, and I can tell he would like to let us in on it. But someone is stopping him."

The four formulated a plan to work together in gathering information. It was decided the boys still needed to go to the meeting tonight to overhear as much of the discussion as possible. The girls would come back to the Hall of Records tonight to gather history on the battle Alexander fought against Norris. They would meet back at the boys' room at ten o'clock to compare notes. Everyone nodded in agreement.

"We've been here too long to do it now, but we still need to find time to go look at the room before the meeting tonight," Jack reminded Maxwell as the four made their way out of the Hall of Records and on to training.

"We have a couple hours between Protection and Flight training," said Maxwell. "We'll just go together and see what we can find. One of us can keep watch while the other searches the room."

As you can well imagine, none of the four Protectors left Messaging with any new skills that day. Their minds were elsewhere. Nathan discussed the placement of items to trigger responses in humans. Our four Protectors' attentions faded in and out. They would catch bits and pieces of training but not enough to comprehend the technique. Toward the end of training, they split into groups to try to position an item and generate the correct response. In every exercise, when our four placed an item, either they chose the wrong item to use or put it in a position in the hologram where it was ignored. Their selections always produced the wrong response from the receiving Protector.

Nathan knew they had not been paying attention. This was one of the easiest Messaging skills to master. He asked the four of them to stay after class and told them they would have to repeat this lesson after dinner.

"Repeat the lesson?" exclaimed Maxwell. "How?"

"Every session is recorded by the behold-a-scope," said Nathan. "You can watch it in this room on this wall." He pointed to the far wall across the room. "It's the same mechanism you have on your walls in your resting quarters; only you must watch this one here. Each room is set to behold one area. Your rooms are set on your earthly homes, and this one is set to record this room."

"Every training room in this facility contains a behold-a-scope," continued Nathan. "The machine senses when the room is over half full and begins recording. When more than half of the occupants leave, it turns itself off."

"I didn't know our training was being recorded," said Eden. "It's completely undetectable."

"Yes, child, you are quite right," replied Nathan. "Unless you check the behold-a-scope before training, you would never know it was recording. It was created to be nonintrusive." Nathan made his way to the back of the room where the behold-a-scope was located.

"Not everyone grasps the instruction and training on the first try, as you four can now attest to firsthand," reprimanded Nathan. He opened a narrow door at the rear of the training room. The children were transfixed on the most translucent piece of crystal they had ever seen. It was shaped like a small telescope positioned in the back of the wall. It had dials that constantly moved back and forth, which the children imagined was the focus. A box attached to the near wall displayed buttons for volume, playback, and record. The children saw no wires leading to this box, but Nathan acted as though they went together.

From the view of the training room being recorded, all that was visible of the behold-a-scope was a small hole covered in glass, similar to a peephole on the front door of a house on Earth. The room containing the behold-a-scope was no more than the size of a large closet. The scope was fixed to the side of the wall and grew larger as it came away. Colorful lights made their way through the translucent tube when Nathan pressed the small, silver button on the bottom. The larger back end of the scope was uncovered, and everyone in the room could watch the picture moving across the opening.

"What's going on inside the scope?" asked Gem.

"Take a closer look," replied Nathan with a smile. Gem leaned over until her eyes were six inches from the large opening.

"It's a training class!" exclaimed Gem without rising back to a standing position. She continued watching the display.

"Excellent, child!" said Nathan. "I'm so glad you are enjoying our little invention. Maybe tonight won't seem so much like a punishment because it's really not. I just want to make sure you know the material. Every day builds on the last. You've got to stay focused." Nathan smiled at all four Protectors. No one smiled back except Gem, who had never stopped smiling since she looked in the behold-a-scope.

"Now, pay attention, all of you," instructed Nathan. "To turn on playback mode, push the button on the wall while you turn the dial beside it at the same time. The dial allows you to fast-forward to the correct training class, which is the eleven hundred hour. When you finish, simply turn off the playback button and it will be ready to record the next morning. I do believe there will be room for all of you to view the training here without being too cramped. But if not, you can go into the classroom and watch the training on the wall, just like you do in your resting quarters. Now, if you will excuse me. I must prepare for my next group."

Nathan walked out of the small room but then stopped and turned to face the Protectors. "Oh, one more thing . . . I will begin training tomorrow with the four of you, showing the group how much you have learned from this session, so don't try to play hooky. I look forward to opening training tomorrow with a demonstration from the four of you." He turned around but kept talking as he walked out. "Pay better attention tomorrow, my young ones. Good day."

With that farewell, he was gone. His temperament was not cross, just insistent. The four knew they would have to return that night to watch the behold-a-scope. "This is just great," scowled Maxwell. "There go all our plans."

"Maybe not," said Gem. The other three looked at her, puzzled.

"What are you thinking, Gem?" asked Jack.

"Nathan didn't say when we had to be here to watch and practice the repeated class. He only said it had to be tonight and after dinner. We can still go to the Hall of Records tonight to do research, and you two can go to your meeting. We will still meet back here immediately after dinner. We will replay the training. Then you guys can go to your meeting, and we will head to the Hall of Records. We will be short on time, but everything should fit, if we hurry. We can practice the Rescue techniques later, maybe back in our room tonight." The other three processed what she said and nodded in agreement. After a pause, she continued, "We were told when we arrived that we didn't even need sleep here; it is only a habit."

"I like my habits," replied Jack. The other three glared at him. "But I can miss an hour or two . . . I guess."

"Gem, it's a brilliant idea," said Maxwell.

13

How to Stay Alive

When the four Protectors arrived at Protection, Joshua had an announcement for the group: "Today, we are going to make some time for the Guidelines of Survival training, which is basically how to stay alive while on assignment. This training will push the Protection class back another hour. We have decided all of you need some factual background information, rather than the rumors you have heard going around the endless table. It's time you heard details that are accurate. Normally, all of this is covered later in your training, but the instructors have heard a great deal of speculation on your part and feel this information will be more beneficial to all of you now, rather than later. Your instructor for Guidelines of Survival is Rachel. She is an expert in the field of Protectors and will be able to answer many of your questions. Rachel, here are your trainees." Joshua took a seat on the front row.

Rachel stood up, smiled at the group, and began, "I would like to introduce a subject everyone wants to know about but you're afraid to ask: the Manips." The children shook their heads yes.

She continued, "The best way to imagine a Manip is to think of an image in a twisted mirror. For every good deed the Protectors attempt, the Manips will try to do evil. When you are attempting a rescue, you can bet a Manip has most likely been there before you to cause the event in the first place. Sometimes an accident will occur naturally, and the Manip then shows up to disrupt your rescue. Even when a Manip doesn't directly cause an accident, they will often try to influence human against human to cause harm. If harm is befalling a human, you can be assured a Manip has been, is, or will be involved. Just a warning to always be ready." Rachel turned the page in her lecture book.

"Manips may try to speak to you directly," warned Rachel. "They may try to tempt you to join their ranks by offering glory, power, or knowledge. It is best not to speak to them. The more they know about you, the more ways they can hurt you. You are to engage them with your weapons, not words. When you find yourself in a battle with a Manip, some will be as skilled in combat as you. Others may be better, or they may be worse. To our knowledge, they are trained in the same manner as you, although we believe all of you are more skilled. Anyone can be a Manip, but not just anyone can be a Protector. When you are given a protection assignment to guard a human, get ready to defend yourself. Manips will be coming your way." Rachel turned another page. Gem raised her hand, and Rachel acknowledged her.

"Do all Manips look alike?" asked Gem.

"They are all different, and it's not pretty," answered Rachel. "Their appearance is distorted according to the life they lived. When we commit evil on Earth, it is hidden on the inside. At this dimension, it all shows."

Rachel didn't elaborate any further. Everyone imagined some scary images in their mind as she continued with her lecture.

"Let's discuss Manip flight capabilities," she said, examining her notes. "They have the same maneuverability and power in the air as Protectors. Speed and strength in flight are developed individually, just like here. Some will be better than others. You can be sure they are training as we speak." Rachel turned another page.

"I want to change topics for a bit and discuss your first assignments as Protectors," she continued. "When you are given your first and subsequent protection assignments, we will always assign Protectors in pairs and sometimes groups of four. Your partner during training will preferably be your partner during your assignments. We do not require you watch your assignments as a pair; you simply have to work together to accomplish the end result. The longer you work with the same partner, the easier it will be to protect your assignment. You will become an extension of each other. There will be occasions when each Protector in your group will be given a human to protect; other times the four of you will be assigned one common goal to achieve." The Protectors sat spellbound by her words.

"On the hilt of every Protector's sword is a hidden button," said Rachel as she lifted a sword before the group. "It is located beneath this covering." She slid a small latch to the side that displayed a button the same color as the hilt. "When you push this button, a signal is sent to the hilt of your partner's sword. After receiving this signal, your partner's sword will give off a slight vibration, which can be detected by only his partner. The receiving partner will feel this vibration, even if his sword is sheathed, and he will hear the sword vibrating, even if he is not holding it. Your partner alone can feel or hear the vibration and will know you are in trouble and need his/her assistance. This will all be covered with you after you receive your swords." Rachel smiled, and the class nodded. "Everyone will get a chance to practice before your assignment."

"I know several of you have more questions. We have saved a few minutes to address as many as possible." The group asked numerous questions, such as, "What if the Manip gets your sword?" This was quickly answered with, "They cannot pick up your sword without being burned at the touch." Or, "Could a Manip push the button on a Protector's sword by touching it with an object rather than their hand?" Rachel answered, "They cannot, because only a Protector's touch can engage the button."

The group of Protectors continued to ask thought-provoking questions, which were quickly answered by Rachel. At the end of the hour, Joshua stood up and told the group to take five minutes to mingle and stretch their legs before they began Protection training. A young man with a United Kingdom flag on his sleeve walked up to the Americans and introduced himself as Jacob Gilbert. He asked which of them was Alexander Justice's grandchild. The other three pointed to Maxwell.

"How do you know about my grandfather?" asked Maxwell. "I just found out myself."

"You've got to be kidding me," said Jacob. "You mean you didn't know?"

"Well, I've found out some things since I arrived here," answered Maxwell, not wanting Jacob to know the whole truth. "But I'd like to know more. What have you heard?" Jacob could see Maxwell wasn't joking.

"Just how great he was," said Jacob. "Unstoppable is what I heard. He practically saved humankind, beginning with my country." Jacob leaned in closer to speak in a low voice as he continued, "Everyone has high hopes for you, Max. They all think you'll be a chip off the ole block." Jacob gave Maxwell an encouraging slap on the back.

Maxwell's expression conveyed anxiety with that last statement and Jacob noticed. "Don't worry, bloke," he said. "I'll back you up anytime you need me. It would be an honor." Jacob smiled with sincerity.

"Thanks, Jacob," said Maxwell. "It's cool of you to say that."

"I mean it, man. Anytime," said Jacob. "See you around." With that quick goodbye and a two-finger salute, Jacob disappeared into the crowd.

Maxwell stood in the same spot for a moment and thought about what Jacob had just told him about his grandfather.

Maxwell felt he had a close relationship with his grandfather, but he would have never guessed he was a Protector—a great Protector. He looked forward to returning to Earth to talk to him about his adventures but he couldn't shake the feeling that his life could be in danger—and his friends' lives as well because they were with him. He knew there was more information he needed to know now and it would be up to the four of them to find it.

14

A Plan Is Formed

Maxwell, Jack, Eden, and Gem stood close together as Joshua called the Protectors to attention for training.

"Protectors, from the look of your Protection training yesterday, we need to do a repeat of session one. Try to be more accurate today and watch the tiny details. Your skills need to be honed. I noticed a few of you are ready to move on, but for the benefit of most of the group, today I will use your talents to assist in the training of your fellow Protectors. If any of you need additional training after this day, we may set up after-hour sessions for you. So, today show me your best, Protectors, or there may be homework for some of you."

Jack leaned over to Maxwell and the girls. "We don't need anything else to do tonight," he said. "Everyone needs to do their best. If we get another after-hour training, we can forget about gathering any extra information or eavesdropping on any meeting. Let's show them what we're made of." Jack leaned his staff into the center of the foursome and the remaining three Protectors knocked their staffs into his in agreement.

The chime rang out, and the four lined up before Anthony, their first trainer from the previous day. Rings were floating at a slow speed before each of them. The Protectors were to charge their rings, fake a move, then stab the ring in the middle with the staff.

"Let's try to master our skills faster today, Protectors," instructed Anthony. "Don't let the fake jab throw off your aim at the center ring. Stay focused." Each Protector started slowly, wanting to make each jab count. Their strategy seemed to work in that they quickly became more accurate. Near the end of their rotation, all four were hitting their rings nine out of ten tries.

"Excellent," said Anthony as he observed the four Protectors' improvement. "Keep up that kind of performance and you will be assisting the instructors." The foursome smiled as the chime rang out for the groups to move to their next station.

After moving, Eden watched the Egyptian Protectors, who were stationed beside them again, just like yesterday. Anthony was now their instructor, and he called the one named Akyl to come up and assist him with the training of the other three Egyptian Protectors. His skill was an undeniable gift. He hit the rings with precision every time. His instruction to the others in his group seemed to improve their performance as well.

"How can he be that good?" asked Maxwell. Gem hadn't known he had been observing, too. "We've only begun our training. He looks like he could teach the instructors."

"He's done it before, perhaps?" suggested Jack, leaning into the conversation.

"How?" replied Maxwell.

"I don't know, but he looks as if he already knows the drills," said Jack.

"Okay, that's it," said Eden, who was also observing. "You guys are finding conspiracies in every direction you look. Can we just concentrate on the one concerning your family, Maxwell, and leave the others for another day?" She glared at them harshly as she took her position in line.

After Protection training, the four finalized their plans for the evening. "Jack and I will scope out the room for tonight's meeting now," said Maxwell. "Then we will meet you in our resting quarters twenty minutes before Flight training."

"And we will go to the Hall of Records to uncover some history on your grandfather. I'm sure it will take more time than we have, but we need to at least make a start," added Eden.

The boys took the GUST to the dining floor on Level Alpha. As they entered the dinner hall, many workers flying here and there in royal blue garments were preparing for a great banquet. The workers didn't appear to be angels because they were smaller in size, although they did have wings and could fly. They seemed especially happy as they worked in the room and around the table and chairs. Many of them sang softly or whistled. Some workers were decorating the hall with fresh flowers while others repaired scrapes and marks on the furniture. They hadn't seen these workers before and were curious as to who or what they were.

"Excuse me," interrupted Maxwell. "I have never seen a creature such as you. May I ask your name?" The creature slowed down to a stop, surprised she was being spoken to.

"I am Tot," answered the creature, smiling. "We are the Helpers from the Above."

"Where's Above?" asked Jack.

"It's another world in the northern dimension," said Tot.

"Do you work here?" asked Maxwell.

"Yes, any time our services are needed, we come," she answered. "Everwell has always been especially kind and protective of our people so we enjoy being able to contribute in return. We are at our happiest when we are helping others." She smiled at them and flew right back to her task of arranging the flowers.

"If they are looking for a challenge," said Jack, "I wonder if they would help clean and organize my room back home?" Both boys laughed and continued on their way.

No Protectors were in the hall eating as it wasn't dinnertime, and the boys didn't see any angels either. The Helpers didn't react to the two Protectors being in the hall and continued working, paying them little attention.

The boys ducked into the same hallway that led them to the previous meeting, but this time, it was well lit, and they could hear voices in the distance. As they passed the physical training rooms, most were full of Protectors with one or two angels assisting in the training.

"Can Protectors come in here and train?" asked Jack. "No matter what the time?" Jack looked at Maxwell as if he would know the answer.

"I would assume so," answered Maxwell, shrugging his shoulders, "as long as you weren't skipping a training session somewhere else." They strolled past the Scheduling and Portal rooms, but the occupants were too busy with their concerns to notice Maxwell and Jack.

"I don't recognize any of these Protectors from our trainings," commented Jack.

"The doors do say 'Scheduling' and 'Port,' " replied Maxwell. "Maybe they are experienced Protectors who are done with their training and are now on assignment." Jack nodded in agreement as the boys continued their walk.

When they arrived at the conference room, it was lit but empty. They had passed several other doors on the way to the room at the end of the hall. All rooms appeared to be meeting rooms just like this one, and all were empty as well. Maxwell thought it would be safe for them to look around since no one seemed to be near. The room contained beautifully carved chairs but no tables or other furniture. It didn't look like the sort of room a Protector would find himself in.

"I don't see anywhere to hide," said Jack despairingly. "We're going to have to be where we were before, out in the hall."

"That is way too dangerous. Anyone could walk up on us or come out of the room," replied Maxwell. "It's a miracle we weren't discovered last time."

Both boys stood in silence as they examined the room. Maxwell appeared to have a sudden epiphany and made his way to the back of the room. To his delight, there in the wall was the tiny crystal glass of the behold-a-scope.

"Yes!" exclaimed Maxwell in a whisper that bordered on a muffled shout. Jack knew the plan before Maxwell had a chance to speak it.

"Perfect," said Jack in agreement.

Maxwell set the behold-a-scope to record, and the boys left the room in a much better mood than when they arrived. They met the girls in their resting quarters twenty minutes before Flight training as planned. They excitedly told how they had set the behold-a-scope and would go back tonight after everyone had left and replay the meeting with little risk of getting caught.

"The only thing that could possibly go wrong," said Maxwell nervously, "is if someone notices the behold-a-scope is on and turns it off before the meeting."

"But they would have to go in the back room to notice this," added Jack. "And that's unlikely since this room doesn't appear to be used in training the Protectors."

"True," said Eden, agreeing with Jack. "I think it's a good plan, unless someone goes to the back room." Eden agreed and disagreed in the same sentence.

"No one will go in," reassured Maxwell. "It's the only promising option. Everything else is too risky."

"So, let's go over tonight's schedule," said Jack, handing each Protector pencil and paper. "Dinner at six o'clock, watch the Messaging training on the behold-a-scope after dinner, allow some practice time, and then leave around seven thirty or eight. The meeting of the angels begins at eight o'clock, so we will research in the Hall of Records until the meeting is over and give them time to clear out. Probably by ten o'clock all should be clear. We go to the meeting room, watch the behold-a-scope, and make it back to our rooms between eleven and midnight to discuss what we know and don't know." Jack looked at each Protector and asked if they had any changes.

"I think we're set," said Gem. "We'd better go." The four made their way out of the room toward Flight training.

When they arrived, the Flight instructors, Matthew and Michaela, were beginning to line up the early arrivals. Our foursome hurried into their positions in formation while the remaining Protectors trickled into the empty slots.

"Ready, trainees?" began Michaela. "Wings extended!" Again, the Protectors heard the familiar sound of a flock of birds. Nearly everyone's wings extended today.

"After observing each one of you yesterday, we have decided that today we will split you into two groups," said Matthew. "We want all of you to show us simple takeoffs and landings. Not too high. After we tell you which group you are in, stand still until we are finished separating you." Matthew continued, "We will capitalize on your strengths by pointing out your good technique, and improving on any weaknesses you may have by acknowledging and changing your poor technique."

"I hope they don't separate us," whispered Eden to the other three.

"The need for two groups should only last for a couple of sessions," added Michaela, as if she had overheard Eden's concerns. "We should have all the kinks worked out and everyone working together as one very soon."

"That's a nice way to say they are weeding out the nonflyers," said Jack. Concern was showing on every face in the room today. Michaela and Matthew walked by every Protector and assigned group one or group two. As Michaela came closer to Maxwell and Jack, a bead of sweat popped up on Jack's forehead.

"Jack, group one," said Michaela. She marked his name off her check-list as she eyeballed Maxwell and Eden. "Maxwell, group one; Eden, group one." Again, Michaela scribbled notes on her list. She looked up and observed Gem a bit longer than the other three and finally proclaimed, "Gem, group two."

The other three Protectors jerked their heads around as if they had just heard a sonic boom. They couldn't believe she sent Gem to group two. Gem was the little athlete of the group. Her takeoffs and landings weren't perfect, but they were up to par with Maxwell and Jack. Eden was on another level from the others, as she had demonstrated yesterday. Gem felt sure there must be a mistake. She mustered up the courage to approach Michaela.

"Excuse me, Michaela," interjected Gem timidly. "I don't want to interrupt, but are you sure I'm in group two?"

Michaela looked down at her list again. "Yes, child. Hurry to your group so we can begin," replied Michaela. Gem was devastated. She couldn't think of any reason why she would be in group two, but this was no mistake. She didn't know what to say to the other three, but her face said it all.

"I'm sure it's only for a short time," reassured Eden. "She will realize this is a mistake soon enough."

"You've got skills, Gem," added Maxwell. "Go show them what you've got."

"Hang tough, kiddo," said Jack. "We're not moving on without you, so don't worry." Gem gave a soft smile to Jack's comment. She walked courageously to group two and turned around to gaze at her friends from her new group.

Matthew quickly got group one lined up. He began with the takeoff and landing practices from the day before. Eden kept glancing over to group two, trying to find Gem to see how she was doing. She could never locate her due to the fast pace Matthew was keeping. After being reprimanded once for not paying attention, she never had another opportunity to get a good look. When Matthew let the Protectors take a couple minutes to get their breath, Eden glanced over to group two. She walked over to Maxwell and Jack.

"I can't find Gem," said Eden, worried. "See if you can locate her." Both boys looked over to group two. She was nowhere to be seen.

"Maybe she's with Michaela," replied Maxwell. "I don't see her anywhere either."

"Michaela being gone does not make me feel any better about the situation," said Eden in a snippy tone. "What if they have already removed her from group two, and she is out of the flyers?"

"Cut it out, Eden! Quit going to the worst possible outcome," said Jack, clearly aggravated. "Gem is as skilled at flying as any of us. They are not going to pass us and fail her. It's impossible. I still think someone made a mistake putting her in group two."

With five minutes left in Flight training, Gem came flying over to group one. She did a perfect landing between Maxwell and Jack. She couldn't hide her expression of pure joy.

"Please tell me you're here to stay," pleaded Eden.

"I am," replied Gem with a smile. The girls hugged, giggled, and hugged again. The boys smiled and gave Gem a pat on the back. They were excited that Gem was back, but thought the girls' giggles were ridiculous. (Boys just cannot comprehend how important it is for a young lady to have another young lady around for conversation and companionship.)

"Tell us what happened!" exclaimed Eden.

"Michaela needed some expert assistants while she was working with group two," said Gem with an exaggerated boastfulness while she blew on her fingernails and pretended to buff them on her shirt. The rest of the group knew by her tone that she was only kidding, and all of them burst out laughing and shoved her. Gem's face suddenly turned serious.

"Actually, she scared me to death," said Gem solemnly. "I thought I was on the next bus bound for Earth. I told her, 'Next time, let a girl know what's going on.' Michaela acted like she didn't understand why I was worried. She felt I should be more confident in my abilities. Maybe I should, but all of this is still really new."

"Gem, that would've worried anyone without knowing beforehand," replied Eden. "We were concerned too—especially when we couldn't find you."

"They had us working one-on-one in separate rooms, not to embarrass anyone," said Gem. She never said whom she was working with, and the Protectors never asked. Each of them privately felt that if it had been them, they wouldn't want anyone to know.

"Well, we're glad we're all together again *but*," said Maxwell as he moved into position to whisper. Everyone closed in to hear. "You still can't fly as fast and high as me, Miss Expert Assistant." And he shot up into the air to prove his point. Jack laughed and followed almost immediately, with Eden and Gem close behind.

After Flight, everyone returned to their quarters to get cleaned up. They needed to change clothes, eat dinner, and plan their evening. Eden and Maxwell's legs were already aching. Jack, with his skateboarding, and Gem, with her trampoline back home, were better prepared for jumping in Flight class. The four hurried back to their rooms in anticipation of the evening ahead.

15

Crystal Lagoon

The boys knocked on the girls' door to see if they were ready for dinner. "Just give us a couple more minutes," replied Eden. Both girls were running around the room, picking up clothes and grabbing papers and manuals on their way out the door.

"Sorry you had to wait on us," added Gem. "We spent too much time exploring." The boys had no idea what the girls were talking about as they closed their door and made their way to dinner. They felt like the girls were leading them into one of those conversations where they don't really tell you what they're talking about so you will continue asking. The boys tried to resist, but eventually Maxwell caved.

"So, what took too much time?" asked Maxwell, puzzled. "Where were you exploring, in your closet?"

"No, not in our closet," answered Gem.

"They don't know about the pool yet," Eden said to Gem. The girls just shook their heads in unbelief. "How could you not go jump in the pool after that Flight workout?" They were really rubbing it in. The girls laughed because they knew the boys had no idea.

"I didn't know there was a pool!" barked Jack. "And why didn't you come and get us before you went?"

"It's all in your manual," replied Eden. "We just wanted to check it out so all of us could come back later. Actually, we had no plans to even swim today. But you do have to admit, with you two, anything that involves checking out a location during food or rest time results in excuses not to go."

"We only took our swimsuits in case they wouldn't let us in without them," added Gem. "It's located on this floor, but if we were going to check it out, we didn't want to come back without going in to see what it looked like."

"They do make you wear your suits to enter into the pool area," Eden jumped into the conversation again. "So, it worked out. After we put on our swimsuits and saw the pool, we couldn't resist jumping in."

"Oh, and it's not called a pool," added Gem. "It's called the Crystal Lagoon. The name is quite appropriate because it's larger than any pool I've ever seen, and when you first look at the lagoon, it sparkles like crystal."

All through dinner, the girls went on and on about the lagoon. They told the boys about the tropical plants with fragrant flowers of every color that surrounded the pool. Ivy (not the poisonous sort) hung down, and thick, green leaves created a canopy over the lagoon. The trees were filled with birds of every kind, singing and flying from perch to limb and back again. The lagoon itself was crystal clear and filled with colorful fish and friendly turtles that would pop their heads up as if to say hello. The water was cool enough to be refreshing, but not so much to give you the shivers, and on the floor of the lagoon was white, soft sand that created a

calm sensation on the soles of their feet. The girls said the waterfalls were the best feature of all. One waterfall even had a smooth marble slide with an occasional flower floating in the clear water, which cascaded down. It was, of course, much better than the waterslides back home.

Vines were attached to some of the surrounding trees, so Protectors could swing out and let go. They would plunge into the lagoon with hoots of joy. This would startle the resting birds, resulting in scolding squawks.

The girls kept talking about the purity of the water. It smelled like fresh-fallen rainwater and was as transparent as glass. Depending on what time of the day you were there, sometimes it would glisten blue like sapphires. At various times, a mist would move out of the tropical garden across the lagoon, cooling the water. And as the mist lifted, the water warmed up again.

The girls said another interesting feature at the lagoon happened as you were leaving. When you stepped out of the lagoon and started down the path that led away, a warm breeze would swirl all around and dry you. By the time you opened the door to leave the Crystal Lagoon area, you were dry top to bottom, hair and all.

"Unbelievable," said Jack, looking at Maxwell. "I want to see that lagoon."

"Me, too," replied Maxwell. "Maybe next time all four of us can go."

"Don't tell us anything else about the lagoon," said Jack putting his fingers in his ears. "Let us find out some of the rest for ourselves."

16

What Was Said

*A*fter another delicious dinner, the four hurried back to the Messaging room to watch the training lecture on the behold-a-scope, which truly, they had paid little attention to the first time around. After watching, they were glad they had repeated the lecture as they realized how many vital details they had missed.

One important point was how their assistance may be needed at times by a human other than the one they are assigned to on Earth. In these instances, the Protector closest to the physical location of the human calling for help will hear the request. The scheduler here at Everwell will also hear the call, but if a Protector on another assignment is very close, they can beat the Protector on call by several minutes, which could make all the difference between life and death.

Your scheduler will let you know whether to answer these calls at that time. Many instances, you are forbidden to help in random calls for help during your first assignment as the call may be too advanced for your skills. After what seemed like the longest hour of their lives, Nathan finally finished the lecture.

The group stood and packed up their notes and handbooks. "That was really interesting about how the cries for help can be heard by the closest Protector," said Maxwell. "I couldn't ignore someone's cry if he needed me. They should never ask us to do that. I disagree with that decision."

"I'm sure they have a very good reason, Maxwell," replied Gem. "New Protectors are probably slow flyers or something of that nature. We probably couldn't make a positive difference if we did show up for an emergency. We might even make it worse."

"Speak for yourself, grandma wings," laughed Jack as he walked by her. Gem stuck out her foot and tripped him.

"There's your grandma wings," said Gem as she walked past him lying on the floor. Maxwell smiled and helped Jack up as the four headed to the Hall of Records.

After they stepped off the GUST and entered the hall, Maxwell began looking for a table around which the group could sit. The Hall of Records seemed especially crowded tonight, or maybe this was typical after training every evening. Maxwell figured this was probably how many of the trainees spent their downtime.

"I'm sure it wouldn't hurt us to spend more time here," said Maxwell as he looked over the crowd. The girls looked at him annoyed.

"What do you think we have been telling you two since the beginning?" reminded Eden.

"Well, we understand now," said Maxwell as he found them a table. He leaned in close and spoke in a low voice as they all sat down. "Everyone just act casual and have a look around. We don't want to arouse suspicions. We need to become familiar with the workings of the Hall so we can look up subjects without too much assistance. Jack, you hold our table while we see what we can find out." The other three Protectors nodded in agreement. Jack watched those browsing around him as Maxwell, Eden, and Gem walked away in different directions.

Several minutes later, Gem returned with a large, tan, leather-bound book tied closed with a thick leather string. The book was titled *Great Battles of the Protectors.*

"That looks like something we can use," said Jack with a smile. "Let's look through it together and see if we can find some information. If it's anywhere, it should be here."

"I'm not sure how complete this volume is," said Gem. "It probably doesn't contain every battle fought by the Protectors. How could it? It would be ginormous!" Jack smiled when Gem used this word. She was right, there had to be more.

"Let me go back and check where you found this book," replied Jack. "I may see more volumes." Gem pointed back in the direction she had come from.

"Go two rows over on the right and three shelves down," said Gem as she shut the cover on the book to show Jack again. "See if there are any with similar titles." Jack hurried over to the row Gem had described while she leafed through the volume in front of her.

Maxwell and Eden returned to the table at nearly the same moment. Eden held a thick edition called *Past Protectors J-K.* "I thought this might contain some information that could be useful," said Eden, showing Gem and Maxwell her book. "What did you all find?" she asked. Maxwell and Gem slid their books to Eden on the opposite side of the table.

"My find is titled *Dangerous Manips of the 20th Century,*" said Maxwell. "I thought it might give us some background on this Norris fellow." Eden glanced at the book Gem had found earlier.

"This looks excellent, Gem," said Eden. "I think we have found a great starting point."

"Jack is checking to see if he can find more volumes," replied Gem. "I was so excited when I found it, I rushed over without checking for others." The next moment Jack returned with three other volumes, also in the Great Battles series.

"I had trouble finding the dates on these," said Jack in a flustered tone.

"The one before was labeled on the inside," said Gem as she flipped open his volumes. He had returned with the seventeenth-, eighteenth-, and nineteenth-century editions. Gem had grabbed the twentieth-century edition of *Great Battles* earlier without even realizing; it was the first one she found.

"The twentieth-century editions are probably all we need," said Jack, looking up from the volumes.

"Probably for Maxwell's grandfather that's true, but Norris may be in earlier editions," added Eden. "Who knows how long he has been here?"

"We probably should go through all of them but spend more time on the recent editions," said Maxwell as he glanced at his watch. It was nine o'clock. The Hall of Records was starting to thin out some.

"Do they ever close?" whispered Jack. Maxwell shrugged his shoulders. Eden spoke up.

"No, they're open twenty-four/seven," she replied confidently, continuing to look down at the books in front her. She instantly looked up and stared at nothing as she spoke. "That's an odd saying to use here, twenty-four/seven. I know they try to keep us on an Earth schedule, but really there is no twenty-four/seven here. There's no daytime and no nighttime; it's all just time."

Everyone at the table just stared at Eden when she said this. "I'm overanalyzing, aren't I?" Dead silence and stares answered her. Eden looked at each one of the Protectors. "Come on, guys, what I said wasn't *that* weird." Everyone burst out laughing. This was followed by looks and *shhhhs* from several workers in the hall.

"Okay, let's look at what all we have here," said Eden, sitting up straight in a let's-get-down-to-business kind of way. The others spread out the various books, scrolls, and parchments before them. "Maxwell, you check out *Past Protectors* and look for your grandfather. Jack, you examine *Dangerous Manips.*" She handed out the various volumes to both guys as she continued. "Let's see here . . . this periodical says, 'Find out what really happened to Elvis.'" Eden shot a condemning glance toward Gem.

"What? I can't help it," said Gem, smiling. "I'm a fan, and I want to know."

"You'll have to find out later," said Eden, tossing the publication to the side. Gem rolled her eyes, then looked over at the paper with longing.

"Okay, Gem, let's try again. Here's a couple . . . *20th Century Chronicles* and *Great Battles I*. And I'll take *Great Battles II* and *III*."

Everyone grew silent with his or her tasks at hand. Moments turned into minutes. Maxwell was the first to speak. "Here is Grandfather," said Maxwell excitedly and then read, "Alexander Justice began Protector training at twelve."

"Like grandfather, like grandson," interrupted Jack. "Same age as you." Maxwell shook his head in agreement. In his mind, he had already made that connection. Maxwell continued reading.

"Alexander Justice had an uneventful training period," read Maxwell. "He showed no signs of being exceptionally skilled in any area. He was given a simple first assignment in protection, which turned into a serious situation. He handled the difficult circumstances with expertise far beyond his training. He was hence given more difficult assignments with the most demanding conditions. No Protector who had come before him had accomplished so much so quickly. Alexander Justice is truly an example for us all." Maxwell continued to stare at the page and then looked up. "That wasn't much help."

"So much for like grandfather, like grandson," laughed Jack as he wadded up a piece of blank paper and threw it at Maxwell's face. Maxwell grabbed the same wad of paper and hurled it back at Jack with twice the force. Both boys laughed and continued throwing the same wad of paper back and forth with the girls watching and wondering what just happened to make them lose focus so quickly. This was followed by more looks and shushing from those around them.

"Stop it, the two of you," scolded Gem. "We don't need to get kicked out of the Hall and told never to return. We need to keep looking. Eden, have you found anything?"

"Yes, actually, I have," she replied. She relayed to the group how Maxwell's grandfather had been able to intercept the Axis war plans time and time again. He had been instrumental in infiltrating their intelligence briefings to destroy them from the inside. She told nothing of the trouble Norris had experienced because her version had been what Alexander had been able to record. "It also says your grandfather lost his sword, which was never recovered during his last altercation of the war, and the Manip named Norris may possibly have it." Eden raised her eyes to meet Maxwell's gaze.

"I might need to pay this Norris character a visit," said Maxwell.

"May I remind you? This Norris character took the sword from your grandfather, who is supposed to be one of the greatest Protectors ever," interrupted Eden. "Maybe this is a clue we need to stay as far away from him as possible."

"Girls," said Jack, ignoring her warning. "I'm with you, buddy," he added with a poke of his elbow at Maxwell. "Oh, and there is something about Norris in my book, too," added Jack, looking down at the page. "It says his rank was that of lieutenant general of the Manips, but now he seems not to be leading as many underlings as before. It also says that in the past fifty years, another Manip general named Spear has assumed some of Norris's command." Jack looked up at the others.

"That's an interesting development," responded Maxwell. "Sounds like someone may have an ax to grind."

"It sounds like he has a score to settle, Maxwell," said Gem, "because of your grandfather. You need to stay clear of him." Maxwell didn't comment. He appeared to be lost in his thoughts.

"It's getting close to ten o'clock," interrupted Jack. "We should go soon."

"Okay, everyone, here's an idea," said Maxwell in an energetic tone. "Take Eden's assignments as well as whatever books, scrolls, and parchments you have in front of you. Try to learn everything you can about my grandfather, Norris, the battles fought, and their details. Each day, we will pool the information we have gathered and discuss it at evening in our quarters. These books and scrolls cannot be removed from the Hall, so anytime you have free time, come up here to research. Talk to no one until we find out what is really going on. We don't want to raise suspicions. Everyone agree?"

"Agreed," answered everyone in a hushed tone.

At just after ten, the four Protectors made their way to the dining hall with the excuse of a late-night snack. When Jack poked his head into the hallway leading to the meeting room, all was clear. "It's deserted," said Jack.

"Let's hurry before someone comes," urged Eden as everyone rushed into the hallway and closed the door behind them. They moved as quickly as possible down the hallway but kept in mind the need for silence. Maxwell peeked through the window of the meeting room. The lights were out, and the room was empty.

"Don't turn off the dark," instructed Maxwell. "Head for the room in the back. We should be fine with only the light in there."

As they entered the small room, all the contents were in the same position as when they had previously left. Obviously, no one had checked the behold-a-scope before the meeting.

Eden started the machine while the remaining three grabbed their seats. The voices began speaking aloud on the behold-a-scope as Eden joined the others.

Pontier, the angel in charge from the last meeting, was leading this one as well. Raphael and Josiah were there, as well as many of the other instructors. Hampton was seated beside Pontier at the front of the room. Jack couldn't help thinking how much Hampton looked like a bodyguard or bouncer, just daring anyone to say a cross word.

"Let's get on with the business at hand," said Pontier sternly. "For those of you not at our last meeting, we are here to discuss the special circumstances with this group of trainees. We welcome comments from the instructors who have now had the opportunity to work with these Protectors for a few days."

Raphael's wing tip did a ripple whereby to call attention to himself. "Yes, Raphael?" said Pontier, recognizing the angel.

Raphael stood up and raised his concerns: "I would like to add, at the beginning of this meeting, that we do not want to underestimate our adversaries like last time. There appears to be a personal grudge involving a Manip and he may not be through . . . He may not be through until he rids the Protector program of all of them." The room rumbled with discussion. Raphael took his seat.

"Let us hear from some of the instructors," continued Pontier. "Matthew, Michaela, how is Flight training proceeding?" Both instructors stood.

Matthew spoke first. "Fine, Pontier. He is progressing very well. Not an exceptional flyer yet, but I have high hopes for him in the future."

"He wants to learn," added Michaela. "He gives his all and should be in the top 10 percent at the end of his training." Pontier acknowledged their comments, and they both sat down.

"Joshua, how about Protection?" asked Pontier.

"He's good," answered Joshua while standing. "His ideas can be unconventional and sometimes harebrained, but they work nearly every time." He returned to his seat.

"Weatherly, Collin, how about Rescue?" asked Pontier.

"One of my best trainees." answered Weatherly. "He still needs to work on his technique, but he is only just beginning."

"He has successfully rescued most of his test subjects," added Collin.

Rachel waved the tip of her wing to be acknowledged. Pontier called on her and announced to the room that she was the Policy and Procedure instructor. She stood.

"He asks a lot of questions," said Rachel. "He will figure this out. I recommend telling him the facts up front." Nathan, the Messaging trainer waved his wing, was acknowledged, and stood.

"I knew his grandfather," said Nathan. The four Protectors watching the behold-a-scope exchanged wide-eyed looks. This was the first solid clue that they were most likely discussing Maxwell. Nathan continued, "His grandfather would not accept special treatment, and I'm sure this young O'Malley won't either." Maxwell quietly cleared his throat upon hearing this. The other three looked at him but said nothing.

"We do not know if this Manip has had his fill of revenge," added Nathan. "From my past experience with Manips, I have never seen any of them have their fill. This young man and his companions need to be assigned to light duty and kept close to Everwell where we can monitor them." The group murmured in agreement. Pontier turned to Tillie, who was seated in the second row.

"When you hand out their first protection assignment in the next few weeks," instructed Pontier, "you know what you must do. We do not want a repeat of the blunder that happened earlier."

Tillie stood to address Pontier. "I understand," replied Tillie boldly.

Nathan said nothing more and resumed his seated position.

Pontier continued, "I want each instructor/trainer to keep me informed of his progress. Three days before their assignments are handed out, I want to see Matthew, Michaela, Rachel, Joshua, Collin, Weatherly, and Nathan in my office. We will make final arrangements at that time. I give you all leave to go." With that, Pontier dismissed the group but added at the end, "Rachel, I would like to see you now."

The group got up to leave. Rachel made her way to the front of the room as the behold-a-scope went black. The four Protectors *ughhhed* in unison at missing Rachel's conversation with Pontier. Everyone sat still, waiting on Maxwell to say something. Finally, he stood up.

"We'd better go," he said. The four Protectors walked silently back to their rooms. Everyone was in deep thought over what they had just seen on the behold-a-scope. The other three felt it was Maxwell's place to begin the conversation. This was all about him, and they didn't want to overstep.

Maxwell's mind was racing. He still had so many unanswered questions. But one thing was clear now; Norris wanted revenge on his grandfather. He was proud his grandfather was able to put a kink in Norris's plans, but what was all the "underestimating our adversaries" and "not another blunder" talk? Norris had obviously succeeded in hurting his grandfather in some way. He felt the need to check on things back home as soon as he and Jack were back in their rooms.

When they arrived at their respective doors, the girls said goodnight. Maxwell was glad no one forced him to talk on the way back. He needed time to think. He couldn't imagine what the other three were thinking. Just being associated with him could put them in harm's way because they were on his protection team. He knew their lives were in just as much danger as his.

As soon as the boys shut their door, Maxwell turned on the behold-a-scope on his wall. It was evening back home on Mackinac Island. Maxwell's grandfather was walking some of his horses back inside the barn. He had prepared each stall with fresh hay, then filled their feeding bins with grain and buckets of fresh water.

"He looks fine," said Maxwell out loud, sounding very relieved. Jack looked up to see Maxwell's grandfather working.

"Your grandfather still looks like a sturdy guy, Maxwell," said Jack. "If Norris could have gotten to him already, I'm sure he would have. Something tells me, he can handle himself." Jack smiled and gave Maxwell a reassuring pat on the back.

"Turn on the darkness," said Maxwell. "For some reason, I'm extremely tired this evening." In reality, he didn't want to talk; he just wanted to be alone with his thoughts.

"We all are," agreed Jack as he switched on the dark. Before he fell asleep, he could hear Maxwell muttering in his restless sleep. Jack closed his eyes, hoping for a quick end to this day.

17

No Time for Foolishness

When Eden and Gem met the boys at breakfast the next morning, Eden silently mouthed the words to Jack, "How's he doing?"

"He's quiet," Jack mouthed back. The girls understood Maxwell wasn't ready to talk. Today was favorite meal day. Whatever food happened to be your favorite back home was before each Protector for their morning and evening meal. Everyone was eating in uncomfortable silence. Jack told Maxwell his pecan pancakes looked great. He nodded in agreement.

"I would like to add that your Fruit Loops look delicious as well, Jack," said Gem. Both girls snickered at his selection. Maxwell noticed them laughing, but he continued sitting there stoically eating his meal. As everyone was trying to get their composure and not laugh, Maxwell slipped one of his pancakes with just a hint of syrup onto the napkin in his lap. He tore it into three pieces.

When everyone was composed and bored silly, Maxwell said, so softly everyone had to get especially quiet to hear, "I would like all of you to know . . ."

Everyone stopped eating and watched as Maxwell continued, "That I am especially fond of maple syrup!" Maxwell began pelting the three with pieces of pancake and syrup, starting with Jack. This gave the girls a moment to take cover, all the while grabbing the food in front of them in retaliation. Gem's eggs, grits, and toast mixed with Eden's New York-style bagel topped with cream cheese and blueberry jam joined the flying debris. Jack's colorful Fruit Loops and milk topped off the entire mess.

Of course, let's not forget, other Protectors were seated on their right and left. By chance—or not—some food must have landed on some of the other groups. Either way, the food fight spread swiftly down the endless table like falling dominoes and within minutes, the immaculate dining hall was covered in food.

"Enough!" shouted Josiah, walking into the hall. All throwing of food ceased. "Each and every one of you involved in this unacceptable display will clean up this mess immediately." He spoke slowly and precisely.

You could hear a pin drop as he continued, "Your training begins in thirty minutes, and you will not be late. I will be back to inspect this dining hall at that time. If it is not acceptable . . . well . . . let's just hope it's acceptable." Josiah stomped out of the room.

"He's not going to send us home for blowing off a little steam with a food fight, is he?" said Eden in a whisper as a piece of pancake unstuck from her face and fell to the floor. The other three burst out laughing then muffled themselves.

The mid-size group of about fifty Protectors tried not to smile as they quickly cleaned up the mess and hurried off to training. They never saw Josiah afterward, and he never brought it up again. He acted like it had never happened and the Protectors were relieved. Nevertheless, the tension had been broken for the moment and their questions temporarily forgotten.

The morning training sessions went without incident. Maxwell seemed to possess a new determination to master every task. It wasn't that he was more skilled in the techniques compared to the previous days, but his willingness to redo them over and over was a new characteristic. The other three Protectors noticed, too.

"I don't think we can keep up with him," whispered Jack to the girls on the way to training a couple days later. "It's like he's possessed."

"With his grandfather's spirit," chuckled Eden.

"You're probably not too far off," added Gem. "He has something to live up to now. He wants to show he's got it, too. It's in his genes."

"One thing I do know," said Jack, not in a joking way. "It's not in my genes, and it's killing me trying to keep up."

The next few weeks continued much the same way. The Protectors divided their time between intense training, researching in the Hall of Records, and relaxing at the Crystal Lagoon. The Protectors had noticed a far-off city when they were standing on the rocks at the lagoon. It appeared to be miles away. When they asked Josiah about it, he said the city was inaccessible for them at this time but perhaps for another day. More unanswered questions.

Maxwell had a newfound vigor and seriousness in his training, and it seemed to spill over onto the other three Protectors. Perhaps you have noticed that peer pressure tends to happen here on Earth as well. You hang out with an overachiever, and it's so much easier to improve yourself. On the other end of the spectrum, if you spend your time with an unconcerned do-nothing . . . Well, I guess you know where that will lead.

18

First Assignment

The day finally came for the handing out of the first protection assignments of this rotation. Maxwell was still lying in his bed, waiting for the slow crawl of time to pass so he could start his day. He had hardly slept that night. He wanted so much to live up to his grandfather's reputation and not be a disappointment to his ancestry. Training had gone well. His skills had greatly improved, and he felt he could keep up or even do a little better than many of the other Protectors. A few Protectors stood above everyone, and Maxwell knew he wasn't one of them, but he also knew he wasn't at the bottom. He had no reason to expect he would come face-to-face with Norris, but deep down, he did hope. Just maybe they would meet. He longed for a chance to finish Norris's downfall, which his grandfather had begun. Perhaps he could even retrieve his grandfather's sword and return it to the ranks of the Protectors where it belonged.

Jack began mumbling in his sleep as he rolled over. His talking snapped Maxwell away from his thoughts. His excited anticipation of the assignment to come energized him to grab his pillow and fling it at Jack. His aim was right on target. Jack woke up startled and realized a tossed pillow was the culprit, which he immediately threw back in Maxwell's direction with the same speed and accuracy. Jack sat up in his bed and looked at the watch on his wrist that had been a present from his mother on his last birthday.

"Do you seriously think we need to be up this early?" protested Jack as he flopped back down in bed and rolled over with the covers over his head. Maxwell knew his tactic had worked as he sat up and swung his feet over the side, ready to get up.

"Maybe we will get a better assignment if we are in the front of the group," said Maxwell, coaxing Jack to get up.

"I think they have already decided who is going to get what assignment," groaned Jack. "That's why they call them *assignments*. We already know ours will be a dud. Who cares when we get there?"

"Just get dressed and let's go hurry up the girls," said Maxwell, jerking Jack's blankets off his bed. Jack slowly rolled out of the bed, onto the floor, and there he lay.

After fifteen minutes, which felt like an hour due to Maxwell's prodding, the boys were standing in front of the girls' door. After repeatedly knocking and gradually getting louder, they finally got Eden to open the door. Her eyes were half open and her hair definitely had not been combed and was doing its own thing.

"There had better be something seriously wrong with one of you," griped Eden, "to be waking us up this early." She looked at both boys. Jack silently pointed at Maxwell. Eden's eyes made their way to Maxwell, giving him an angry stare. Gem joined them at the door, in the same physical state as Eden.

"What's wrong?" asked Gem, rubbing her eyes.

"I thought it would be a good idea," said Maxwell talking slowly, trying to be convincing, "if we could get to the scheduling room early, so we may perhaps get a closer seat up front, which will show we are geared up and ready to go, thus resulting in a better assignment." Maxwell gave the girls a half smile. Gem made a disgusted sneer and trudged back to bed.

"We'll meet you at breakfast in twenty minutes," said Eden, more awake now and sympathizing just a bit with Maxwell.

"Please hurry," said Maxwell with anticipation as Jack began pulling him away from the girls' door and on to breakfast. Jack did always live by the philosophy, "If I'm up, I may as well be eating."

When the girls joined them at breakfast, which turned out to be more like forty minutes later instead of twenty, the boys were still enjoying a delicious meal.

"I'm surprised you're not already in the assignment line, Maxwell," said Gem briskly.

"There is no line," replied Jack, without even slowing down his chewing. "We've already looked." Jack laughed with his mouth full and elbow jabbed Maxwell, who didn't laugh. Gem just smiled and shook her head as she and Eden joined the others at the table.

As soon as the girls took their seats, their food swooped down in front of them. Not a morsel was out of place on the plate. Jack leaned over to see if the girls had the same food they'd been served earlier; they did.

"This French toast is the best I've ever tasted," said Jack, stuffing another oversized bite into his mouth. "The bread is soft and thick with a sweet taste."

"It's Hawaiian French toast!" said Eden, smacking Jack's fork away from her plate. "My dad used to make it for me after he came back from serving in the Navy. He was stationed in Hawaii and learned to cook many Hawaiian dishes while he was there."

Maxwell's gaze turned to observe a group of Protectors going down the hall where the assignment room was located. "Look! Protectors are going to get in line for their assignments!" exclaimed Maxwell. "Come on, Jack. Hurry, girls. They will get ahead of us."

"Not this early, Maxwell," replied Eden after she had finished chewing her first bite. "They are probably meeting in one of the other rooms." Maxwell completely ignored Eden's response as though her words had not been spoken.

"Jack and I will save you seats," said Maxwell, jerking Jack's shirt from behind.

"Go ahead," said Gem waving them on. "We'll meet you there as soon as we finish."

Maxwell and Jack hurried through the large, ornate wooden doors and scurried down the hall. When they met anyone walking toward them, they would slow their pace and walk. When they finally reached the scheduling room, it was empty.

"See? I told you!" said Jack shoving Maxwell. "You dragged me away from my favorite meal for nothing."

"Every meal is your favorite meal," replied Maxwell, shoving back and walking away. "Stop thinking about food all the time. Let's get a seat on the front row." Jack was watching Maxwell walk into the deserted room. Seconds later, he followed his friend's path to the front of the room and took a seat.

"I hope we get assigned something interesting," said Maxwell.

"Don't count on it," replied Jack. "This is our first protection case. I'm sure we'll have to prove ourselves." Jack was also thinking to himself that those in charge would want to keep Maxwell safe and close. He knew there was no chance they would get an interesting assignment.

Jack felt it was obvious they were the best team to come out of this training group. There were individual Protectors who were extremely talented, but as a complete team, they were the strongest in their skills.

He also knew Maxwell was the reason for their marked improvement. The only group to even come close to them was the team from Egypt, with Akyl leading the way. He was the most competent fighter, with any weapon, Jack had ever seen.

Jack did wonder about the assignments, though. He didn't understand how the leaders at Everwell could completely overlook some of their best Protectors and keep them under wraps. They would just have to wait and see how it played out. The boys sat in silence as Maxwell kept glancing back toward the door to see if anyone was coming.

After thirty long minutes, the girls came running through the door. Gem started laughing immediately when she saw the empty room with two lone boys on the front row. Eden *shhhhed* her, but even she let out a giggle or two on her way to her seat. Maxwell completely ignored the girls and didn't turn around. Jack smiled at the girls as they took their seats beside him.

It seemed like an hour, but it was really only twenty minutes before a few other Protectors began filing through the door at the back of the room. Excitement was in the air and the four Protectors could feel it. Maxwell kept fidgeting in his seat and every time he would move, Jack would look at him. Finally, Jack could take no more.

"Relax, Maxwell," said Jack. "You're driving me batty. I never gave the assignment much thought until this morning, but now you're making me nervous."

"Sorry, but it's almost time," replied Maxwell. The room was filled to near capacity now, and the sounds of nervous chatter could be heard all around.

Suddenly, the back of the room got quiet. Maxwell jerked his head around to see six adult figures walking to the front of the room. Two of the figures Maxwell recognized from the beginning of training. One of them was an individual from the angel meeting room at the end of the hall, when he and Jack had taken their first look around. The other they had seen in Scheduling when they walked by. He had never spoken to either of them.

"I would like to have everyone's attention!" said Josiah in a commanding voice from the front of the room. "I would like to introduce two individuals to you today. Most of you have not had the pleasure to meet them, but you will be in contact with them a great deal from now on. Our head schedulers are Tillie and Amanda."

"Tillie will hand out your first assignments and all future assignments," continued Josiah as the Protectors sat perfectly still, absorbing every word. "You will have no input regarding your first assignments, but future requests will be considered." Tillie smiled and nodded at the Protectors.

"Amanda will be your contact at Everwell throughout your assignment," continued Josiah. "If any additional help or resources are needed during your assignment, you will contact her.

"We try to schedule you on a protection assignment within your own country, due to your familiarity with customs and the geography," said Josiah. "It is not always possible, but whenever a native Protector is available, they will be first selection on the assignment.

"When the assignments are handed out, your team of Protectors are to leave together immediately. Upon leaving this room, you will go outside into the hall where a trainer will be waiting on you. Every group has a trainer designated to assist in preparation for their assignment. Trainers will make sure each of you has your assigned weapons and instructions."

Josiah then looked over in Tillie's direction. "Tillie, let's get started." He made his way off the small stage, and Tillie moved to the lectern to get right to business. He held a small, shiny silver metal board in front of him, similar to a clipboard but with no clip or paper. Maxwell assumed it listed the assignments. Tillie cleared his throat.

"First group, United Kingdom," said Tillie. The four British Protectors sat up straight with anticipation. "You will be protecting the prince during his armed services deployment for the next two weeks and will accompany him during his holiday immediately following. You are dismissed." The British Protectors hurried to the back of the room and out the door to their trainer.

"Next group, Egypt," continued Tillie. "You will be protecting two archeologists who are digging for a tomb in the Valley of the Kings. They have many obstacles before them and will need your protection and guidance to navigate their way." The Egyptian Protectors, led by Akyl, burst out of their seats and made their way into the hall.

"Next group, China," Tillie proclaimed. Once again, he didn't call Maxwell and his three friends. "A young scientist is conducting experiments in Beijing. These experiments will be very valuable in finding a cure for cancer. It is important that his research not be interrupted. The human race has waited much too long for this cure." Out the door the Protectors from China sped.

One country after another was given their assignment. Some were more glamourous, some more dangerous; some were neither glamourous nor dangerous, but all seemed quite important. The four American Protectors waited anxiously, but country after country was called before them. Finally, they were the last group of Protectors remaining in the room.

"I'm glad we got here early," Jack said, leaning over to Maxwell. "It really helped our place in line." Jack nudged him again, smiling. Maxwell knew he was just ribbing him. He knew, deep down, Jack could care less if they were early or late.

"They are saving us for last for a reason," replied Maxwell. "That much is obvious. It must be a top-secret assignment that even the other Protectors cannot know about." Tillie cleared his throat again. The boys picked up on his hint and stopped whispering.

"Last but not least, the United States," said Tillie, glancing down at his metal board. "We have a group of senior citizens in Colorado at an assisted living facility. They keep getting injured and are constantly getting into trouble. We need the four of you to watch over these four individuals and also keep an eye on all residents in the entire home." Tillie looked up from his notes and descended the stage to leave the room. Maxwell raised his hand.

"Yes, Maxwell?" said Tillie, turning to look at the young Protector.

"I don't want to complain," began Maxwell, standing up and speaking in an irritated tone. "But is that it? Out of the entire country, *that* is the best assignment for us, watching senior citizens at an old folks' home?"

Tillie stared at him but said nothing, so Maxwell continued, "How dangerous can it be? Are you afraid one of them will go too fast on their scooter?" Maxwell plopped back down in his seat and looked away from Tillie. Tillie walked closer to Maxwell.

"Young O'Malley," said Tillie in a stern, reprimanding tone. "All of our assignments are equal in importance. If you succeed in your first assignment, you will be in the minority. At this time, you may not know all the details involved in your assignment, but rest assured, great care has gone into a selection that is right for your team. You need to have a positive attitude and have faith in our leadership that we know best where your services are required. The excitement level may be less than your liking, but I can assure you, the task ahead is quite significant." Tillie then continued walking toward the door.

The four Protectors sat in silence. On his way out the door, Tillie winked at Josiah, who had witnessed the entire scene and was waiting for the four.

"Hurry along, Protectors," called Josiah from the back of the room. "I will be your trainer for today and have much to cover with you before you leave." The Protectors dragged themselves back to Josiah and out the door. Maxwell knew why they had saved them for last. It was to keep the other Protectors from laughing when they were given their assignment.

19

The Portal

The Protectors followed Josiah through a crowded hallway to a room marked Intelligence Prep. The large, open room contained multiple tables, each encircled by five chairs, many of which were already occupied by Protectors and their trainer.

As they made their way between the seats, they observed Protectors listening intently as their trainers were going over the specifics of their assignment. Maxwell overheard bits and pieces of details as they passed the individual tables. His heart sunk with disappointment with each table he passed. How could they give him such a lousy assignment when he had given his all and made such an improvement? He couldn't get past his belief that he and his friends were one of the better Protector groups. So, why had they had been given such a simple assignment watching senior citizens?

He knew his attitude was dreadful. Eden and Gem would both tell him he should be grateful he was even selected to be a Protector and to stop being such a baby. The girls were already acting like they would enjoy the assignment. Eden was saying she loved it because she missed her grandmother back on Earth and thought it would be interesting. Gem agreed; her grandparents were greatly involved in her life back home, and she knew how much fun they could be. They were both laughing and behaving carefree as they followed behind Josiah.

At least Jack felt the same way he did. Jack knew this was a stinker of an assignment and that their bad luck was probably due to Maxwell's grandfather. The two of them would just have to keep their eyes open for excitement. Maybe another person in this town would require their protection services as well. If Everwell wouldn't give them an interesting assignment, he would simply find one for his team. He would share his idea with Jack as soon as he had the opportunity. Josiah sat them down at an open table where four Protectors had just left.

"Listen closely," instructed Josiah. "And ask questions if you do not understand any detail as I explain it. First thing, when we leave here, I will take you to get your armor and swords in the Weapon room. You will wear your armor and carry your sword with you at all times. Every sword has a twin weapon because Protectors are assigned in pairs. Maxwell and Jack are a pair as are Eden and Gem. If you get separated from your partner, your sword is able to track its twin weapon. As long as you keep your sword with you, your partner will forever be able to find you. Never lose your sword, or you will be on your own.

"After the Weapon room, you will be taken to the Portal room. The Portal room is where you exit Everwell and enter Earth's dimension while on assignment. The portal propels you at the precise angle and speed to enter the spirit dimension of Earth, which is the same dimension you are in now at Everwell. It is the dimension in which you will protect your assignment and battle Manips. Just like the Protectors, the Manips also patrol in this dimension. This means you can see them and vice versa. So, be prepared for battle. It will happen. I know all of this has been covered in your training, but I like to remind new recruits.

"If you need to assume human form and cross from the spirit dimension, you, as a rookie, must have permission from Amanda," said Josiah firmly. "She approves all dimension crosses during your first assignments. When you have more experience, we will allow you to cross back and forth on your own."

"What if a Manip crosses dimensions while we're fighting?" asked Maxwell. "Can we not pursue?"

"Not during your first assignment," replied Josiah. "We know this is a big disadvantage, but we can't risk someone seeing you from Earth. It already happens much too often even with experienced Protectors. I know our reasoning is difficult for you to understand, but it's for the best in the end." Josiah's expression was dead serious.

"Now, we need to go over the specifics of your assignment," continued Josiah. "Maxwell, your assignment is Adele Jamison." A hologram still picture of an elderly lady, emitted from Josiah's handheld tablet in the middle of the table, appeared in front of Maxwell. It could be viewed by any seat at the table. "She is sixty-nine years old and the ring leader of everything at Golden Acres Nursing Center in Durango, Colorado. They are about to begin their softball season, and every year, more and more of their players are suffering substantial injuries. Adele pitches for the team, so I don't need to tell you, she gets her share of those injuries."

"Jack, you will be watching Kenneth Woods," continued Josiah as Adele's face on the hologram changed to that of an elderly man for Jack to view. "He is seventy years old and a retired postman. He plays shortstop on the softball team, and last season alone, he broke two fingers and his nose." Jack smiled at this news.

"I bet he's a tough player," said Jack, still smiling and shaking his head in agreement. "This assignment is looking up already." Maxwell looked at him like he was crazy.

Josiah ignored both of them and continued, "Eden, your assignment is Essie Hudson." Eden smiled with excitement as Kenneth's hologram changed to Essie's face. "She is seventy-two and a retired school teacher. She plays first base on the team and catches about 98 percent of the balls thrown to her. No matter how she must jump, dive, or stretch, she will try to make the play. She's quite good." Josiah was smiling as if he remembered seeing her play. Good luck with that one. You're going to need it.

"Gem, you're assigned Betty Miller," said Josiah with some finality as the last face appeared as a hologram. "She is also seventy-two years old, and a retired horse trainer, who has trained horses that ran at Saratoga Springs and in the Kentucky Derby. She is the softball team's catcher, which means she has been struck by balls, slung bats, and rammed by players running for home plate." Then he looked squarely at Gem for emphasis. "If you can, just try to keep her out of the runner's way so she will not get knocked over so much. She will feel much better the day after the game if you succeed. She gets pounded season after season but always comes back for more."

Josiah turned off his tablet and looked at the Protectors before continuing, "Protectors, those are your assignments. Keep your charges as safe as possible—not an easy task."

"What was Adele's profession?" asked Maxwell. "You told us everyone else's profession but hers. What did she do for a living?"

"That's a good question, Maxwell. Let me see," replied Josiah. He reopened his tablet, looking for the missing information. He flipped through several views before finding it. "Here it is," said Josiah with a pause. "It says bird-watcher. She worked for the Audubon Society." Three of the Protectors stared blankly.

"I've heard of it," said Gem. "It's a large organization that works to conserve and restore natural ecosystems, especially those focusing on birds and wildlife." The other three Protectors looked at Gem like she was from another planet. "What? I like songbirds," she added.

Maxwell's attitude lifted after the assignment was given. It wasn't the task he was hoping for, but at least it shouldn't be boring. It sounded like these senior citizens were an active bunch.

Josiah took them to the Weapon room where they would be fitted with breastplates and swords. They waited outside the door until the Israeli Protectors in front of them finished their fitting. Each of them came out of the room wearing spotless white armor and grasping the hilt of their sword, which hung about their waist. Josiah led his group of Protectors into the room and introduced them to Azariel, the weapon authority at Everwell.

"Azariel, let me introduce the American Protectors." Josiah introduced each Protector individually, finally presenting Maxwell, who just happened to be the last in line. Azariel shook hands with Maxwell, the same as he had with the others, but this time he forgot to let go. He seemed to be studying Maxwell's face. He suddenly released his grasp, after realizing his lengthy handshake, and hurried over to the breastplates.

When Azariel returned, he was carrying four silver plates of armor. All were covered in dings and scrapes and appeared nowhere near the quality of armor the Israeli Protectors displayed as they left the room. Their armor had looked brand new.

Azariel decided to fit the girls first and handed Gem a visibly worn piece of armor. Gem pulled hers over her head as Azariel walked over and hooked it on each side. After he had latched the last clasp and stood back, the breastplate molded itself to Gem's body and became a perfect fit.

"Now, let's take this off," instructed Azariel. "I will put it in the flames to seal the fit." Gem obeyed. She unlatched the armor and pulled it over her head. Gem handed the armor to Azariel, who then disappeared into the next room. When he returned minutes later, the scrapes and dings were gone. The color was a pearl white, just as the Israeli Protectors had worn, and looked brand new. You couldn't tell it had ever been previously used. When Gem tried on the armor, the fit was perfect.

"This armor will change colors depending on your surroundings," added Azariel as he tweaked the breastplate. "If it is night, it will be black; if you are in the woods, it will be green and brown. If it remained white all the time, it would be difficult to sneak up on your adversary." Gem kept turning left, then right, in front of the mirror. She loved her new armor.

The fit for Eden and Jack followed the same format. Azariel chose one of the breastplates and then tried it on them. After the clasps were secured, the armor transformed to a perfect fit. Both times, Azariel returned with polished, pearl-white breastplates, which fit perfectly. When Azariel walked up to Maxwell, he spent some time studying his proportions. He walked behind Maxwell, raised his arms to shoulder level, and measured below his arm.

"I think I will make a change on the armor selection for you," said Azariel. He expanded his wings and flew up to the highest shelf in the farthest corner of the room. Numerous breastplates were piled in a heap. Azariel mumbled to himself as he dropped breastplates, clanging and banging into one another, as they fell to the floor beside the one he had previously chosen for Maxwell. He was digging for just the right one.

Unexpectedly, the clanging ceased as the Protectors heard Azariel exclaim, "I knew you were here!" He returned with a very worn yet still white breastplate. It had many dings and scrapes, even more than the earlier ones, yet it still retained its color. "This should fit perfectly," said Azariel as he pulled the armor over Maxwell's head and clasped the latches. Maxwell held his arms out, waiting on the armor to adjust. Oddly, nothing happened. The armor didn't size itself as there was no denying the fit was perfect.

"What's wrong with mine?" asked Maxwell, fearing his armor was defective. Azariel smiled, knowing he had been successful in his choice.

"Actually, nothing at all," replied Azariel excitedly. "I have never before chosen an armor that did not adjust, even a little. The Protector's armor is a very personal piece of protection. It does not adjust itself unless it is reassigned to a new body." Azariel stood still, deep in thought, examining the fit. "I believe the armor thinks you are its previous owner. This is really quite remarkable. You must have the same body type and mannerisms of the previous wearer. You have fooled your armor. That is very rare indeed."

Azariel muttered to himself as he walked around Maxwell to admire his handiwork. Maxwell couldn't help wondering if the armor had previously belonged to his grandfather. He looked at the other three Protectors, who were looking back with knowing expressions. He knew they were thinking the same. He gave a half-smile, acknowledging their thoughts.

"I now need to flame the breastplate to remove the battle scars," said Azariel, still fidgeting with Maxwell's armor.

"Will the scarring and dents affect the performance of the armor?" asked Maxwell, running his hands down the battered front of the breastplate.

"They will not affect its performance in any way," replied Azariel, surprised by his question. "Firing is for purely cosmetic reasons, just for looks. Most Protectors prefer their armor sparkling when they first take ownership. The previous owner sustained no significant injuries in this breastplate."

"Then I wish to take ownership just as it is, battle scars and all," said Maxwell. "But what if the Protector comes back and his armor is gone?"

"He won't be back," Azariel answered empathetically but matter-of-factly.

"Why not?" asked Maxwell, responding quickly and hoping for a speedy reply.

"Enough questions," interrupted Josiah, putting an end to this conversation. "Each one of you must be fitted for your sword."

"Follow me," instructed Azariel, obeying orders. The four Protectors followed Azariel to a stone pool in the corner of the next room. Water poured from an unknown source in the rocky wall, down a small waterfall, and into a pool surrounded by more stone. The pool was waist high to the Protectors, so they could lean over the stones and touch the water. Eden walked up to the edge of the stone pool and reached out her hand.

"Halt!" shouted Azariel. Eden froze like a statue with her hand still extended. "Do not put your hand in the fountain until you have heard my instructions and I tell you to do so." Everyone's eyes grew wide with wonder at what would come next. "Who is partnering with whom? Is it the two girls and two boys?" asked Azariel. Gem stepped forward to be beside Eden at the pool.

"We are partners," said Gem, putting her arm around Eden's shoulder.

"Are you right-handed or left?" Azariel asked Eden.

"Right," replied Eden.

He then looked to Gem.

"Left," said Gem.

"Eden, when I tell you, put your right hand into the pool," instructed Azariel. "Gem, likewise, upon this same instruction, put your left hand into the pool. Insert them beneath the water up to the wrist, fingers open. Hold them submerged and as still as possible until I tell you to bring them out of the water or until they come out on their own." The girls exchanged puzzled looks.

"Under no circumstances are you to remove your hands out of the water until told. Do you understand?" repeated Azariel. The girls nodded they understood. They both stepped up to the edge of the pool. They were so close to the water, some spray splashed up on them from the fountain. The boys inched in closer behind the girls so they could see what was happening.

"Get ready," instructed Azariel. "Hands in the water, *now!*" The girls shoved their selected hand into the water and remained perfectly still as instructed. The water got cloudy and heated up. After a few moments, their hands couldn't be seen under the water. The water swirled around their hands like a whirlpool. It felt like pinpoints were touching them all over their hand, top and palm. It wasn't painful, just odd. Faster and faster the water swirled until the girls wondered how long they could keep their hands still. They were growing tired. Finally, they both saw a flash of light beneath the water and felt a blast of heat from the pool so strong it blew their hair. They both staggered back but not enough to pull their hands out of the water.

Simultaneously, both girls felt something in their grip. It didn't scare them. It felt like it belonged there, like an extension of their hand. They felt pressure on their palms as they raised them out of the water. The hilt of a newly forged sword rested in the hand of each girl.

As both hands slowly rose from the water, the shimmer of steel was visible. Higher out of the water, both hands rose until it was obvious they were holding nearly identical swords. Except for their grips, which perfectly fit the Protector's hand, every inch of the sword was identical. From the jewels in the hilt to the cut of the steel, all the way to the tip of the blade, no difference was noticeable.

The girls stepped back from the fountain so the boys could go next. They followed Azariel's instructions flawlessly and likewise lifted their hands out of the water with two matching swords, which, by the way, looked nothing like the girls' swords. They had less jewels, and both had battling figures carved in the hilt. Again, the swords were identical except for the grip.

Maxwell and Jack exchanged swords. They didn't fit each other's hands. "At least we won't get them mixed up," joked Jack. The girls exchanged swords as well and found the same to be true.

"It doesn't fit!" exclaimed Eden in amazement.

"Everyone get their correct sword," instructed Azariel. "Now, I want to demonstrate how to use your sword to locate your partner."

The four Protectors turned to face Azariel.

"Hold your sword out in front of you, flat side up," he commanded. The four Protectors did as they were told. "One feature all Protectors' swords have in common is the small locator light at the base of the metal next to the hilt, just at the beginning of the blade."

Azariel pointed to the locator light on each of their weapons. He showed them how to activate the light by pressing the locator button hidden at the end of the hilt, which caused their partner's sword to vibrate. It was small and circular, about the size of a quarter coin. On the locator light, an illuminated red arrow went straight from the bearer of the sword in an outward direction, pointing either straight ahead, right, or left or back. This light led the holder of the sword in the direction of their partner's sword, no matter how far apart.

"Jack and Gem, I want you to take five steps back and two steps left while all four of you activate your locator lights," instructed Azariel. The illuminated bars on their locator turned in the direction of their partner's movement. "If you can't locate your partner and want to find him, you know you are heading in the correct direction if you keep the red bar pointing straight ahead of you. If the bar is pointing right, your partner is to the right of you. If you turn right, the bar should point straight ahead. You should now be heading toward your partner's location. Are there any questions?" Everyone seemed to understand the locator.

"I think we are ready," said Josiah, who had been silent through most of the instruction. "Thank you, Azariel, for your direction."

"My pleasure, Josiah," replied Azariel, looking at Josiah, then turning to the Protectors. "God be with you, Protectors, on your first assignment and every assignment thereafter." Azariel smiled and then bowed his head in farewell as Josiah and the Protectors left the room. They passed another eager group of Protectors waiting at the door to enter.

"Now, let's head for the portal," said Josiah. The four Protectors gathered around him as they were walking so as not to miss any information. "Amanda is your contact here while you are on assignment. If you want to communicate with her, all you need to do is think or say her name. She will answer telepathically. The communication channel to Everwell is opened with names. She hears your thoughts after you say or think her name, and she will reply with your name. Do not worry about talking to another person with the same name; she knows when you are trying to contact her. You will continue your communication back and forth until you are finished, and the sign-off response from both of you is said. That response is, 'Is that all?' from Amanda and 'That is all' from you. These phrases thought or spoken in succession will close the communication channel. She will cease to hear your thoughts and you hers until you call her again. This is a new feature and is quite handy when you find yourself in a tight spot and need help. You need only ask for it, and assistance will be sent as long as you remain in the same dimension. If you change dimensions, we lose the communication channel.

"Likewise, if she needs to contact you, she will speak your name, and then you must acknowledge her by thinking or saying her name in response. The four of you need to check in with her each evening and give her an update on your assignment. It can be done together, but we prefer you do this individually. We do understand that sometimes that scenario is not possible." Josiah stopped walking and looked at each Protector. "Do you think you're ready to begin?" he asked.

The four Protectors were apprehensive yet excited. They couldn't wait to start their assignment. Maxwell was still a bit disappointed over not receiving a more exciting mission, but at least he would be out helping someone and not stuck here at Everwell. From the sound of things, the senior citizens did need some protection. One positive aspect of their situation is how little they could mess up on this assignment. Even if they happened to miss a rescue here or there, what's the worst that could happen? A ball would hit someone. And that's hardly ever life threatening.

Josiah walked the Protectors into the Portal room. They got in line behind the African Protectors, who were already talking with the operator in the room. Jack spoke to Jamir, who was standing in the back of his group.

"Good luck protecting the diplomat and his wife from a kidnapping attempt," said Jack. "Keep them safe."

"Thank you. Same to you," replied Jamir. "What assignment did you get?"

"Oh, there's no time to go into that now," interrupted Maxwell. "Look, it's your turn." Maxwell pointed to the front of the line. Jamir turned around. His group was walking forward. He waved goodbye and hurried forward. The American Protectors watched as the Africans prepared to enter the portal.

Just from watching, the Protectors thought the portal worked similar to the GUST by using airflow. They saw four connected, large, clear pipes, approximately three feet in diameter. The Protectors had not yet been introduced to the operator of the portal, but they observed her feverishly working. Josiah told them her name was Finnae. The Protectors watched her lower a transparent piece of thick plastic—which wasn't plastic at all because it was too clear—into the four tubes. This cut off the flow of air through the tubes.

Finnae asked the African Protectors to lie down in the tubes on their stomachs, headfirst with their arms at their sides, flat against their body. Finnae's instructions couldn't be overheard by the Americans, due to the wind noise when the clear barrier was lowered. She spoke to the African Protectors as she showed them hand signals. Afterward, she walked back to the clear barrier in each tube and lifted it. One by one, they were propelled forward, *poof*, gone in an instant.

"It was so fast! I barely saw them moving forward!" exclaimed Maxwell. It was quiet again in the room with the clear barrier in the lifted position. Air was moving through the tubing at super speeds, but the clear tubing muffled the noise.

Josiah leaned over to the four Protectors and explained, "Portal openings are located all over the Earth, which break the dimension barrier. They open spontaneously for just a few seconds. Finnae has developed a system that alerts her when the precise conditions occur just before portals open up. She uses this technique to predict the locations of approaching openings. On rare occasions, Finnae has been able to move a portal to a specific location to pick up Protectors, but that takes a great deal of planning on her part. She is extremely talented at her job. Actually, we do not even need a portal to break the dimension barrier, but you must be going at faster speeds than those available to humans or even most of us. That is why we use the tube in this room to propel the Protectors at the exact speed needed to break the barrier. This way, we can send you anywhere you are needed whether there is a portal there or not."

Josiah introduced the Protectors to Finnae. "So where are we heading?" asked Finnae.

"Durango, Colorado, in the United States," answered Josiah. Finnae went back to her controls. She looked in a book that resembled an oversized atlas. She punched in some coordinates, and the entire room moved to a different angle. The floor and walls adjusted themselves to the movement of the portal so that when it stopped, you couldn't tell the room had shifted, even though everyone knew it had.

Finnae then went over to the tubes and dropped the clear barrier. The wind noise picked up again. "Climb in, headfirst, belly down." Her instructions were then repeated verbatim, just as she had given them to the previous Protectors. She was talking loudly, almost yelling. Although she was talking over the blowing air, everyone could hear her clearly.

Jack jumped in the first tube, followed by Gem in the next, then Eden, and Maxwell last. The boys had already decided, without telling the girls, that they were going to be first and last, no matter the mode of transportation. If they landed in a pile of Manips, they didn't want them to get the girls first. This was all very chivalrous, but they knew the girls would have never allowed it if they had known.

"Put your arms flat against your body, elbows locked," reminded Finnae. "This helps the aerodynamics and the speed. These coordinates should drop you very near the Rocky Mountains. Be careful when you first come down out of the sky, especially if you are in cloud cover. We wouldn't want you running head-on into one of those big mountains." Finnae winked then smiled. "Have fun and, most of all, be careful." Finnae walked back to the clear barrier. She grabbed hold of the clear divider. Eden shut her eyes. Maxwell smiled. *Whoosh!* All four were gone from the portal.

The Protectors felt a sudden rush of wind as they propelled faster and faster down the tubing into a cloud. Suddenly nothing could be seen as a thick mist surrounded them. They knew they were still in the tubes and their fellow Protectors were beside them. Surprisingly, this kept everyone calm. Deep down, they all felt that no matter what was waiting on them, the four Protectors, together, could handle it. Their bond had grown strong over the past several weeks.

The clouds thinned. Beneath them, they could see the countryside. The sun shone brightly, and all was warm as the Protectors saw the Rocky Mountains in the distance. They experienced an overwhelming appreciation of majestic beauty as they beheld the mountain range. Hawks, hunting prey, could be seen flying in circles below them.

They were still several thousand feet in the air when Jack motioned to the end of the portal tube, just a few feet away. Now some uneasiness could be detected among the group. They barely had time to notice the end of the tube when suddenly they were all flying out in midair (actually, *falling* in midair for a moment), with no support. Their wings had automatically extended out of their backs at the end of the portal tube. All four Protectors did a few somersaults until they regained their balance and some control.

Below, they saw the Los Pinos River winding through the valleys. They followed Gem's lead and dove down to skim the water with their hands. They were in awe of the splendor of nature surrounding them. Eden thought how exhilarating it was to fly over the river with the wind and a splash of water blowing in her face. Nothing she had ever experienced compared with this moment. This area of Colorado was especially beautiful. The scenery combined with the sense of freedom from flying felt tremendous. Flying on Earth was a completely different experience than flying at Everwell.

The Protectors were being drawn to their destination. The portal had sent them to a specific location, and they were still on their way as the river twisted this way and that. The Protectors were getting quite skilled at maneuvering the river. They banked in unison in a bend of the river and leveled in unison during a straight stretch. All at once, they came upon another bend in the river, yet they remained on a straight path. A small dirt road led from the river as an access for loading and unloading boats. The Protectors' flight path left the river, and they proceeded down the dirt road.

They remained flying above this dirt road for another ten miles as they approached an area that seemed to be more populated. Since leaving the river, they had passed three houses, which doesn't sound like much, but at least there were signs of life. Up ahead, they noticed a large, one-level building as the four Protectors found themselves being lowered out of the sky, down to the ground. They were standing on the grass in front of a brick building with numerous windows. It reminded Gem of her elementary school building back home in West Virginia.

"This must be the place," said Maxwell as they made their way to the front door to have a look around.

20

William Carter

William Carter's past occupations included realtor, insurance salesman, and, presently, financial advisor. He had failed miserably at the first job, realtor. He couldn't believe the time those house hunters expected him to spend with them. Prospective buyers would look at one house, not enough kitchen space. He would show them the next house, not enough bathrooms, then the next house, ceilings too high, no fireplaces, no basement, only one garage. *Ugh!* He had to find another occupation where it wasn't necessary to spend his valuable time with demanding people.

Job number two was an insurance salesman. Carter didn't have much going for him, but he was a born salesman. He did quite well for himself selling insurance until the state insurance commissioner's office caught him pocketing some of the premiums and not sending in the paperwork. *I was doing so great*, thought Carter to himself, *until that blasted rain in the spring of last year*. The whole valley flooded in a matter of two hours. His phone rang off the hook that evening. By the next morning, he knew his luck had run out, so he skipped town and took a new alias.

This brings us to Durango, Colorado, and Golden Acres Nursing Center and job number three, financial planner. William Carter knew a great deal about financial planning from his insurance days. Selling a whole life insurance policy is not much different in terminology from selling a variable annuity for investment purposes.

William Carter had an acquaintance, John London, whom he had met during his insurance days. He knew John's behavior could be as shifty as his. He had listened to John pitch to a customer while both of them were vying for new clientele at a professional meet and greet. Carter knew the numbers London was quoting his customers were impossible to maintain long term. Cater introduced himself, picked up London's card, and made a mental note to one day partner with this guy. In a few months, Carter and London got together and hatched this new elaborate scheme.

London would invest Carter's clients' money in an untraceable account for a percentage. This allowed Carter to stay under the radar of the police with all his aliases. After several weeks, when London and Carter both took their percentages, the clients would always have a little less money. Carter constantly had a scheme working where his client turned a huge profit the first quarter, which, many times, would motivate them to invest more funds. The following months would result in poorer returns, but Carter would continually encourage his client to stay the course—until their entire savings was nearly wiped out. Then he would change his location and change his name again.

Senior citizens were William Carter's choice of prey. Most of the time, they didn't keep a close watch on their investments. If they did lose money and happened to get alarmed, Carter could usually tell them a lie to give himself more time. He really knew how to recognize and then target the weaknesses of individuals at nursing centers. Many of the occupants had few visitors, so they were thrilled if anyone came by to talk and wanted to spend time with them. Carter would always bring the senior citizens sugar-filled pastries and cigarettes. Both of these items were discouraged in the center, so Carter would sneak extras onto the grounds. This was no problem for an accomplished liar like Carter, who had been skilled at deception since he was a child hanging out with the troublemakers in his middle school.

One particular day in sixth grade proved to be a pivotal point in Carter's childhood. A fellow classmate, who happened to be very athletic and sure of himself, threw a basketball at a more awkward student who was doing his best to keep up with the jocks. The bully threw the ball in a way he knew it couldn't be caught, which was quite an evil thing to do. As the athletic boy threw the ball, he yelled the name of the awkward boy, who was standing with his back toward him. The awkward boy turned his head to see what the athletic boy wanted and *Wham!* He was hit right in the nose at full speed. If any of you have been hit in the nose by anything resembling the size of a basketball, you know how painful this feels. The athletic boy figured that even if the awkward kid hadn't turned around in time, the ball would've at least hit the back of his head, which would've been equally as funny.

Carter laughed out loud with the surrounding boys while the injured boy ran off the court with tears falling, hiding his face. Carter's athletic abilities weren't any better than those of the awkward boy, but as long as he laughed and went along with their shenanigans, he would be a part of the cool group. Carter felt a slight pull of empathy as he laughed that day in the gym, but the more he laughed, the less compassion he felt.

By this point in his adult life, Carter felt no guilt or blame, no matter what he did to other people. In his mind, many people in the world had much more than he did, so it wouldn't hurt them to spread the wealth. Who cares if they worked hard and saved their entire life to have money in their retirement or to leave something for their children and grandchildren? In his mind, it still wasn't necessary for them to have so much, so he would take a share for himself.

He found many senior citizen centers, bingo halls, and nursing facilities in the Durango area. Carter had been stopping by all of them and was building up quite a list of possible marks. It was still early in his scheme, so no one had invested a great sum of money yet, but he was getting close to reeling in all of them. He liked to coordinate his gathering of sizeable funds so as not to arouse suspicion. It worked better if his victims lost their money at the same time so that no one had time to warn others or alert law enforcement. This gave him time to escape to another town.

Golden Acres Nursing Center was one of the better, more upscale assisted living centers in the area. It was elaborately decorated with beautiful gardens and offered many outdoor activities for the residents. The cost of the facility hovered close to the top of the scale, so it served many well-to-do patrons. Carter knew this center could be his jackpot.

He was settling in comfortably with some of the residents of Golden Acres. Or he was—until he began speaking with one particular older lady named Adele Jamison. She disliked him five minutes after he had opened his mouth. Carter could tell. He had been around long enough to know who he was fooling and who he wasn't. He couldn't understand what he had said or done to turn her against him.

Carter had used all his first-rate con stories on Adele. Maybe he had promised her too much return on her money. Perhaps it sounded too good to be true. Due to their greed, most people wanted his investment promises to be true, so it was easy to lure them in, but not Adele. Carter spoke to her, telling her how his investors doubled and tripled their money in a year. After he finished his proposal, he looked up from his charts and graphs; Adele was staring directly at his face. She was looking hard into his eyes but said nothing—just staring. Carter waited. He raised his eyebrows and looked back with the most innocent face he could muster.

Finally, he lowered his eyes. He couldn't take the stare down any longer. He felt sick to his stomach. He felt as though she could see inside him and could peer into the slime-covered darkness of his soul.

Carter hurried as he rustled his papers together and put them back into his faux leather folio. He told Adele, "Think about my offer, but don't think too long. You wouldn't want an opportunity like this to pass you by." She just kept staring at him in silence.

The next day when Carter went back to Golden Acres to speak to some of his potential clients, many of them seemed distant to him. He knew Adele Jamison was to blame. He would just have to avoid her watchful eyes. All of his contacts at Golden Acres had not abandoned him. He would now have to be more discreet in his selections.

21

Golden Acres

"We need to split up and locate our assignments," said Eden to the other three Protectors. They all nodded in agreement. "Let's meet back here at nine o'clock tonight to report our findings to Amanda at Everwell. Gem and I will search this wing of the building." She pointed to the left side of Golden Acres.

"Jack and I will start on the other end," added Maxwell. "We'll see you inside." The boys flew to one end of the building and the girls to the other. As they passed through the doors, they seemed to be drawn to their assignments. Jack and Eden both gravitated to the lawn at the back of the building. There they found Kenneth and Essie playing bocce against some other residents of Golden Acres. Gem found Betty knitting a shawl in the recreation room in front of the television, her favorite game show blaring loudly. She tried to quickly answer the questions out loud and beat the buzzer just as though she were on the show herself.

Maxwell located Adele's room by checking the mailboxes at the front desk. Her room number was 108, but when he arrived, he found it empty. She was nowhere to be found. When he left her room, he walked the entire complex, but he always felt the pull to go back. He decided he should return to her room and double-check to make sure she hadn't fallen in the closet or bathroom.

On his way back, he passed the other Protectors in their various locations. They had all located their assignments, but his charge was missing. *It's strange the other Protectors knew exactly where to find their assignments but mine has vanished. Yet, I can feel her presence,* thought Maxwell. Out loud, he said, "Where could she be? Why can't I find her?"

Maxwell had been out on the back lawn with Jack and Eden when he saw a small-statured lady with short, dark hair streaked with gray returning from a brisk walk. He recognized her; it was Adele. His first thought was how she looked and behaved younger than her sixty-nine years.

"There she is!" exclaimed Maxwell. Jack and Eden both looked up as Maxwell flew to be beside his assignment. Adele looked upward as Maxwell flew down beside her. He knew the assignments couldn't see their Protectors in the spirit dimension, so her glance must have been coincidence, but the look was unnerving. She kept looking over her shoulder in his direction. *She is looking right at me!* he thought. He looked behind himself to see what she could be staring at.

As if Adele could read his thoughts, she looked away from Maxwell and toward her teammates. She waved her hand to get their attention and began running at a trot in their direction. Maxwell followed her but couldn't help thinking how unusual it was to see someone her age jogging. He wondered what kind of strange person he was protecting. Maybe this assignment would turn out to be more interesting than he had previously thought.

22

Where Is She?

That evening, the four Protectors reunited on the outside lawn to take turns giving Amanda their first reports. One by one, they basically gave the same statements about finding their assignments with nothing eventful to report. This hadn't been a game day, so injuries hadn't been an issue—unless you count Gem removing a piece of soap off the shower floor so Betty wouldn't fall.

When Maxwell took his turn giving his account, he told Amanda about his difficulty in locating Adele. He explained he couldn't understand why he was drawn to her room when she wasn't there. Why had the other three Protectors in his group easily found their assignments while he found an empty room? It made no sense. Amanda told him he was new at this skill and not to worry about it. After all, he had eventually located Adele, and she was fine.

Amanda completely dismissed this detail, so he reasoned perhaps he was being overly sensitive. *If she isn't worried, then I shouldn't be either.* Tomorrow their assignments had a ballgame on the schedule. Maybe, with luck, he would find someone to protect, in the game or out.

All the Protectors' assignments had turned in for the evening. Amanda sent every Protector back to their charge's room to watch him or her through the night. She wished them a successful day during the game tomorrow. The Protectors told each other goodnight and returned to their assigned rooms for a long night of nothingness.

After several hours of sleep, Adele was stirring, ready to get up and begin another day. The night had given Maxwell a chance to look over her apartment since the Protectors required no sleep while they were on assignment. Her apartment was small but neat, not cluttered. She had a small couch, one chair, a small television, and bookshelves on nearly every wall. Her books were mostly how-tos, ranging from playing better softball, to cooking Southern style, to fencing. Other strange titles were mixed into her assortment. She had many titles on geography and some on aerodynamics. He wondered if she might have been a pilot in her younger days.

Adele had obviously traveled extensively, her being a bird-watcher, which explained the geography books. She had several history books on Leonardo da Vinci, which didn't seem odd. He would be interesting to most. Maxwell pulled the da Vinci book off the shelf to take a look. Adele had bookmarked the page of his studies concerning winged flight. This must have been of interest to her due to her bird studies. She had underlined a passage on the mechanics of winged flight and how the bird's wings moved at different stages of flight. Da Vinci's drawings did have some of the same characteristics of Maxwell's wings. Maxwell chuckled as he looked at the picture. *Maybe Leo was a Protector, too,* he thought.

Maxwell spent a great deal of the night looking through her swordsmanship books. He silently practiced some of the techniques demonstrated in the books and felt he had improved his skills with just one night of practice. With several more nights of repetition, he should be able to outmaneuver Jack a time or two. Jack would wonder where he learned these new skills.

Adele was a unique assignment. He had been with her part of one day, and all he knew about her was what she liked to read. *What kind of a profession is bird-watching?* he thought. At least the other assignments had normal jobs. She didn't seem to be wealthy enough to be a bird-watcher without being paid for her employment. Very few companies would pay someone to watch birds when there were enough people out there who would watch them for free.

"Well, Ms. Adele Jamison, what are you hiding?" Maxwell mumbled under his breath. "You're going to have a tough time keeping it from me." He repositioned the Leonardo da Vinci book back on the shelf. He heard her get out of the bed and walk to the closet to get her robe.

As Maxwell checked on Adele, she was heading for the kitchen. He leaned against the wall, out of her way, so he could observe her. She put on a small pot of coffee and poured a bowl of cereal. She opened the front door of her apartment and picked up the morning paper. After her coffee finished brewing, she sat down at her table for two with her paper, coffee, and cereal, just as she had done every morning since her arrival at Golden Acres.

Maxwell decided very quickly that nothing was happening here. He wanted to check on the other Protectors and see how their night had been spent. He found Gem and Jack outside as their assignments did their morning walk on the jogging track. Eden flew out to join them. She said her assignment, Essie, was watching the morning news shows.

While they were outside discussing their evenings, the Protectors heard cries for help inside their heads. All four turned their eyes at once in the direction of the cries. Several angels or Protectors—they weren't sure which from this far away—were flying in the direction of the calls.

"It sounded close by," said Gem. "That's the first time I've heard a cry for help."

"I'm surprised they even let us hear them, being rookies," added Eden. "I know they don't want us leaving our assignments, being new to protecting."

"That's ridiculous," grumbled Maxwell. "We should be able to help anyone who needs us. I bet the person who wants help wouldn't care if we were rookies or not."

"It looks like they have it covered," said Jack. "What time is the game?"

"Noon," answered Eden. "Right after lunch. They are planning a short batting practice this morning. I overheard Essie telling the project coordinator at the activity center. We probably should stand in with them during practice, too."

"I'm going back to check on Adele," said Maxwell. "See you at practice." The four went their separate ways and returned to their assignments. When Maxwell returned to Adele's room, she was gone. The empty cereal bowl and coffee cup were in the sink and the newspaper was still on the table.

Not Again! thought Maxwell. *How is she doing this? I'm not sensing anything on her location. My radar must be defective because I'm picking up zilch.* He looked throughout the residence building and found nothing. Maxwell flew out to the jogging track where Jack and Gem were waiting on their assignments.

"Adele has disappeared again," said Maxwell despairingly. "I'm not sensing anything on her location. What kind of Protector am I if I keep losing my assignment?" Maxwell did a standing three-sixty. "Nothing. I sense nothing," said a panicked Maxwell.

"Calm down, Maxwell," said Jack, putting his hand on Maxwell's shoulder. "I'm sure nothing is wrong. She's probably out visiting a friend or running errands with one of the other tenants. We'll help you look."

"I'll get Eden to help us, too," added Gem. The three flew away toward the residence hall to begin the search.

Gem and Eden rejoined the guys outside Adele's room. "Double-check her room," instructed Jack to Maxwell. "We'll begin searching each of the other rooms. If she's nowhere to be found here, we'll search the outlying towns." Jack, Eden, and Gem split up to begin searching each room in the building.

Maxwell disappeared through Adele's door. To his shock and amazement, she was sitting at her kitchen table, reading the paper, just as she had been earlier. It looked as though she had never left. *I must be losing my mind,* thought Maxwell as he retraced the previous minutes over in his mind to convince himself that he had been here earlier and she truly had been gone.

Maxwell scanned the scene before him and glanced back at Adele's face. He could've sworn he saw her smile in his peripheral vision, but she sat there now as solemn as a judge. *Great! Now I'm imagining things,* thought Maxwell. He flew out into the hallway to tell the other Protectors. This time he did see a smile. He saw three of them.

23

First Sighting

Maxwell rejoined Adele in her room. She pulled on her warm-up suit over her clothes, grabbed her lucky bat, and picked up her ball mitt. The well-worn mitt looked like the only one she had used her entire life.

The mitt had been her father's from high school. Adele had no brothers, only two older sisters. Since she was the only one to show interest, her father decided she would be the one to learn his secrets of the game. She thought of him every time she picked up the mitt.

Adele's father, Charles, had passed away in a car accident. He worked out of town on an oil drill rig throughout the week and then drove home to be with his family every weekend. This particular week, he had worked over a couple hours, so it was dark for his drive home. He swerved to avoid an animal crossing the road and ran into a ditch on the side of the road. The ditch was shallow, so he was able to keep driving. When he attempted to steer out of the ditch, he gave the wheel a sharp jerk, which flipped the car upside down in the opposite lane. Another vehicle quickly came around the curve, slamming into his vehicle and killing him instantly. Adele and her family were devastated. She had never gotten over his death.

Maxwell watched Adele pause and smile when she picked up her mitt, hooked it on the handle of her bat, and flipped it up to carry it on her shoulder like a soldier with his rifle. He thought the way she carried her bat reminded him of a young person, not a senior citizen. Maxwell stayed close behind her. *You're not getting away from me again, mysterious lady,* he thought to himself.

The entire team had a productive practice, with everyone hitting the ball well. A couple of ground balls got past Kenneth at shortstop, but that's expected in a senior league. Most of the players could still wallop the ball but were a little slow in fielding. Jack thought it made the game more exciting when you have slow runners because there was always a chance to get them out no matter how far they hit the ball. None of us move like we did when we were young (as you, the reader, will experience one day, too).

It was half past ten when the players noticed the heat of the day. "Let's call practice, grab a light lunch, and meet on the field in an hour," said Betty, Gem's assignment. The rest of the team agreed and headed back to the residence building.

Jack flew over to Maxwell and said, "Well, are you ready for our big test in protecting?" Maxwell rolled his eyes and laughed.

"It's the only assignment we've got, so we need to make sure no one gets hurt," said Maxwell. "But don't get me wrong; I never want another assignment like this again. While the team is in their pregame huddle, we should get together and go over what to expect. Tell the girls to be beside the dugout at eleven thirty. Adele is going inside. I don't want to lose her again. See you at pregame."

Maxwell followed Adele, who was walking toward her wing of the building. As Maxwell followed about ten paces behind her, Adele abruptly stopped walking. She didn't turn left or right; she just stood still, looking forward. Suddenly, a softball came soaring over her head and landed directly in the spot where she should have been standing had she not stopped.

"Heads up!" called Essie, jogging up to Adele, even though the ball was already on the ground. "Sorry about the close call. I never dreamed Kenny could hit the ball that far." Adele reached over and picked up the ball.

"I'm fine, Essie," reassured Adele. "Tell Kenny he better hit like that in the game if he wants to make it up to me." Adele smiled, gave a wink, and then tossed Essie the ball. "Go rest. I don't want the two of you tired for the game." As Essie waved for Kenny to follow her to the residence building, a scream erupted from the practice field.

Betty came running as fast as her little legs could carry her. "Snake! Snake!" she screamed. "It's a rattlesnake! I almost stepped on it!" Betty was breathing hard, gasping to get more oxygen. "I can't believe it didn't bite me," she added. "It was right beside me and lunged for me. Then the back end of the snake snapped backwards a foot. I still can't believe it missed me. I've never seen a snake go backwards before. Maybe I scared it as much as it did me." Betty was visibly shaken.

Kenneth ran for the maintenance man while Essie and Adele tried to calm Betty down. Maxwell looked out in the field. Gem had just let go of the snake across a ravine, out of the boundaries of the ball field. She was just as excited at successfully protecting her assignment as Betty was scared. Eden had flown out to congratulate Gem as Jack stayed beside Kenneth and the maintenance man while they made their way out in the field to look for the poisonous snake. It was nowhere to be found. The snake had swiftly slithered away as soon as Gem released its tail.

Maxwell gave Gem a thumbs-up and then looked over to Adele. He had almost forgotten about her sudden stop moments ago, which had kept her from getting smacked in the back of the head with a ball. Had she known that ball was going to hit her? Or was it dumb luck? He knew she couldn't see out the back of her head. He ran the different possibilities over in his mind as he followed her into the building.

Adele laid down her equipment upon entering her apartment and went straight to the kitchen. She got some leftover homemade chicken salad out of the fridge and made herself a sandwich. Maxwell watched as she made the sandwich with whole wheat bread and poured herself some carrot juice from a container in the fridge.

That looks like something Grandfather would eat, thought Maxwell, chuckling to himself. Maxwell remembered eating many lunches with his grandfather while helping in the stables. His grandfather was always drinking goat's milk, barley juice, or beet juice. He would eat or drink anything considered healthy, even if it smelled bad or looked disgusting.

"The body is God's temple, Maxwell," his grandfather would always tell him. "Take care of it, and it will last you a lifetime." Maxwell imagined his grandfather lecturing him on nutrition as he watched Adele eat.

I would never have imagined that Grandfather was such a great Protector! thought Maxwell. He had always been more strong and fit than others his age, but Maxwell always attributed that to his work in the stables. In Maxwell's eyes, nothing was ever too difficult for his grandfather; he could handle any unforeseen problem. Maxwell had never seen him overwhelmed or shook up. Well, never until . . . Benjamin died.

Maxwell's grandfather took his grandson's death especially hard. He barely spoke to anyone for weeks. Gradually, he returned to his old self—or nearly, but it was slow in coming. Maxwell had spent hours each day with his grandfather while growing up, so the change was still obvious to him. When Maxwell mentioned his concerns to his parents, they dismissed them, saying it was just the way of his grandfather's generation.

Maxwell snapped back to his present surroundings as Adele walked out of the back room in her ball uniform and picked up her equipment. He realized he was starting to enjoy his protection assignment. He knew there was more to Adele than what met the eye. He was determined to discover her secrets, one way or another. Maxwell decided to keep quiet about his suspicions to the others. They already thought he was imagining things. All he needed was them making more fun of him. He would investigate on his own.

Maxwell followed Adele out onto the field with the two of them the first to arrive. Adele tossed the ball into the air a couple of times, catching it in her glove. All of a sudden, she hurriedly snatched the ball, jerked her head around, and stared toward the empty road leading to Golden Acres and the softball field.

"What's she looking at?" Maxwell said to himself. "I can't hear anything, and I see nothing. Maybe she's expecting visitors." Maxwell convinced himself this must be the reason, even though her quick glance toward the road seemed more of an alarmed reaction. By this time, Kenneth was walking onto the field with Jack hovering close behind.

"Hey, Dele! Throw me a ball," called Kenneth, waving at Adele. Adele didn't react. She continued looking down the empty road. Kenneth walked over to her. "Did you forget your hearing aid, ole girl?" teased Kenneth.

"Sorry, Kenny," replied Adele as she turned to face him with a half-smile. "My head was in the clouds again. You know I wander off sometimes."

"I know you do," answered Kenneth, smiling. "It's fine. Are you all right? You seem worried. That's not like you on game day." Maxwell noticed that she did seem worried now, but she hadn't in her apartment. He wasn't buying her head-in-the-clouds story.

Adele removed any trace of concern left on her face and emphatically said, "Are you kidding me? We're going to clean Meadowbrook's clocks today!" She laughed and put her glove up to receive a toss from Kenneth.

Essie and Betty were joining them on the field. Maxwell and Jack looked over to see Eden and Gem standing on the edge of the field. The girls threw their hands up to acknowledge the boys' looks.

While Maxwell was watching the girls, he didn't notice a car driving up the road that had previously held Adele's interest. The driver of the vehicle slammed on his breaks and slid to a halt in the gravel/dirt mix of the parking lot. Everyone turned to look toward the screeching brakes, but it took a minute for the dust to settle. The driver's side door squeaked open and out stepped William Carter, the sleazy investment planner. Kenneth, Essie, Betty, and several others all waved at William and said hello. Adele did not. She continued staring at him silently, with her hands folded in front of her. After a moment, she turned her back to him and told the others to warm up.

William returned the greetings to the other senior citizens as he climbed up the bleachers and sat on the highest step. As the dirt continued to settle around Carter's car, Maxwell noticed shadows coming out of the dust. They didn't appear to be human, but they may have been at another time. Maxwell looked over to the other Protectors to see if they had seen them too. They did. Jack, Gem, and Eden were heading toward Maxwell.

"What kind of freaky things are they?" asked Jack.

"They're Manips," answered Eden. "I saw drawings in my books. They are even uglier in person."

"They came in with the man in the bleachers," added Gem. "He gave me the creeps when I first saw him."

The Manips had spotted the Protectors. Zantos, one of the two figures, cursed his luck at seeing the Protectors who were now guarding Carter's waiting prey. "Carter should have put more pressure on the old people to sign away their savings," said Zantos, to the other Manip. "Now his work will be more difficult."

Zantos had not seen these Protectors before. "They must be new recruits," he said to Dover. All Manips were on high alert over the rumor of Alexander Justice's grandchild being in the newest group. "Maybe we've lucked out and one of the four Protectors will turn out to be Justice's heir." They could report this new information to Norris, their commander, as soon as they returned to headquarters. Perhaps this day wouldn't be a complete waste.

Both Zantos and Dover snarled a laugh and conjured visions of grandeur. If they could discover that, in fact, one of the Protectors was their greatest rival's offspring, then report the news to Norris, lavish tribute and glory would be theirs, with their entire society chanting their names: "Zantos! Dover! Zantos! Dover!" Over and over, they'd be hailed, then envied.

Then, suddenly, flying beings were all around them, interrupting their daydream. They were surrounded by the four Protectors.

"Leave this place now or prepare to be removed!" shouted Maxwell with his hand on the hilt of his sword.

"What have we here?" replied Zantos with a calculated, evil tone. "Let me guess, a foursome of newbie Protectors? You must be at the top of your group if they put you all the way out here with such an important assignment. Not every Protector gets to guard the elderly. They live such peril-filled lives." Zantos and Dover both threw their heads back and laughed hysterically—if you want to call it a laugh. It was more like a mix between a cackle and a shriek. Then Dover became serious very quickly.

"What are your names?" asked Dover. Zantos cringed at the question. He knew they would need to be more subtle to find the Protectors' identities. Maxwell drew his sword with the other three Protectors following his lead.

"Never mind our names!" exclaimed Maxwell. "Consider yourself warned to never come back here again. And keep your friend on the bleachers away from these people. If we see your face again, it will be your last memory as a Manip."

The Manips said nothing as they stared back, hatred in their eyes. They knew they were outnumbered. Even though they didn't know the abilities of these four Protectors, they knew their chances were slim to beat them in a fight.

Eden moved out of the way to give the Manips room to exit. Zantos hissed at Maxwell as he flew by. He hated him already. "Another time, newbie, another time," said Zantos. "Better keep your friends close by. I'd hate for one of you to come up missing one night. My name is Zantos, by the way. I'm not afraid to give my name. Goodbye, mysterious chicken rookies."

Zantos thought the dig at being a coward might prod the Protectors to give their names, but none of them spoke. Zantos and Dover gave another shriek of laughter as they flew away. The Protectors stood motionless until they were out of sight.

"That was interesting!" exclaimed Jack. "So much for a dull assignment."

"Maxwell, I don't like his threats toward you," said Eden, concerned. "Jack, make sure you're close to him always."

"I'll guard our elite Protector," replied Jack, putting his right hand up to his forehead in a salute jester toward Eden. Both boys laughed off the seriousness of the suggestion.

"You'd better heed Eden's warning," added Gem. "That's not going to be the last we see of either of them."

"We agree, we agree," said Maxwell, trying to calm the situation. "But I'm pretty sure the threat was meant for all of us, not just me."

The four turned around to see the ballgame beginning. Maxwell noticed Adele returning her gaze to home plate after looking off in the direction where Zantos and Dover had just flown away. He knew none of the other Protectors had noticed Adele because they were busy watching their assignments.

I'm going to find out what you're hiding, thought Maxwell on his way to join Adele at the mound, *right after I take care of Zantos.*

The game progressed with few mishaps. Eden had to lift Essie's glove about two inches or she would've caught one of Kenneth's throws in her teeth. Jack had to slip one of Kenneth's legs out from under him to prevent the ball from hitting his face after a bad bounce off an infield dirt clod.

Gem, on the other hand, had to do very little for Betty, the catcher. She was a retired horse trainer, and there wasn't much on that baseball diamond she couldn't handle. The players on the other team ran fast toward home plate, but Betty held her position at the plate. She was plowed into several times, but she never dropped or boggled the ball. The four Protectors decided to cover the entire field, helping the other players prevent injuries as well. They even protected the opposing team's players while they were in the field and their assignment wasn't batting. These extra duties kept the Protectors busy the entire time and helped sharpen their protection skills.

The Golden Acres Gators won the game, six to zero, against the Meadowbrook Frogs. It would've been closer if anyone on the other team had been fortunate enough to get past Betty on home plate. Adele had no mishaps, but she struggled in her pitching. The other team had been on third base many times but could never make it home to score. In fact, Adele had walked more players in this game than she had ever walked in her life. If the Protectors had not been in the game to prevent some of the injuries, the Gators may have been beaten. Adele apologized for her terrible performance on the pitching mound.

"I don't know what happened to me out there, guys," said Adele. "I just couldn't concentrate today."

"We've all been there, honey," said Betty, putting her arm around Adele. Her face and arms were smeared with dirt.

"Hey, we won in the end!" added Kenneth. "And, I don't know about the rest of you, but I didn't get injured even once!"

"Me either," said Essie.

"Speak for yourselves," corrected Betty.

"It's your own fault," chimed in Essie. "You need to get out of the way when the other team is running home. You can still get 'em out if you tag them. I swear. Sometimes I think you stand on that home plate to see if they have the nerve to knock you off. You give them your 'I dare you' look."

Essie scrunched up her face, imitating Betty, and assumed the stance Betty takes when she's defending the plate. Everyone laughed at her, even Adele, despite her foul mood.

24

A Stranded Stranger

The Protectors huddled together after the game while their assignments were in their dugout discussing the game.

"Whose turn is it to give the report to Amanda first?" asked Gem.

"It's mine," answered Eden.

"Be sure and tell her about the Manips following the insurance guy named Carter," reminded Gem. "They may want to put extra assignments on him."

"He's only one guy," said Jack in an aggravated tone. "I think we can handle him."

"He has two Manips with him, Jack," replied Gem. "It's our first assignment. I want to be extra careful."

"Fine. Go ahead and report every detail," said Jack. "But I want to voice Maxwell's and my opinion that we four can handle this minor situation without extra help. Isn't that right, Maxwell?" Maxwell was nonresponsive. Jack nudged him to get an answer.

"Absolutely," answered Maxwell in a not-paying-attention sort of manner. He was trying to see into the Gators' dugout. "I don't see Adele," he said, thinking out loud, worry in his voice. The other Protectors turned to look.

"No, she's not there," said Jack. "Probably went on inside, Maxwell. She played pretty lousy. Maybe she's not feeling well."

"She was fine before the game," replied Maxwell. "If she slipped away from me again . . ." He didn't finish his sentence. Maxwell flew as fast as his wings would carry him to Adele's apartment. Nothing. She was gone. Maxwell was heading back outside when he met Jack and Gem walking in behind their assignments.

"She's gone again!" exclaimed Maxwell excitedly.

"Maybe she just went for a walk, Maxwell," said Jack. "You're making a big deal about keeping up with her."

"Why can't I sense where she is?" replied Maxwell. "The rest of you can feel the location of your assignments. Why can't I?"

"Who knows?" said Gem. "But I'm sure it's nothing to worry about. We are all new at this. Adele always shows up, and she's never gone for long. Maybe your sensor is on the fritz." Maxwell smirked at Gem's last remark. He turned to continue outside.

"Maxwell, check on Eden if you're going out. She should be almost done with her report to Everwell," said Gem, calling after him. Maxwell nodded in agreement as he headed out the door.

Maxwell's eyes scanned all directions as soon as he exited the building. *Where could Adele be?* he wondered. He saw Eden standing at one side of the softball field, gazing off in the distance. She was giving the day's report to Amanda. Maxwell saw her turn her eyes toward him.

She stretched out her wings and flew in his direction.

"Amanda wasn't happy about the Manips," said Eden, matter-of-factly. "She's going to talk to Raphael about moving us." Maxwell could tell Eden regretted giving Amanda the complete report. "She said no other report was needed this evening from the other Protectors. She wanted to go ahead and contact Raphael."

"Why would they move us after seeing two Manips?" exclaimed Maxwell. He wasn't in the mood to be treated like a child. "We have our training. They should let us use it!" Maxwell spoke with authority, but then remembered he couldn't even find his assignment. He quickly calmed down as he told Eden about Adele being nowhere inside.

"I'm going to circle the grounds and see if I can find her," said Maxwell. Eden could hear his anxiety as he spoke.

"Don't be gone long, Maxwell," warned Eden. "Everwell was extremely upset over something happening here, and that worries me. We may be in the middle of a mess and don't even know it. Watch and see. Adele will show up. Just go back in her room and wait for her. That's the safest decision."

"I'll do one loop around Golden Acres and be back within ten minutes," promised Maxwell. "Don't worry." He reassuringly touched Eden on the shoulder as she walked by him. She produced a worried smile. Maxwell floated upward to get a better view.

"Ten minutes, Maxwell!" shouted Eden before she entered the building. Maxwell waved back to her, acknowledging the reminder.

Upon his first glance, Adele was gone. She was nowhere to be seen. It had only taken him a couple of minutes to complete one circle around the grounds. He decided to expand his loop to get a more thorough search. He reasoned he had only been away less than ten minutes, so he still had extra time.

He flew to the outskirts of the Golden Acres property where he could see a winding river running parallel to one side of the property line. The river ran a mile to the west with the Rocky Mountains rising up directly behind. Adele was nowhere in sight, so Maxwell turned to fly east.

"Help! Help!" Maxwell heard screams. "Somebody! Please! Anybody!" The shouts were coming from the direction of the river. He turned around to find the source of the cries. It didn't take him long.

A man was standing on a boulder in the middle of the rapids on the river. He had no boat or floatation device with him, which left him stranded. Maxwell searched the sky and the area surrounding the man. He saw no response from angels or other Protectors.

What should I do? Maxwell wondered. His training had been clear: first assignment Protectors are not to respond to emergencies. He could jeopardize his Protectorship, but wasn't that why he was here, to help? He heard the cries again. He looked around, still no response. He knew he had to help.

Right away, Maxwell flew in the direction of the stranded man. His eyes scanned downstream, then upstream, for additional clues while accessing the situation. He saw the man's kayak turned upside down and caught between two rocks in a small rapid farther down the river. The man must have been alone on the water, which was his first mistake.

Upstream, Maxwell spotted a fallen dead tree trunk half in the water and half out. He decided if he could free the log, it might just be long enough for him to float downstream and position it between the man's boulder and the river's edge. The stranded victim would never be the wiser of how he truly got rescued. He would believe he had just been lucky the log came along when it did. On downstream, out of sight, Maxwell could free the kayak and drift it to the river's edge where the man was sure to find it.

Maxwell flew upstream and positioned himself behind the log. He shoved with all his might. The log moved rather easily. He had never before realized his power had increased because he was a Protector. He freed the log from its constraint, and it floated downstream with little difficulty.

Maxwell stayed with the log to guide it to the desired position. He would lodge it against the stranded man's boulder first, then ease the opposite end over to the river's edge. Maxwell enjoyed Rescue training the best. It was his specialty. He couldn't wait to tell the others about his first real rescue.

Without warning, the log picked up speed. It began moving quickly with the current, too quickly. Maxwell panicked. He had to slow the log down but he couldn't swim against this current. Even with his newfound strength, it was too strong for him to handle. At this speed, the log would collide into the stranded man's boulder, possibly knocking him and the boulder into the water. Racing through Maxwell's mind were visions of the boulder crushing the man or, worse yet, making the man fly off into the rapids. Not only would he not rescue the man, he would probably cause his death.

Without pausing to think, Maxwell climbed on top of the speeding log, lying flat with his belly down. He wrapped his arms and legs around the log with his wings outstretched above him. He knew he couldn't slow the log down while it was in the water. The current was too swift. His only hope was to raise the log out of the water.

Maxwell began flapping his wings with every ounce of strength he had left. He was still a bit winded from his futile effort of trying to slow the log while still in the water. His wings moved slowly but steadily at first, as if they were utilizing all the surrounding air. Then they moved faster and faster still. After just moments, the wings were moving so fast they couldn't be seen.

Maxwell was unaware he was being observed. *This Protector has remarkable skills,* thought the observer. *He has the intuition of a seasoned Protector, not that of a beginner.*

Maxwell noticed the log slowing down. He wanted to just barely raise the log above the water's touch so the stranded man wouldn't be aware it was not traveling via the current (although the water was speeding around the log on all sides if he had been paying attention). Maxwell attempted to keep the log moving forward at a fairly fast speed while trying to maintain control.

The stranded man noticed the floating wood moving in his direction. He stretched out an arm to try and secure the log heading toward him. When it was almost to the boulder, Maxwell lowered that end of the log into the water. It nudged against the boulder ever so gently as Maxwell glided the other end of the log in the direction of the water's edge. Maxwell lowered the other end completely into the water as it grounded onto the river's bank and held firm.

The stranded man on the boulder was already making his way excitedly across the secure log on his way to the riverbank. But Maxwell knew he wasn't yet finished in his rescue; he needed to find the man a way out of here. Maxwell glanced downstream and spotted the suspended kayak. It was out of the man's view, so Maxwell towed the kayak to a rocky shore that would be within the man's eyesight after he reached land. When the man caught his breath and stood up to get his bearing, he should easily be able to spot and walk to his yellow kayak.

In the back of Maxwell's mind, he knew he still hadn't located Adele, not to mention he was overdue on his allotted time to search the grounds alone. He needed to get back to Golden Acres, *now*.

No sooner had Maxwell thought of his next move than he was tackled from behind and shoved under the water. *Wham! Mumph! Gurgle!* He had no idea what was attacking him. *Wham! Mumph! Gurgle!* He knew it was strong and had both of his arms pinned where he couldn't reach his sword. *Wham! Mumph! Gurgle!* Maxwell tried to use the water to his advantage. He kicked and twisted enough to get turned around to see his attacker. It was the Manips, both of them, the same two he had seen earlier on the ball field. They had him, and they were holding on tightly.

The man who had been rescued noticed a great deal of splashing in the water downstream, which helped draw his attention to his lost kayak.

He was so excited to see his lost means of transportation, he simply dismissed the splashing as a school of fish in a feeding frenzy.

One of the Manips holding Maxwell kept going for the sword on his side. As soon as the Manip would loosen his two-handed grip on him to grab his sword, Maxwell would likewise reach for his sword. It appeared to Maxwell that he was stronger than the Manips as it took both of their arms to hold one of his. Both Manips were unable to loosen their grips and draw their swords to kill their catch. When one of the Manips let loose with one arm, Maxwell would move the entire pile to the left or right, attempting to free himself. They struggled back and forth, above and below the water, with neither side gaining advantage. Maxwell could feel himself tiring.

He needed a diversion. *No,* he thought, *I need help.* Suddenly, one of the Manips restraining him took the brunt of a force as strong and swift as a falling tree, pinning him under the water. It took Maxwell just an instant to realize one of his arms was free. The next moment, Maxwell saw what he assumed was one of his Protector friends and the former Manip, who had been under the water, rise up out of the water with swords flashing and the splash of water so thick he couldn't tell which friend had saved him. Steel desperately striking steel, back and forth they went.

Maxwell saw all of this commotion happening in his peripheral vision, but he took the opportunity to grab his own sword to attack the single Manip still clinging to one of his arms. When the Manip realized Maxwell had one arm free and his sword drawn, he immediately loosened his grip and hurriedly flew away, abandoning his partner.

"Chase after it!" yelled the other Protector still fighting the remaining Manip. "Don't let it escape!" Maxwell sped after the fleeing Manip. He realized the Protector wasn't one of his three friends, but the voice sounded familiar. Maxwell couldn't see the Protector's face during the sword fight, but he thought he may have been at training with her. Perhaps she had been one of his instructors.

Maxwell was closing in on the Manip. He saw it look back to get his approaching position. The Manip flew toward the bank of the river, then around a bend into the forest. Maxwell lost sight of him for just seconds. As Maxwell was coming out of the bend, the Manip was nowhere to be seen. "Where did you gooooooo—?"

Whack! Maxwell was hit with the branch of an evergreen that had been pulled back and released at the precise moment he came out of the bend. Maxwell went spiraling down to the grass and landed with a thud.

As he lay on the ground motionless, he strained to bring his eyes into focus. The limb had smacked hard, sending him tumbling, and he was still shaken. Maxwell scolded himself for allowing the Manip to bait him into a blind spot. Now, he had managed to get away and would most likely return with reinforcements. He needed to pull himself together and get back to the other Protector, who may need his help.

Maxwell managed to rise up above the trees to see if, by chance, the Manip would still be in sight. Nothing. He made his way back to the location where the Protector had helped him. From the sky, he saw one person standing alone on the bank of the river. It was the Protector; the Manip wasn't with her. Perhaps her Manip had escaped as well. As Maxwell descended, he still couldn't make out her face; she was too far away. He watched her walk toward a sword lying in the mud beside a pile of charcoal with worms devouring the ashes.

Maxwell landed in the clearing. The Protector, with her back to Maxwell, reached down to pick up the jagged sword. She turned to face him.

"Did you catch it?" she questioned with authority. Maxwell just stared, open-mouthed. He couldn't believe his eyes. It was Adele.

"Well, this explains a lot!" exclaimed Maxwell.

"Did you catch it?" she asked again in an agitated voice, ignoring his comment.

"No," he answered defensively. "It hit me with a branch when I wasn't looking and—" Adele cut him off.

"We don't have time for you to explain." She sounded determined. "We've got to get you out of here." She slipped the fallen Manip's sword in her belt.

"Don't you mean *we* have to get out of here?" replied Maxwell. "Why would you need to get just me out of here?" She ignored his questions.

"I assume you are okay to fly?" asked Adele, appearing concerned. Maxwell had a large gash above his eye where the branch had smashed him in the head. It was still bleeding. Adele was examining the cut.

"I'll be fine," replied Maxwell. "What's going on here? Why am I protecting a Protector or angel or whatever you are?"

"Let's get away from here to somewhere safe," she answered. "I'll get you cleaned up, and then we'll call Everwell to report the attack."

Maxwell crossed his arms in defiance. He wanted answers.

"I'll talk to you after we're safe. I promise. But now, we have to hurry," said Adele convincingly.

She flew straight up into the air, then turned around and paused. She looked down at him waiting on the ground. Maxwell looked up at her watching, then felt very foolish. He realized she was right and flew up to meet her.

"We have a sanctuary right over this mountain," said Adele, pointing forward. "I'll get your head cleaned up and report in. We'll go from there."

"I'd like to start with what in the stars is going on!" exclaimed Maxwell.

"Follow me," instructed Adele, still ignoring his comments.

25

Sanctuary

$\mathscr{A}$dele flew over the mountain ridge, then dropped rapidly over the edge, causing Maxwell to struggle to keep up with her. He still couldn't believe Adele had ties to Everwell. Nothing about this assignment made sense. She seemed to be more than a Protector but he knew he hadn't seen her during training. Plus, she didn't carry herself like an instructor, more like a soldier. Who was she?

Maxwell noticed her course of flight descending. He lowered his gaze to the ground and noticed a small cabin amongst the pine trees. It looked dark and broken down, as if it had been deserted for years.

Adele landed on the front porch, and Maxwell followed closely. She walked over to the window to peer inside. "It's empty," she said.

Maxwell looked in the window after Adele. It looked worse on the inside than on the out. Everything was broken and trashed, with rats scurrying throughout. They would probably be bitten as soon as they entered. He didn't want to go inside. Anywhere would have been better than this cabin. Maxwell voiced his objections.

Again, Adele ignored him. Maxwell tried to think about the positive. If he could get Adele to answer some of his questions, maybe it would be worth entering this forsaken place. He made his way to the front door while Adele did one last scan of the outside area. With a *thud*, he walked right into the front door.

"It's locked," exclaimed Maxwell, now rubbing the other side of his head. He jiggled the doorknob again. Definitely locked. Unfazed, Adele walked past Maxwell and turned the knob. The door clicked open. "How did you—?" said Maxwell. Adele entered the cabin, giving Maxwell no response.

The cabin was small but cozy. It looked completely different now that they were inside. He saw no mess, trash heap, or rodents as the view from the window had displayed. The furniture was quaint and aged but well maintained. It sat on a large, barely worn Persian rug, which covered a hardwood floor, and in the living area, off to the side, was a wood-burning fireplace with a beautifully carved wooden mantle above. The kitchen sat at the far end of the room with no door. Off to the right, he saw two closed doors, which Maxwell assumed led to bedrooms or a den, and a staircase leading to the second floor. To Maxwell, it seemed dark inside. Adele saw him searching for a light switch.

"There's no electricity," said Adele. "We'll light these oil lamps." Maxwell saw the lamps conveniently placed all around the room. They were made of polished brass with glass shades of various tints. "Get some wood for a fire from the box on the back porch through the kitchen. I'll get these lamps on," instructed Adele.

Maxwell asked no questions. He now knew better. There would be time for that later. He was wet, cold, and bleeding, but he knew he was with someone who would help him. Adele carried an aura of calm competence, which was soothing. He wanted to no longer cause her any aggravation. He would do whatever she instructed. If he stopped fighting her, maybe she would be more willing to share her story.

"Won't someone see the smoke from the fire?" asked Maxwell as he stacked logs on top of the kindling. Adele was lighting the last lamp in the room as she turned to look at him.

"This cabin is a sanctuary," she answered. "Sanctuaries are located all over Earth in inconspicuous locations. They were placed here for Protectors' needs of any kind, such as medical care, protection from an enemy, research, or transportation." Maxwell wondered about all of these examples, but he asked no questions. He had her talking, and he wanted it to continue.

"Manips cannot see sanctuaries. It looks like a bare spot in the woods to them. We can shroud them in the spiritual dimension from the Manips but not in the physical dimension from humans or vice versa. In one of the dimensions, reality must show itself. That is why we make this cabin unappealing for humans. From the outside, to a human, it would simply look like a run-down cabin surrounded by woods. Also, the earthly law of physics doesn't apply to sanctuaries due to it being an object brought here from another dimension. No smoke can be seen escaping from the chimney. No light is seen through the window. The food here never runs out or spoils, and the firewood box is never empty. Water from the spicket is the purest found on this planet, and when you sleep here, you will be more rested and reenergized just as if you were at Everwell."

"Why were we never told about sanctuaries during training?" asked Maxwell, still examining the cabin.

"We have never needed to use them with rookie Protectors," answered Adele. "Your first assignments are always more cushy, never dangerous, even though some do sound exciting. When you are receiving your first assignments, it may sound like it's terribly important business, and we do this to build your confidence. But once you arrive at your designated location, we make sure the assignment isn't more than you can handle. Sanctuaries are explained during your second or sometimes third rotation, depending on your team's skill level. That is, until now." Adele stopped talking for a moment, staring off into the fire, deep in thought.

During the silence, Maxwell wondered who Adele really was. As the firewood sparked and popped and the flames climbed and rolled over the logs with a strong heat, Maxwell turned to Adele. "You must be a Protector," he said. "You seem very capable of taking care of yourself. So, why am I protecting you?"

Adele stopped staring at the fire and looked at Maxwell, weighing her words. She sat on the sofa, leaning forward with her elbows resting on her knees. She noticed the blood still trickling down around Maxwell's eye. He kept wiping it with his sleeve and smearing it into his hair. Between the blood on his clothes and in his hair, he looked a sight worse than he felt.

"I'm protecting you," she answered. She immediately left the room to go into the kitchen, returning with a bowl of water and napkins to stop the bleeding. Maxwell waited for her to return, even though his mind was racing.

"Why would I need to be protected?" asked Maxwell, not letting on that he had an idea why. "This is the craziest nonsense I have heard since I got here, and I've heard some pretty unbelievable things. Have you been able to see me all along?"

"Yes," she answered. "Once you have been a Protector, you never lose the ability to see the spirit realm. It can be quite disruptive at times. The spirit realm appears fainter when you are in your earthly dimension, but you do notice when others show up. Now, that's enough of that subject. Let's move on. Have you heard about your grandfather yet?" asked Adele. Maxwell could tell she suspected he knew.

"Yes," he answered. "He was a great Protector during WWII and helped the Allies win some of their battles."

"Not just *some* battles," she corrected. "The *pivotal* battle, which was followed by many other smaller battles. Your grandfather was key to the Allies winning the war. The Axis powers were on the path to conquer Europe before your grandfather disrupted their plans."

Adele stood up and walked into the kitchen, returning with a bowl of fresh-cut fruit and a glass of sparkling water with ice chips. She sat the food and drink in front of Maxwell. He scooped up the bowl and glass while she returned to the kitchen for a second time. He wanted her full attention, so he waited for her to return before he spoke. She returned with a bandage to patch his head, along with cups of coffee and hot cocoa.

"I really need you to tell me what's going on," begged Maxwell. "I need to know every detail, not just half of the story."

"Sit back, rest, and enjoy the food and the warmth of the fire. Everything inside these walls contains healing properties, including the food and the fire," said Adele. "I will fill you in on the details that I'm aware of. You will be healing as we talk. All Protectors heal faster in a sanctuary. I do need to contact Everwell and alert them of your situation first." After standing, Adele paused to think.

"No!" insisted Maxwell. He had reached his breaking point. "I've patiently waited long enough. No more excuses." Adele turned to look at him.

"It is most likely they will move you immediately," replied Adele, second-guessing her decision. "Then whoever is chasing you will eventually find you at the new location. It's better we face them now with the slim chance they still don't know who they've found. I've always felt you should have been told all the facts of your situation beforehand."

"What facts? What situation?" asked Maxwell solemnly. Adele rejoined Maxwell on the sofa, tucked her legs beneath her, and took a sip of hot coffee before she began.

"Your grandfather and I joined the Protectors in the fall of 1940. The Nazis were marching across Europe and had already invaded Poland, Denmark, and Norway." Adele took another sip of coffee. "We were trained at Everwell, just as you and your friends were. Our first assignments were more critical because nearly everyone's assignments during that stage involved the war effort. The world had not seen evil that rampant for decades. It was a dangerous time for the entire planet. Humankind's freedom and survival depended on the Allies winning the war.

"Your grandfather was a standout from the beginning. He was a nat-ural-born Protector. He had the talent, brains, and courage to pull off any task assigned to him. I was honored to serve with him."

"So, you served with him?" asked Maxwell.

"We were paired as partners. We were together for many assign-ments."

"Tell me about your assignments," said Maxwell.

"We began our protection assignments by guarding Jewish children. We would find them a safe haven in which to hide or would find a way to smuggle them out of their country. We couldn't save them fast enough. Too many were still dying. It was your grandfather's idea to protect the children by bringing down those at the top of the Nazi war machine. His idea was to go on the offense. He wanted to stop reacting to their moves by making them react to some of his.

"Mind you, none of this was cleared with Everwell. He made this decision without consulting anyone in authority. He did tell the three of us on his team. Philip, Millie, and I had to cover for him by continuing our protection of the children. We knew it was a risk, but we believed in his idea, especially with him at the helm. We had faith your grandfather could accomplish whatever he set his mind to. He had never let us down." Maxwell listened intently and said nothing. He just soaked in every word.

Adele continued, "In December of '41, the war in the Pacific began, which meant we had even more to deal with. We were hiding and smug-gling children while your grandfather was sabotaging the Nazis and spying in the Pacific Rim. We were all working around the clock. It was obvious to everyone at Everwell when our group had returned back home to our earthly lives and were out of rotation because of your grandfather. You could see the difference by watching the newspaper headlines and by listening to the news on the radio. What ground he would gain for the Allies would go back and forth while we were rotated out." Adele paused for a moment, taking another drink.

"By January of '43, Alexander had convinced those in charge at Everwell to let the four of us stay on full time. They agreed. It had never happened before, and it has never happened since. We missed almost two and a half years of civilian life. When we returned home, we hadn't really missed a thing. We could remember everything that went on while we were gone. Everwell had been concerned the memories might not keep for that long, but they did. It wasn't that strange having two memories, but it does seem like you have been alive longer than your chronological age."

"What happened to you during those two and a half years?" asked Maxwell.

"That is for another time," answered Adele. "I will tell you this much. It all ended with your grandfather crushing Norris's plans. Everything fell apart for the Axis powers after that confrontation."

"How did Grandfather defeat Norris?" asked Maxwell. "You have to at least tell me that story."

"Why in a sword fight, of course," answered Adele, smiling.

"I need details!" exclaimed Maxwell. Adele jumped up off the sofa and picked up her sword. She had Maxwell stand opposite her, holding his sword at the ready.

"First, he slashed left, then right," said Adele, demonstrating each move in front of Maxwell. "Norris counterattacked with a slash and a swipe of his blade." Adele showed Maxwell the blocks used by his grandfather and the return jabs and thrusts of his sword. In one final swoop, Adele plunged forward as though she was going in for the kill. She stopped centimeters from Maxwell's neck and held the sword in midair as she smiled. Maxwell just stared wide-eyed, unsure of what she had just showed him. "It really wasn't much of a fight," said Adele. Now Maxwell smiled.

"Grandfather was too much for him?" asked Maxwell, standing back upright. "Did he disarm him by some sort of trickery? Did Grandfather get information out of him before he put an end to him? Or did he knock him in the noggin and take him prisoner?" Maxwell was flailing his sword in the air, imitating his grandfather's imagined fight. He looked to Adele for confirmation, then lowered his sword. "Are any of my ideas similar to what really happened?" he said.

Adele stared back at Maxwell and blinked. "Not even close," she answered. "Sit back down." Maxwell collapsed backwards onto the couch, his disappointment showing. Adele continued, "I don't have time to tell you everything, which would take hours. But I will tell you about your grandfather's last encounter with Norris.

"Alexander was surrounded and trapped on all sides. Even with his gift for combat, he was no match for Norris and his Manips. There were too many of them. So, he did the next best thing; he outwitted them. He created a diversion by throwing the hilt of his sword directly at Norris. No one expected this to happen. Norris didn't think; he just reacted and caught the sword before it hit him. He was seared by the hilt. He screamed in agony but couldn't release his grip. It was all the distraction your grandfather needed to escape the room he was trtapped in. During this covert operation, he had discovered key intelligence to aid the Allies, which helped turn the direction of the war. It didn't happen overnight, but gaining this information eventually led to the final blow and the Axis powers' ultimate defeat."

"You left out so much," complained Maxwell. "Talk about the condensed version! We still have plenty of time. Can't you tell me more?"

"Time is the one thing we don't have," answered Adele firmly. "What I do have time to tell you is the Manips have not regained the evil control lost at the hands of your grandfather. They have gained ground in certain areas but not like the scale during WWII. They know who is most to blame for this loss of their control, and they would like nothing more but to avenge this loss. That is where you come in." Maxwell noticed Adele was getting more adamant when she spoke.

"If the Manips find out who you are related to, you will be public enemy number one," she warned. "Norris, especially, will stop at nothing to get revenge for his shame and embarrassment by harming you. Those in authority at Everwell didn't want you to be selected as a Protector, but that is one area where they have no control."

"Who did select me?" asked Maxwell.

"All selections are made by higher authority in the land across the divide," answered Adele. "The only way you cannot be a Protector, after you are selected, is by your refusal of the offer. You accepted, so we must try to keep you as safe as possible while you perform your duties."

"I'm not performing any duties," scoffed Maxwell. "You are watching me."

"Actually, you are," corrected Adele. "The rest of the occupants of Golden Acres are not former Protectors. William Carter is not an honorable man, and he is out to swindle these kind, trusting friends of mine. It is the job of you and your protection team to stop that from happening."

"What concerns me is how much you look like your grandfather when he was younger," continued Adele. "I don't know if the Manip that got away noticed the resemblance, but we should plan for the worst scenario. Protectors are rarely pulled from their assignments, except for three reasons. One, your rotation time is over; two, the threat has been eliminated; or three, the need for your protection is greater somewhere else. Since this is your first rotation, your skills are not so specialized that you would be moved to a greater need position, although Everwell could use this as an excuse to move you to what they deem a safer location. We both know your rotation time is not up, so that leaves us with option two, to extinguish the threat, which is William Carter. Your first priority should be dealing with him. You need to find a way to expose him to the group for what he really is, a swindler.

"If the escaped Manip recognized you, the powers of darkness will design a plan of action to capture or kill you. We are going to be ready for them if and when they do attack. You need to gather your friends and bring them up to speed with what you know."

"I will get started on our defensive strategy and maybe even an offensive response to their attack," said Adele, thinking out loud. "We will assemble together in my apartment at eleven o'clock tonight. Your wounds are almost healed. I'm going to get back to Golden Acres and begin planning. Stay in the cabin until you are fully healed." She looked him over. "It should take less than an hour. If you leave without a complete healing, it will take you days to get better." Maxwell nodded in agreement.

"Have a look around," added Adele. "You will find many interesting items in this cabin. Everything here, in the sanctuary, is for the Protectors' use. Take any items you think you may need because the next time you visit, the items will have changed. Different items will randomly be exchanged in and out from time to time. You will learn most of this on your next rotation."

"Be careful flying back, Maxwell," said Adele, holding Maxwell's arm for emphasis. "I don't believe the Manip has had time to report his findings and return. You should be safe, although it doesn't hurt to be overly cautious. Fly low to the trees, out of view. Stay on alert until you get to Golden Acres."

Adele opened the door, turned to Maxwell, smiled, and gave him a big hug. "Don't worry, Maxwell," said Adele. "We'll be ready when the time comes. I'm not going to let Norris harm you, too." She gave him another squeeze, then turned and closed the door behind her.

You, too? Maxwell thought about what Adele had just said. *She said, "I won't let him harm you, too." Had Norris hurt his grandfather? Was it another Protector? Who had he hurt?*

Maxwell began doubting what he heard; maybe he was hearing things. He reasoned, *She probably said, "I'm not going to let Norris harm you." After all, I did bump my head.*

Maxwell felt the spot on his forehead where the cut had been. It had already scabbed over and was nearly gone. "I'd better have a look around now, or I'm going to be healed and will need to head back," said Maxwell aloud as he scanned the different objects in the room.

26

In the Doldrum

Zantos and Dover had simply been out to observe their shadow, William Carter. Shadows were the human prospects the Manips would cultivate. You, being from the human world, probably assumed Manips assist their Shadows. That isn't the case. Unbeknownst to the humans, the Manips guide them to their desired actions. They are called *manipulators* for a reason.

Any deed Shadows perform to forward the cause of evil is due to the Manip motivating them. The Shadows believe their actions are the result of their own grand ideas, but in reality, they are nothing more than puppets. They have surrendered all good judgment for one reason or another. Some lose their way for fame, some for pride or jealously, and some, like our friend Mr. William Carter, for greed.

After escaping the Protector, Dover made a rough landing upon returning to his doldrum. He walked inside, still shaken. Norris, his commander, was sitting in a dark corner. Dover couldn't see the upper half of Norris's body, only his legs and shoes. Even in the darkness, he could detect the smoke rising from Norris's cigar. Dover never understood why Norris continued to smoke in the spirit realm. He knew no satisfaction or calming effect could be derived from the nicotine-infused stogie because satisfaction and calm could never be enjoyed by Manips. Norris just couldn't break his smoking habit.

Dover thought his boss might be happy with his news. He knew he would receive backlash over losing Zantos but not so much if his boss had other concerns to focus on.

"Where's Zantos?" barked Norris.

"There's been an incident," replied Dover nervously. Norris stood up. A dim light showed on his twisted face as he inhaled his smoke. He began a careful walk toward Dover. Dover began slowly backing up while trying to explain.

"We were working with William Carter, just like you told us to do," continued Dover. "Carter decided to prepare his paperwork so signatures would be all he needed from Golden Acres occupants. He included all the fine print on each contract so they would have no recourse for action after he charged them his astronomically high service fees. Carter's satisfaction with himself for devising such a plan was evident by his smile.

"Zantos and I felt he did not need our input during the paperwork; he already seemed so pleased with himself. So, we decided to have a look around the area to see if anyone could use a little trouble. We found a kayaker on the water and decided to have a bit of fun." At this point, Dover had backed into the wall as Norris had continued inching closer.

Dover decided to speed up his story: "Zantos dumped the kayaker while I tried to tangle his feet in the rocks beneath the water. Unfortunately, he managed to escape and climb up on a rock in treacherous water. We moved the kayak out of his reach and took a spot in the trees to watch the show. Out of nowhere, here comes a Protector. He positioned a fallen log so the kayaker could free himself from what would've been almost certain death." Norris was within arm's reach now. An angry growl came from deep inside his throat.

Dover began talking faster: "The Protector managed to get him and his kayak to shore. He appeared to be alone, so Zantos and I both attacked him. We thought it would be an easy kill, but we found out rather quickly he was not alone. Another Protector flew down—again from nowhere—and began fighting Zantos. She was older and quite skilled. I thought Zantos would be the stronger opponent.

"Meanwhile, I was having difficulty battling my adversary. His skills were remarkable. I could see Zantos losing his fight. As soon as I had a moment to flee, I did so. I witnessed Zantos's demise before I left for good. The Protector he was battling was relentless. She never let up. She fought like a Protector from the past—old-school style."

With both hands, Norris gripped Dover's neck, squeezing. Dover knew he had only one breath left. "The Protector who saved the kayaker and fought with me looked like Justice himself!" Norris immediately stopped squeezing Dover's neck.

Norris and Dover's faces were three inches apart. Even though Dover's neck was still in Norris's grasp, all he could think about was how Norris's breath smelled like dead toads.

"I bet he's one of Justice's relatives," stammered Dover as his eyes began watering from the stench. He saw in Norris's eyes the thought of what if, the thought of possibly taking revenge. He released his grip.

"He definitely had his skills," added Dover, still trying to convince his boss.

Norris's face returned to red as he gritted his teeth and grabbed Dover's neck again and hissed, "If you have purposely misled me . . . You will wish it was you, rather than Zantos, that perished by the sword of the Protector."

Dover backed even closer to the wall and stammered, "Never would I ever mislead you, chief."

Norris's face went from scarlet back to his normal shade of gray. He took a seat at a table in the center of the room. "Sit down, fool!" ordered Norris. "Tell me every detail about your assignment at Golden Acres. I want to know if you have ever seen these Protectors before today. Leave nothing out. I will assign Trumble to be your new partner. He is more experienced than Zantos and is better skilled in battle."

Dover sat down and began at the beginning. He told Norris about putting the idea in Carter's mind to scam the elderly. Carter embraced the idea; his conscience never gave it a second thought. He opened the phone book and circled the care homes close to his location. Golden Acres offered more amenities, which always resulted in higher cost; thus, those residents should be wealthier.

As a first step, Carter volunteered with the seniors at Golden Acres. He interacted with them almost daily to build their trust. His plan was to control their investments by first showing fraudulent profits; then, he would hit them with huge service fees after the beginning months. Depending on the group, maybe he would skip town with all of it. If he left the country, he knew he could disappear, especially if he had plenty of cash. He had been toying with the idea of going to the Cayman Islands to put his money in an untraceable bank account. He knew he had time to decide and enjoyed planning his getaway.

Dover told Norris how the Protectors had just showed up one day at a softball game. "Who sends four Protectors to guard senior citizens at a softball game?" Dover fumed. Norris sat in silence, still puffing his cigar, soaking in all of Dover's details.

"This is to remain between us," said Norris, breaking his silence. "It is not to be told to Recco. It may not even be another Justice. I don't want to face more humiliation if it turns out to be some overly ambitious young Protector. Do you understand?" barked Norris.

"I u-u-un-n-der-st-t-t-and," stammered Dover. In reality, Norris hoped to regain his former rank of second in command directly below Recco. Recco cared less about revenge and more about his overall plan for the complete destruction of mankind. Norris believed the more members of the Justice family that were disposed of, the more quickly both he and Recco would get their wish.

"Send for Trumble," instructed Norris. "Have him meet us here at the doldrum without delay. It will be your first priority to discover our up-and-coming Protector's identity. *If* it is a Justice heir . . . I will personally destroy him." Norris displayed a rare smile.

27

The Items in the Cabin

Back in the sanctuary, Maxwell decided to listen to Adele's advice and have a look around. He opened the wall cabinets to the left of the fireplace lined with unfinished wooden shelves upon which sat everyday random items. These items included a ball, a hat, glasses, and lip gloss, and other trinkets. When Maxwell saw the lip gloss, it reminded him of his mother back home who always carried some with her. He opened the container and smelled. "Strawberry, just like Mom," he said and smiled. A clip-on earring (only one), a necklace with a shield pendant, a bowl sitting beside a pitcher, a belt, and many more items were on the shelves, too many to list here. Each item was insignificant and looked like nothing special.

Maxwell picked up many of the items. He looked beneath them, rolled them around in his hands, and even gave them a good shake.

Nothing happened. After replacing the items, he noticed a single book on the top shelf. The binding was blue leather with worn gold edging but no title on the spine. Maxwell picked up the book. He found no title on the front cover either. He opened the book to the title page, which had turned yellow. Maxwell saw the word *Sanctuary*.

"Be careful with me, I'm old," said a voice coming from the book. Maxwell jumped, being startled, and dropped the book. The book landed with the pages open on the floor and the cover facing upward. Maxwell walked around in front of the book and looked all around it, but he heard nothing. He reached down and carefully picked up the book. Eyes and a mouth appeared on the front cover. "Ow! You hurt me. Please hang on to me tightly," said the book. The eyes observed Maxwell as he raised the book in front of him. "Well, what are you waiting for? Open me," instructed the voice.

Maxwell sat the book down on one of the shelves in the cabinet, and with both hands, he gently opened the book. "What are you?" asked Maxwell.

"I'm the operating manual for this sanctuary," answered the book.

"Why are you talking?" questioned Maxwell.

"We all talk when we're touched," answered the book.

"We *all*? Are there more of you?" asked Maxwell.

"Every sanctuary has an operating manual," answered the book. "My name is Woodrow. I am here to assist you. We are all assigned Protector teams. I assist the Americans. When you change locations, a sanctuary will move with you, and I will move along with it—unless you work out of the country. Then, you will use that country's sanctuary." Maxwell stared at the book. He removed his hands from it. The book's eyes and mouth disappeared from sight. He quickly jerked his hands forward and grabbed the book again. The eyes and mouth reappeared.

"If you want to have a conversation, you need to keep your hands on me," instructed Woodrow. "As I was saying, one manual per sanctuary, but you'll find a library upstairs. It is small, mind you, but full of conversing, interesting books just like me. I get used the most, and none of us are labeled on the outside. So, I am kept downstairs for easy access."

"Why does the sanctuary need a manual?" asked Maxwell.

"So you will know what items are located in this sanctuary and how to use them," stated Woodrow. Sanctuaries are always being filled with new items, and I am automatically updated as they arrive. Can you imagine trying to figure out the functions of the items on your own?" Woodrow rolled his eyes and chuckled. "That would be fun to watch."

Woodrow cleared his voice, getting back to business. "I can instruct you audibly, or you may read me in silence. Which do you prefer?"

"Out loud, please," replied Maxwell, more comfortable now. Maxwell kept one hand on the book and picked up several of the items, one at a time. He started with the pitcher and the bowl. He held the pitcher in his hand, looking inside. It appeared empty.

"The pitcher is a never-empty container of drinking water, and the bowl is, likewise, never empty of nourishment. When you go to sleep at night, put out the pitcher and the bowl. When you awaken the next morning, both will be full. The pitcher will contain pure water, and the bowl, most days, will contain freshly steamed rice. Some days the bowl may contain soup; other days it may be bread. It will always be just what the body needs on that particular day. Your protected will never thirst or go hungry as long as they are in possession of the pitcher and bowl. This item does, however, have one stipulation. The possessor can tell no one of its abilities. The minute he tells another human, the pitcher and bowl will reappear back into the sanctuary, out of their reach. The pitcher and bowl refill each day until the protected no longer has need of them; at that time, they return themselves to the sanctuary."

"What a great idea!" exclaimed Maxwell. "I'm sure there are many who could use the pitcher and bowl."

"It is one of our most frequently used pieces," replied Woodrow.

"Are all the items props for our assignments?" asked Maxwell.

"Heavens, no," answered Woodrow, "take the mind ball for instance." Woodrow rolled his eyes in the direction of a small, red ball on the shelf. Maxwell picked it up. "This ball is for the Protector's use. You control the movement with your thoughts. Not only is it great fun to toss with the other Protectors, but it can also come in handy when there's an unaware Manip, located across the room, who needs to be knocked on the side of the head. It has been used in many successful skirmishes. After being thrown in battle, the mind ball will always return to your hand, and it cannot be used against you. If you remove it from the sanctuary, it will only obey your thoughts until you return it. If you do not touch it for seven days, it will disappear and return itself to the sanctuary. Therefore, it can never be lost."

"That is incredibly cool and definitely going with me," Maxwell placed the ball in his pocket. He picked up a pair of antique eyeglasses. "My grandfather has a pair of these. Are they reading glasses?"

"Not reading glasses," answered Woodrow, "they are reality glasses."

"Reality glasses?" replied Maxwell, puzzled. "What do they do?"

"When a Protector looks through these glasses, they see the true self of the person before them." answered Woodrow. "It shows the purity of heart. If you ever wonder if you're being deceived, put on these spectacles. You will know the truth." Maxwell pocketed the glasses.

An empty pouch sat on one of the shelves. It had the Protector's crest on the outside with a long leather strap. Maxwell picked up the pouch and looked at Woodrow questioningly. "This is unique. What does it do?"

"It's a hidden satchel," replied Woodrow. "It cannot be detected, nor any of its contents, when it's on a Protector's body." Maxwell had heard enough to know it was something that could prove useful. He tossed the satchel over his head and filled it with his newfound treasures. Maxwell picked up the lip gloss and showed it to Woodrow.

"That is healing lip gloss. It is not for you. Healing is nearly always done by female Protectors since they have natural healing abilities, so first-aid items are developed with them in mind. One kiss from a female Protector wearing this lip gloss and the recipient is healed of all ailments. It works on humans and Protectors, but it can only be used once; then it is gone. A new one reappears instantly in the sanctuary after it's used. Only a female Protector can remove it from the sanctuary." Maxwell returned the lip gloss to the shelf. He picked up the belt.

"How about this?" asked Maxwell.

"That holds up your pants," said Woodrow.

"What's special about that?" replied Maxwell briskly.

"Not all our items are special," said Woodrow, "but all of them are useful." Maxwell tossed the belt back up on the shelf. "Pick one more item; then you must go," added Woodrow. "You are now healed and must not tarry. You are needed."

"Okay, one more," said Maxwell as he scanned the items. He picked up the necklace with a shield pendant.

"That is the necklace of safekeeping," said Woodrow before Maxwell could ask. "When you put the necklace around your neck and wind the latch, you cannot be harmed until the latch works its way around and touches the shield pendant. You cannot speed up or slow down the latch. It must work its own way around to the pendant. When you are about to go into battle, it is a good idea to wind the latch. You can transfer the protection to another person by removing the necklace from your neck and putting it around another. The protection will not restart. It will continue from the point at which you transferred the necklace. The less active you are, the slower the latch will move. Likewise, the more active you become, the faster the latch will move. Once your latch touches the pendant, the necklace will disappear from your body and reappear in the sanctuary. Keep it off your neck until you need its protection."

Maxwell placed the necklace with the other items in his satchel. "Goodbye, my friend," said Maxwell to Woodrow, holding the book in front of him. "I hope to see you soon. I'm Maxwell, by the way."

"Goodbye, Maxwell," replied Woodrow. "Stay safe and Godspeed to you."

Maxwell returned Woodrow to the shelf. He eyeballed a few of the other items, but he knew he had to go. "Until next time," he spoke aloud as he closed the cabinet door. He made his way over to the front door of the sanctuary, went out on the porch, and surveyed the area for Manips. The surrounding woodlands were clear. Maxwell closed the door, expanded his wings, and flew toward Golden Acres to tell his friends about his adventure.

As soon as Maxwell flew into the air, his mind began racing. He thought about his newly acquired items and how best to use them. He forgot to watch his altitude and stay low, under cover, as Adele had told him. Maxwell realized this blunder when he was almost back to Golden Acres.

"No one is out here anyway," Maxwell said to himself. "That Manip is gone for good." His better judgment caused him to lower his altitude anyway.

Eyes were watching Maxwell return to Golden Acres. He had been easy to locate. Dover and his new partner, Trumble, had returned to the area of the woods close to where the altercation had taken place. They were positioned in the treetops as Maxwell flew by, just above them. The Manips did nothing. They were there to observe.

"It looks like a Justice," growled Trumble, showing some authority to Dover. Both of these Manips had been around when Alexander was a Protector. They remembered his time of service, no matter how they would like to forget. Trumble paused while he studied his subject. "But I don't think he is related to him; he's too careless. Justice would have never been so reckless in flying after a confrontation with a Manip; he's alone and not concealed. This Protector acts as though he hasn't a care."

Dover and Trumble never took their eyes off Maxwell. "He does look like him, though," said Trumble in a murmur. "We need to find out this Protector's identity and stay on task with your previous assignment. We are here to assist Carter in swindling these people at Golden Acres. If all of the Protectors assigned here are this carefree, we will have no difficulty."

"I think it's his inexperience," said Dover convincingly. He didn't want Trumble to get the wrong idea and think of himself as commander of this duo. "But this Protector looks nearly identical to Justice when he was young." Dover looked at Trumble sternly.

"We need to follow the Protector and observe, just like Norris said. If we do find he is a Justice heir, we will notify Norris," continued Dover. "Trumble, you follow up on our Shadow; make sure he is not trying to back out on his double-cross. He can be a lazy sort at times. With a little luck, we will be able to succeed in our swindle, thus making the rest of some people's lives very difficult, and leave the world with one less Protector—and possibly a Justice Protector at that." Dover smiled an evil smirk at Trumble.

Dover lagged behind and kept out of sight from Maxwell as Trumble flew off to check on Carter. Maxwell landed at Golden Acres and walked inside the building. Dover followed closely, all the while looking over his shoulder for Adele. She had an uncanny ability to know when he was on his way to their location. At times, he even wondered if she could sense his thoughts.

28

A Plan Is Hatched

ack at Golden Acres, Maxwell assembled the other three Protectors in the activity room where the seniors would meet to work puzzles and watch television shows together. He was unaware of the Manip up in the ceiling tiles, listening to his conversation. Maxwell filled them in as much as possible in the limited amount of time he had remaining before they were to meet Adele. She wanted to meet with them at eleven tonight, and it was already a quarter 'til. He had only caught them up to his grandfather serving as a Protector with Adele during WWII.

Gem smelled a burning odor. She was concerned one of the seniors may have started a fire while cooking. It never entered her mind that it could be a hidden Manip she smelled. Only some of the Protectors, oddly enough, had the ability to actually smell the Manips. Adele had this ability as well, but Gem hadn't learned about her talent while in training. Everwell chose not to cover this little-known fact because so few Protectors possessed this capability. It would be discussed during later advanced sessions.

"We need to start making our way to Adele's room," said Maxwell, interrupting Gem's fire concerns. "None of us smell anything, Gem. I'm sure if there were any problems, the alarms would go off."

"So, Adele served as a Protector with your grandfather?" asked Eden. "That would explain a few things."

"You have no idea how good she is with her sword!" exclaimed Maxwell. "I would have been toast without her at the river. She saved my life."

The Protectors continued on their way and arrived at Adele's door. Jack took the initiative, reached up, knocked three times, paused, and then knocked two more times. The other three looked at him, puzzled. "I just thought this secret meeting called for a secret knock," answered Jack with a grin. Maxwell punched him as boys will do, and the girls just shook their heads. Adele answered the door without mentioning the strange knock.

"Come in, quickly," said Adele, looking down the halls, first left then right, making sure they hadn't been followed. Dover waited until she had closed her door before he left the building. He had strong suspicions she had some manner of detecting him, so he took no chances. He had his confirmation that Maxwell was Justice's grandson after eavesdropping on the Protectors' conversations. Now he needed to find Trumble. He had a plan of his own.

Only Maxwell had previously been inside Adele's apartment, so the other three Protectors were taking in their surroundings. The four spread themselves out in her living room, and Adele stood up in front of them.

"I'm sure Maxwell has brought all of you up to speed about me," she waited a moment as everyone shook their heads yes. "I am no longer a full-time Protector, but I do help out when I'm needed. William Carter is going to steal many of these trusting people's retirement savings if we don't stop him. The only way to prevent him from coming back again and again is to expose him," said Adele emphatically. "Do any of you have an idea?"

"I think you should tell your friends what you know about him," suggested Eden.

"I have no proof," replied Adele. "Their first response will be, 'How do you know Carter wants to swindle me?' "

Eden felt she was still in training at Everwell. She believed Adele most likely had a solution, but she wanted the Protectors to solve the problem on their own. Eden sat in complete silence, contemplating a plan.

"I know what we can do," said Maxwell, standing up before the group. Adele took a seat. He had everyone's attention.

29

Exposure

William Carter arrived the next morning at Golden Acres in an excellent mood. He walked with a spring in his step as he hummed a cheerful tune. Today was going to be the day. In six hours, he would have complete control of several senior citizens' life savings. His plan amounted to transferring their balances to his offshore accounts and then getting on a flight out of the country in the morning. He had spent the previous evening packing most of his belongings for the next day's getaway.

The activity room at Golden Acres was empty when he arrived. He pulled two tables together, then put two chairs on one side and four chairs on the opposite side. He wanted to sit close by the individual signing his paperwork and keep the onlookers farther away. They could be close when it was their turn to sign but he didn't want the tagalongs to have extra time to read each other's paperwork. His contract stated very clearly that the investor was guaranteed no specific return. In extremely tiny print, there was even mention of a "small chance of losing the entire investment."

"That would, of course, depend on how much risk I decide to assume on the account," said Carter with a smirk as he reviewed his paperwork. The print, which stated all the required warnings, was a great deal smaller than the rest of the font on the contract. You would need a magnifying glass to read the little type.

Carter had found several businesses in Brazil he wanted to invest in. The fact that they were bars would have no bearing on the client. By the time he did his investing, it would all be in his name anyway.

When William Carter looked up, Essie had already walked into the room. Essie loved Mr. Carter's cheerful demeanor and how he was never too busy to spend time with the seniors. Essie didn't realize it was her kind and trusting personality that only saw the good in people. She believed Mr. Carter was the sort of investment manager she could entrust with her savings. She wanted someone who really cared about her and others her age—not some stuffy accountant who always watched her bottom line and made her keep track of every penny.

William Carter stood up from his chair, smiling, and came around the table to greet Essie. "How's my favorite girl?" he said with a convincing look.

"I'm well," answered Essie, blushing. "So nice to see you again, Mr. Carter." She put her hand out for him to shake, but he kissed it instead. Essie giggled like a schoolgirl. Carter knew she would be his first pigeon. He hurried around the table and pulled out her chair beside his.

"The best seat in the room!" exclaimed Carter.

"Shouldn't we wait on some of the others to arrive?" asked Essie, looking around behind her to see if any of the others were coming in the room yet. She saw no one. His rush made her just a bit uneasy.

"Why wait?" replied Carter. "This will give you more privacy concerning your finances." Essie couldn't argue with that logic. It made sense to get started, but she couldn't shake the knot in the pit of her stomach.

Essie sat next to Mr. Carter and looked down at the paperwork he had placed in front of her. He told her he already had her name and address filled out on the appropriate lines. All she had to do was sign. Carter told her it was "your standard investment form," which it was not. She picked up the pen.

The next second, Adele came bursting through the door and startled Essie so, she dropped the pen, which rolled down on the floor. Betty and Kenneth were right behind her, chattering like squirrels.

"Not so fast, Essie!" exclaimed Adele in a serious manner. William Carter held his breath. Essie looked up and smiled at her friends. "No jumping ahead of us and hogging all of the investments." Adele winked at Essie and smacked her hand in a playful sort of way. William Carter, relieved, exhaled as silently as possible.

Carter watched Adele as she made her way behind him, behind Essie, and circled around to take her seat in front of him. Why she chose to walk around them first puzzled Carter. He felt like prey being circled before the kill. Beside Adele sat Betty then Kenneth. Unknown to Carter, the Protectors had entered the room and were standing behind their charges.

Essie picked up the ballpoint pen that Mr. Carter had so graciously picked up off the floor for her. Her eyes grew large in anticipation. Again, Adele spoke up abruptly, "Essie, you have read that contract, haven't you?"

William Carter closed his eyes as she spoke.

"Most of it," answered Essie, looking up at Adele and then at Mr. Carter, who had just opened his eyes.

"Of course, of course," agreed Mr. Carter. "We want nothing signed before it has been read." Adele was ruining everything, but he felt he could still salvage the situation.

"This print appears quite small," added Adele. She put the glasses, which were on a chain around her neck, up to her eyes. "Oh, yes, that makes the print so much better." Adele took her reading glasses off her neck and handed them to Essie. "Try these. It will make the reading easier."

"Okay," replied Essie, still smiling. She took the glasses and put them on. William Carter furrowed his brow and rubbed his eyes. He was clearly distressed, though no one picked up on this detail except Adele and the Protectors.

"This does make the print clearer!" exclaimed Essie excitedly. "Mr. Carter, could you give me another minute? Let me scan this document for just a moment." Essie looked up and saw Carter's face through the glasses Adele had given her.

She nearly fell out of her chair from jumping backward. His smiling face was gone and replaced with angry, glaring eyes. His nose had become a pig's snout, inhaling and exhaling with snot blowing in, then out. His mouth was dripping with foamy saliva, like a wolf waiting to pounce. Essie pushed back her chair slowly. She stood up, still wearing the glasses, not taking her eyes off Carter.

"I believe I have changed my mind," said Essie, backing away. William Carter stood up from his chair. Essie backed up even farther. "I'm not feeling well. I think I will go back to my room to lie down." She removed the glasses from her face.

"What about your investment?" boomed Carter. "You don't want to miss out on this opportunity!" He showed no concern for her health or her need to lie down. Essie turned to walk out of the room.

"Are you okay, Essie?" asked Kenneth. "Do you want me to walk you back to your room?"

"No, I'll be fine," replied Essie. She spoke slowly and steadily, never taking her eyes off William Carter, even though his face had returned to normal after she took off the glasses. She could not forget the hideous look of the creature within him. Essie handed the glasses to Kenneth and hurried out of the activity room.

"I'm going with her," whispered Eden to Jack. "She may need comforting." He nodded in agreement. Kenneth took Essie's seat on the other side of the table next to William Carter.

"This print is tiny," said Kenneth, solemnly picking up Essie's paper off the table. "You're not trying to hide anything from us, are you, cowboy?" Kenneth broke his stare at William and laughed. He jokingly elbowed Carter in the ribs. Carter forced a chuckle as he held his side in pain. Without thinking, Kenneth tried on the glasses Essie had handed him. He read the fine print and looked up, confused, at his two friends across the table.

"As you can see, everything is in order," said Carter nervously. Kenneth looked over to Carter and reacted similarly to Essie, but his reaction was more startled than scared.

"I've changed my mind, too," said Kenneth in a stern and unyielding tone. He removed the glasses and tossed them on the table next to Adele. William followed Kenneth around the table to the opposite side, pleading for him to come back.

"Stop pressuring me!" shouted Kenneth, pointing his index finger at Carter. Kenneth's tone had changed. His joking demeanor was gone. Carter could not imagine what had happened. Why were these old-timers backpedaling on him?

Dover and Trumble were observing from the hallway. They were out of view from the Protectors, but the Manips were watching the happenings. They saw Kenneth take off the glasses and toss them back to Adele. The Manips knew the glasses were charmed. They both were sure of it. They had seen special items used by the Protectors many times before. They whispered among themselves, and then Dover entered the activity room while Trumble went down the hall. Of course, no one, except the Protectors, saw Dover enter the room. They drew their swords. Dover knew there were too many to fight so he never went for his weapon.

"Don't mind me," said Dover waving his hand nonchalantly at the Protectors. "I'm just observing." He laughed nervously as his voice trailed off.

After Kenneth had tossed the glasses and reacted so unexpectedly, Betty didn't even need to look at her contracts. The reactions of her dear friends were enough to make her shake her head no. She stood up and walked to the back of the room with Kenneth. They were whispering to some of the other occupants of Golden Acres as Kenneth kept pointing at Carter.

Adele continued to sit at the table, smiling at Mr. Carter. She calmly picked up her glasses and hung them back around her neck. Carter was not smiling back.

"You did this!" he snarled at Adele.

"What did I do?" Adele threw her hands up as if she had nothing to hide.

He could feel the red-hot anger climbing up his neck onto his face. "I don't know what you did or how you did it, but I know it was you." His voice was loud and angry.

Adele looked at him like he was insane, which only infuriated him more.

Kenneth and Betty, with the other senior citizens, went out the door into the hallway and headed back to their rooms. They were still mumbling and looking at Mr. Carter. The remaining three Protectors remained with Adele since Dover was still in the room. With the room empty, as far as he could tell, except for him and Adele, William Carter could no longer restrain himself.

"Do you know how much time I spent with your over-the-hill, decrepit, gray-haired, senile friends?" said Carter in a steady but angry voice. He could barely control his rage.

"I thought you enjoyed spending time with them," replied Adele in a still cheerful manner. "I love being with my friends."

Mr. Carter stood up silently, put his papers back in his portfolio, and leaned over the table toward Adele. He rested his two hands on the table in front of her and lowered his head three inches from her face. She didn't budge.

"Rest assured; you will pay for this, Adele Jamison," he said in a whisper. "You will pay."

"I look forward to it," she replied, closing the gap between them even more. The Protectors still had their swords drawn and pointed at Dover. He remained still.

William Carter forcefully kicked his chair back, which fell over and crashed to the floor. He stomped out the door and headed for his car. Dover followed him and mouthed to the Protectors, "You will pay."

Dover followed Carter to the right and disappeared down the hall that led out of the building. This reminded Maxwell that the other Manip had not been seen recently and had disappeared down this same hallway, which was where some of the residents' apartments were located.

"Jack, Gem, go check on Kenneth and Betty," instructed Maxwell. He began to worry they should've left earlier to make sure everyone was okay. Both Protectors hurried down the hall.

Adele stood up and said to Maxwell, smiling, "We did it!" She was ecstatic. "It's been too long since I've had an assignment go this well. Solidify, so I can give you a big hug." Maxwell obeyed. She squeezed him like he was her own grandchild.

"Now, maybe we can get back to Everwell and get some answers about my grandfather," said Maxwell. "Or better yet, maybe I'll just go home and ask him myself."

"How is your grandfather?" asked Adele kindly.

"He's okay," said Maxwell. "A good deal quieter since grandmother died last March third, but he seems to be adjusting. He spends more time at work and with our family, that part we love. And he's not like some widowers who can't wait to pull that wedding ring off and look for a replacement. That's not grandfather. He lost his one, true love when grandmother died. But, he doesn't have to worry about being alone; he knows we will always be there for him."

"He's lucky to have you," said Adele, putting one hand on his shoulder.

"And I'm lucky to have him," replied Maxwell.

"Yes, you are," continued Adele as Gem and Jack came half-flying, half-running into the room.

"Eden's gone!" they both gasped. "The Manip took Eden. He didn't touch Essie, Kenneth, or Betty, just Eden," added Gem breathlessly.

"How do you know the Manip got her?" asked Adele.

"We found her sword," answered Jack. "It looks like they struggled in the hallway outside Essie's room."

"Let's hurry and see if we can follow the Manip with Carter," instructed Maxwell.

"I'll stay here and contact Everwell," said Adele. "Don't let them ambush you." The three Protectors ran outside. They looked in every direction.

"There!" shouted Jack. "I think I see him." He pointed way off, above the trees, a figure heading into a dark cloud. All three Protectors immediately went airborne as the figure disappeared in the cloud.

"Keep flying!" shouted Maxwell. "We can still catch it."

"We won't be able to see anything in the clouds," added Gem.

"We have to try," replied Maxwell. All three Protectors disappeared into the cloud in the same space the Manip had entered. The group slowed their speed. They couldn't see anything but themselves.

"We'll cover more area if we split up," commented Jack. They all agreed, as time was of the essence. Maxwell gave the search coordinates.

"Jack, you take the right side of the cloud. Gem, you've got the middle, and I'll take the left. If you see anything, call out, and the other two will come." Both nodded in agreement and flew off carefully.

Maxwell moved cautiously to the left. He had already lost sight of the other two Protectors. He didn't want to fly too fast and crash into one of them. After five minutes of searching, he found nothing. Maxwell wasn't 100 percent sure he was even in the correct area of the cloud.

He looked straight ahead and thought he saw a dark figure, but it wasn't moving. After watching for another moment, it remained still. Shapes were hard to distinguish in the dense cover of the cloud. He would move closer, cautiously.

He inched forward. The shape still didn't move. Scenarios ran through Maxwell's mind. If it were a Manip, why didn't it run away or attack? Maybe it hadn't seen them pursuing. Maxwell knew the odds were in the Protectors' favor: three to one. Maxwell continued to move closer.

"Stop right there!" The Manip's voice cracked like that of a long-time smoker. "We have your friend." Maxwell realized this Manip had been placed there as a lure for them to follow.

"Hand her over or die!" shouted Maxwell, drawing his sword.

"Of course," answered Dover, surprising Maxwell with his answer. "We don't want her. We want you." Maxwell stared at the Manip, wondering what to do next. "Meet me two miles downriver on the left bank next to the large boulder. Our doldrum will appear there in one hour. We will make the switch, her for you. Come alone."

"What's a doldrum?" asked Maxwell. Dover laughed, rolling his eyes as if a doldrum was common knowledge and Maxwell was an idiot.

"Don't you worry what a doldrum is, Justice offspring," said Dover, still laughing. "Just be there *alone*. If you do not do as you are instructed, your friend will no longer be in the protection business." Dover released a bellowing laugh as he backed away into the clouds and disappeared.

Gem and Jack had heard the laugh. They were both beside him within seconds. Maxwell filled them in on Dover's instructions. "They want to trade her for me," said Maxwell.

"I want Eden back just as much as both of you—if not more. She is my friend," said Gem forcefully. "But giving you to these Manips in exchange is madness. They will kill you for sure." Gem stopped speaking. She was visibly distraught. Her eyes scanned the clouds, looking there for an answer.

She looked back at Maxwell and Jack. The answer had come to her. "We need to talk to Adele!" she exclaimed. "She helped us with our plan exposing William Carter. She will help us with this." Everyone nodded in agreement. They followed Gem back to Golden Acres.

Adele had been waiting on them when they knocked on her door. She answered the door so fast, she must have had her hand on the doorknob during the knock. "Did you find her?" she asked. She knew the answer by the look on their faces. Again, the story was told about the exchange. Adele just stood there, a concerned look on her face. She contemplated their next move.

"Well, I guess I should begin by explaining the doldrums to you," said Adele. "It's the Manip version of our sanctuary. I have personally never been inside one, but I have seen them from the outside. Unlike our sanctuaries, which are stationary unless we decide to move them, the doldrums appear out of thin air and remain in a specific location for one hour. After one hour, they disappear and reappear in another predetermined location for another hour. We think they loop around the same spots, sometimes seven or eight locations, until they decide to switch things up. We have never been able to discern a pattern. They can reappear in five or ten hours; it's completely random. There are instances, after it leaves its location, it will reappear the following hour; other times, it will be days, or it may never return. What I am telling you is, no one has ever been able to predict when the doldrums will arrive or where.

"They are also easier to enter than our sanctuaries. No one can go into our sanctuaries unless they are a Protector, an angel, or a heavenly being—unless we invite them in. A doldrum has two doors. One is an entrance; one is an exit. You cannot enter an exit, and you cannot exit an entrance. We have no idea why. The doors of the doldrum cannot be locked, but they are usually heavily guarded. I say *usually*, not *always*."

"We think a doldrum exists for each team of Manips, but we aren't sure. Most of the time, you will be given your sanctuary location at the beginning of your assignment. The four of you didn't receive this information because this is your first assignment. It was supposed to be straightforward and simple, so the sanctuary should've been unnecessary."

Maxwell raised his hand to interrupt. "How do the Manips know where their doldrums will appear?" he asked.

"It seems to be a feeling or instinct," answered Adele. "We've spent many years studying Manips and doldrums. We've never been able to intercept any communication between them or find a map of the doldrums' locations. Now you understand why no locks are necessary for their doors. You would have to be exceptionally lucky to find the location of a doldrum. Then, if you did find one and went in, you would need more than luck to get yourself out. No one has ever lived to tell the tale of what the inside of a doldrum looks like. When you enter, unless you're a Manip, you don't come out. No one has ever come out." Her voice trailed off slowly as she spoke the last sentence. It seemed she remembered a specific occurrence that substantiated this fact. Adele paused as she stared forward, not looking at anyone.

"So," her glance returned to the Protectors again, "we must keep you out of that doldrum at all costs. If Eden is in the doldrum, most likely they will not exchange her for you. During the exchange, they will cause a disruption and attempt to kill her while grabbing you. They may even have stashed her somewhere else but will bring her out to exchange in front of the doldrum. We need to be ready for both scenarios."

"I will need to contact Everwell again," added Adele. "Even though the Manips said to come alone, you cannot. I do not value one Protector's life over another." She grabbed Maxwell's hand. "I know how much all of you care for Eden. I want you to know we will do everything possible to save her, but we never give in to the demands of Manips. They can't be trusted." Adele was firm with her words.

"I'm going to recommend a plan to Everwell to surround the doldrum with more experienced Protectors as well as angels," continued Adele. "If the Manips bring Eden out . . . *when* they bring Eden out, we will storm the doldrum. These Manips will not be able to compete with the best we have to offer." Adele raised both her hands and placed them on the shoulders of Gem and Jack reassuringly.

"What do you mean 'more experienced Protectors'?" asked Gem. "Does that mean we will not be there?"

"That is exactly what I mean," answered Adele, looking at each of the three Protectors individually. "We will even use a decoy for Maxwell."

"We have no time to contact Everwell!" shouted Maxwell. "The Manip told me to be there in two hours." Jack and Gem looked at each other. They knew Maxwell had told Adele the wrong meeting time. He had already told both of them he had to be at the doldrum location in one hour. They both held their tongues. They knew Maxwell had a plan, and it didn't include letting more experienced Protectors attempt to rescue their friend.

"We have more than enough time," responded Adele briskly. "Give me the coordinates; then let me worry about getting the area surrounded."

"Actually, we are down to about an hour and three-quarters now," replied Maxwell as he jotted down the location for Adele. "It's close to the area on the river where you helped me earlier." He handed Adele a piece of paper with the correct coordinates.

"That will be easy for me to find," answered Adele. "Have faith, Protectors. If anyone can bring your friend home, this group will." With that statement, she removed a plant, which was sitting on a white pillar in her living room, and placed it on her windowsill. She climbed up on top of the pillar and stood there.

The three Protectors watched Adele as they tried to figure out what she was doing. "I'll explain this exit another time," she said as she put her hands, fully extended with palms together, above her head. Gem thought she looked like a person about to dive into a swimming pool. Instead of diving, she bent her knees down and jumped up. She never came back down. She was simply gone.

Jack jumped up on the pillar. "Where'd she go? I'll follow her." Jack jumped in the air just as Adele had done. He came back down on the pillar. He jumped again. This time, he missed his landing and went tumbling onto the sofa. He looked at Maxwell and Gem. "What did I do wrong?"

"Well, for starters, your hands weren't together," suggested Gem. Jack began arguing back that his hands were, indeed, in the right place.

"Get up, Jack," said Maxwell, putting his hand out to help him up. "We're going after Eden. We need to hurry."

"Hurry and do what?" replied Jack.

"I'll explain on the way," answered Maxwell as he checked both directions going out the door. He wanted to be sure Adele was nowhere in sight.

30

At the Cave

$\mathcal{E}$den sat on what was once a large chunk of rock that had been crudely cut into the shape of a chair. She had watched Dover chip out the piece of the stone with his fist and fingernails. These Manips were strong and reasonably skilled. She had altered her opinion of their stupidity in just the few minutes she had been with them.

Eden went over the recent events in her head. She had entered Essie's room to make sure she was safely home. After Essie settled in, Eden left her apartment to make her way back to the activity room. One of the Manips had been waiting for her in the hallway. She remembered pulling her sword out of its sheath, then everything went black.

She woke up on her side, still in the hallway and pinned to the ground with both hands bound in front of her. Trumble jerked her off the ground just as Dover was turning the corner, coming toward them.

"You get to be our hostage, little lady," whispered Trumble into her ear as Dover walked up beside them. His breath smelled like a restaurant trash dumpster from one of the alleyways back home in New York City. Eden tried to hold her breath as he spoke, but it happened too fast. The smell engulfed her. She jerked her shoulder away from Trumble in time to be grabbed next by Dover.

"Let's get her out of here," barked Dover, "before the others come." They hurried outside, with Eden struggling the entire time. "Don't take her to the doldrum," instructed Dover. "Use the cave. I want to make sure we have someone alive to trade when he shows."

"*If* he shows," replied Trumble.

"He'll show," answered Dover. "If he's really a Justice, he will be there. The others will come looking for her soon. We need to get into the clouds. Can you handle her alone?"

"I captured her alone, didn't I?" smirked Trumble as he grabbed Eden's arm and pulled her behind him.

Eden listened to their entire conversation. Trumble and Dover did nothing to try and disguise their plans. She knew she was being traded for Maxwell. She hoped he wouldn't be knuckleheaded enough to actually trade himself for her. With Adele, Jack, and Gem's assistance, they should be able to come up with a plan to free her. She resolved to stay alert and watch for cues from her friends at the exchange. Or perhaps it would be Adele at the switch, if there were to be a switch.

Dover had arrived later at the cave to find Trumble waiting with Eden. She hadn't been able to discover why Dover was delayed in his return. He and Trumble stood whispering just outside the cave entrance. They were being more secretive now.

The Manips did appear to want to trade Eden. She figured they probably wouldn't kill her until the trade, so perhaps she could escape. If she

could just get her hands free. Eden glanced down to see what material had her bound. It was like nothing she had ever seen before. She had been wiggling her hands since she arrived at the cave but no progress had been made. The binding was neither looser nor tighter. It would seem she could stretch the material only to have it snap right back as secure as ever.

When Eden first looked at the binding, it took all her self-control not to overreact. The material flickered like a strap of fire, but she felt no heat. The strap was an inch thick with small flames lapping from the binding.

Dover saw her looking at the binding. He stopped talking to Trumble as he walked over to Eden, smiling. "You know it's a lava line. Don't waste your time struggling," said Dover. Eden looked down at her hands, puzzled.

"She doesn't know what it is!" laughed Trumble as he came up beside Dover.

"It's impossible to untie yourself, so you may as well stop trying," added Dover. Eden stopped moving her hands.

"Unless you know how to release lava line . . . you're trapped," laughed Trumble as he turned to walk away. Suddenly, he stopped and turned back around to continue, "But once you know the release, it couldn't be easier to get out, *if* you have the right resource." Trumble couldn't resist a riddle. It was his weakness.

"Stop talking so much!" yelled Dover as he slapped him in the back of the head. Trumble shot Dover a dirty look but did as he was told.

Eden decided she would sit still, save her energy, and observe the Manips until the trade. Perhaps she could find out more about the release of the lave line or maybe even what they were planning after the switch.

Minutes ticked by. All Eden could make out was a mention of Norris now and again: "Norris will be so proud. Norris will promote us for sure. Maybe we should tell Norris our plan. No, he would only take the credit. A surprise will be better for everyone."

Eden remembered the portrait in the Hall of Records, *The Defeat of Norris*. It had to be the same person. If Maxwell's grandfather had defeated him, she knew this would be a life-threatening situation for Maxwell to find himself in. The bits she had heard from the Manips amounted to really bad news. The only positive aspect of the situation was Norris might not be aware of what these two Manips were planning. She held out hope that just maybe, Adele and the other three Protectors would plan some kind of surprise attack and they would only have to deal with these two.

31

The Exchange

axwell, Gem, and Jack arrived at the rendezvous location fifteen minutes early. The three landed together in a huddle.

"I don't like this plan, Maxwell," complained Gem anxiously. "I regret agreeing to go along with you."

"Plan? This isn't a plan," agreed Jack. "We're doing just what the Manips told you to do, Maxwell. That's not a plan. We should've let Adele go ahead and take charge." Gem and Jack were coming unglued as the meeting time approached.

"Not exactly," said Maxwell as he exposed the hidden pouch he had picked up at the sanctuary for the two of them to see. "The Manips will not be able to find the pouch. It's the only chance we have to get Eden and me back safely." Maxwell removed the protection necklace from the pouch and put it around his neck. He double-checked the pouch to make sure the other item was there.

"Oh, good," added Gem, not easily convinced. "You're going into a doldrum with a necklace, a pouch, and a ball. No worries. Eden would freak out if she knew this was the plan."

"Everything will work out fine," said Maxwell. "It's because of me that Eden was captured in the first place. I'm not going to let her be harmed. That is my first priority."

"Maxwell," said Jack, shaking his head in disagreement, "it's not *because of you*. You act like you are at fault. They simply want you instead. Eden was an easier grab without Adele around."

"Either way," replied Maxwell, "I don't want her hurt when it's me they want." Gem admired Maxwell's courage and confidence. He talked like failing wasn't an option. She thought of him as a big brother and wished she could be more like him. Back home, she always tried to put on a brave, self-assured front, but deep inside, she worried. She always worried. She decided to stop complaining and try to follow Maxwell's example, at least for the next few moments. He was right; they were here, and their best hope was him.

The three Protectors noticed the Manips and Eden coming toward them out of the sky. They were relieved Eden wasn't in the doldrum. Several moments later, a small building made of mirrors appeared in the clearing before them. Almost immediately after it appeared, the outward view of the building blended into its surroundings. The Protectors were having difficulty seeing the doldrum as the Manips landed in front of them with their captive.

"You were told to come alone!" barked Dover.

"They are here to see that a fair trade takes place and you don't try to keep both of us," answered Maxwell. "They will not interfere as long as you do what was agreed upon."

Dover leaned over to Trumble. Eden overheard them whisper. "We'll have to turn her over to them," said Dover. "Change of plans. I guess only one Protector will die today."

"We can take them, Dover," said Trumble, trying to convince his accomplice. "We can kill four instead of two."

"The Justice heir is the one we need today," commanded Dover sternly. "Just be patient. We'll surely get another opportunity to finish them." Eden continued to stare ahead as if she had overheard nothing. "Leave your sword with your companions!" shouted Dover to Maxwell.

As Maxwell unsheathed his sword, he called out his demands: "One of you will remain where you are, as will one of us. One of you will walk Eden toward us, and one of my companions will walk me to you. We will exchange in the middle. Then the two of you will remain in the clearing with me until my friends are out of sight."

"No deal!" replied Dover. "You are not making the decisions here! There would be three of you at the exchange to my one Manip if we do what you suggest. That is not acceptable. You come alone."

Maxwell leaned over to his two companions. "I can't go alone," he explained. "If I am unarmed, nothing will stop them from killing us both."

"You must stand firm on this, Maxwell," said Jack. "If not, Eden will be killed for sure. You can never trust a Manip. You must always assume they will double-cross you. The only way to overrule them is a show of authority. Tell them no." Gem agreed.

Maxwell stepped forward and replied in a powerful voice, "Two will walk out from both sides. One will remain on each side or no exchange. Of my three, only one will be armed; thus, only one of you can be. Two unarmed Protectors against a large warrior Manip, such as yourself, will pose no threat. We don't want a conflict. I only wish to exchange myself for Eden and for you to let my friends leave unharmed."

Both sides were silent. The two Manips didn't speak to each other. After moments, which seemed like forever to Maxwell, Dover spoke,

"Bring your accompanying Protector with you." Trumble looked at Dover.

"I hope you know what you are doing," said Trumble quietly.

Maxwell leaned over to Gem. "Let Jack go with me today, Gem." Her face showed the disappointment. "He's older and bigger. Size is all these Manips understand."

She knew he was right. Maxwell continued, "If things start going terribly wrong during the switch, don't hesitate to charge ahead and show them what you're made of." She smiled and nodded in agreement. Maxwell was pleased she didn't argue with him. She put her arms around his neck and squeezed him tightly.

While holding him, she whispered in his ear, "Don't be a hero, Maxwell. Just get out alive. We are a team of four, and we are unstoppable as long as we are together. Promise me." She pulled back from her hug so she could see his face.

"Me . . . a hero?" answered Maxwell with a laugh. "I don't think you know me as well as you think."

That was his answer: a joke. He did not promise her, and she knew it. Maxwell turned to Jack, anxious to get started.

"Are you ready?" asked Maxwell.

"I was born ready!" replied Jack as he drew his sword and stepped forward.

"You might want to put your sword back unless they draw theirs," suggested Maxwell.

"I don't care," answered Jack. "I hope they do fight us. That's how I would like this to go down."

"Then Eden would be the first one killed, Jack," replied Maxwell. "We have to carry through with the exchange. Did you bring Eden's sword?" Maxwell looked around Jack to see if anyone remembered to bring it.

"It's in my belt," answered Gem putting her hand on the hilt.

"After the switch," instructed Maxwell, "and after Eden and Jack are in the clear and on their way back to you, do what we discussed." Maxwell talked quickly, trying to go over their plan one more time. "Wait until they are at least halfway back. Make sure you can run to Jack and Eden more quickly than the Manips can get to them. When you are sure you can reach them first, start running and bring my sword. I will delay the Manips as long as possible. Try to reach Eden and Jack, arm them, and head in my direction as fast as possible."

"You know they could harm you," replied Gem.

"They won't see it coming," answered Maxwell. "I think I can disrupt things enough to give you extra time and maybe even free myself and run toward you. We'll just have to see how things go."

"I'll do my best, Maxwell. I want us all to go back together," said Gem.

"I know you will," replied Maxwell.

"Hurry up!" yelled Trumble from the distance. "We'll all be dead by the time we finish this exchange."

Jack leaned over to Maxwell and whispered, "That's the idea for some of you." Maxwell cracked a smile in response.

Maxwell started walking toward Eden, Dover, and Trumble, with Jack somewhat behind him to the side. As soon as the two Protectors stepped forward, Dover shoved Eden toward them. She stumbled and fell as she took her first step.

"Look where you're going, Protector," laughed Dover at Eden's misstep. He shoved her again. This time she picked up her pace to be out of Dover's reach. As the Protectors and Manips were approaching each other, Dover snarled, "Halt!" Everyone stopped. "Justice heir, start walking toward me, and I will send this Protector over to your escort."

"When I start walking, she better be walking also," warned Maxwell.

"Begin the exchange!" barked Dover.

Maxwell walked forward. Eden anticipated Dover's shove, so she stepped out a second before he pushed. To his disappointment, he was unable to knock her down a second time. The two Protectors slowly walked toward each other. Their eyes met. As Eden passed Maxwell, she mouthed, "I'm sorry." Maxwell just smiled because Dover's gaze never left him. She passed on by.

As Eden approached Jack, she jumped behind him, which startled Dover. He, in turn, grabbed Maxwell by the arm and jerked him in his direction. Dover drew his sword, which caused Jack to draw his. Conditions escalated quickly.

"Save your celebration until you've gone," yelled Dover. "Or you may have nothing to celebrate." He snarled as they backed away. Dover stopped and patted Maxwell down to be sure he had no hidden weapons. Maxwell held his breath as Dover went over his hidden pouch, which was under his shirt. Dover found nothing. Maxwell didn't want to make any moves to hinder Dover's search or make him suspicious, but he needed to delay Dover as long as possible.

Jack and Eden walked back toward Gem, where she waited anxiously. She had already picked out a spot on the grass with a patch of dandelions, which seemed to be just over half the distance. From Gem's perspective, they were walking in slow motion. In reality, Jack hurried Eden along as he quickly told her about their plan.

Maxwell and Dover walked back to Trumble as Maxwell carefully glanced over his shoulder at Jack and Eden. Gem had not started running for them yet. Dover noticed Maxwell's glance and shoved him forcefully forward. Dover's strength surprised Maxwell. His shove had propelled him at least three yards. Maxwell tried to slow down, but the situation sped up instead. Dover trotted forward to catch up with him.

Gem continued watching Jack and Eden walk toward the dandelions. She could wait no longer. They were almost there. Gem took off running with the speed of a doe.

Dover looked back toward the Protectors and saw the one previously waiting in the background running toward the other two. Trumble had noticed too and was already running for Dover and Maxwell. Instead of turning and running back to try and catch Jack and Eden as Maxwell feared, Dover shoved Maxwell even harder toward Trumble. As soon as Trumble reached them, Maxwell had both Manips pulling him toward the doldrum. He knew it was unlikely his friends were going to reach him in time.

Maxwell glanced back as he struggled against the Manips. His friends were in pursuit with their swords drawn, and they were gaining ground. Maxwell's glimmer of hope disappeared, however, when Trumble and Dover grabbed both his elbows and lifted him off the ground into the air. They held him firm as they flew a straight path for the doldrum.

"Get the door, Trumble!" shouted Dover. Trumble increased his forward motion, which surprised Maxwell. He saw no key, no latch, nothing but a doorknob. Trumble turned the knob, then held the door open for Dover to pull Maxwell through. Trumble slammed the door shut.

Maxwell didn't see Trumble lock the door, so maybe his friends could still reach him. He gazed intently at the door, knowing his friends could destroy these two Manips if they could just get inside.

Outside, Jack, Eden, and Gem knew they had been gaining on the Manips. It appeared they would catch them until the Manips took off flying into the doldrum with Maxwell. The Protectors followed suit in the air, but the mirrored doldrum caused them to lose focus. They would think the building was in one area, but it was only a reflection. They had discovered it worked best to look for a distortion in the landscape. At times, they couldn't detect any distortion and lost sight of the doldrum altogether. The Protectors had no doubts of the doldrum's location when they saw a door open in the distortion and their friend taken inside.

"Head for the opening!" shouted Jack.

Inside, Dover slammed Maxwell into a wooden chair and secured his hands behind his back with a lava line. Maxwell saw Trumble fumbling with an antique dial hanging on one of the dingy walls. Dover screamed at Trumble, "Turn it now, you imbecile!" Trumble growled as he gave it a spin. The house shook with a twitch and a quiver. The scenery outside their window disappeared, then reappeared looking different. It looked barren, like a desert with orange sand.

From Maxwell's view, which was limited because he was in the middle of the room, he could see no vegetation or wildlife, just sand as far as the eye could see. Maxwell's heart sank.

"Why did you land us here? Idiot!" screamed Dover running to the window to get a better look.

"I didn't *choose* the Desert of Despair," explained Trumble. "I just gave the transporter a spin, and we landed here."

"Now we are stuck here for the next hour," complained Dover. "Until the doldrum can put us back on our regular schedule."

"Why can't you just spin it again?" asked Maxwell, thinking he may as well find out all he could about the doldrum while he was here.

"Why can't you just *shut your mouth*?" Dover screamed at Maxwell. "Why can't you just spin it again?" he mimicked in a baby voice as he approached Maxwell.

"Because all the doldrum locations are preselected for us, doofus," interrupted Trumble, jumping into the conversation. "If you select a location by turning the transporter dial, you must wait one full hour until you can get back on the schedule. They don't like us picking the locations, but they understand sometimes things happen. Sometimes, we need to leave town in a hurry." Dover glared at Trumble.

"Are you sure you told him everything, you fool?" said Dover sarcastically. "You know it is strictly forbidden to discuss doldrums in the presence of a Protector. Don't tell him anything!"

"It's not like he will be leaving here to tell anyone what I just said," corrected Trumble. Dover thought for a moment, considering Trumble's argument.

"Good point," said Dover, smiling. He walked over to Maxwell. "Do you see anything in this room that looks like it doesn't belong here?" Dover's eyes led Maxwell's gaze to the fireplace. Above the mantle, hung on hooks, was the most magnificent sword Maxwell had ever seen. It was longer than his with sapphires in the hilt.

"That was your grandfather's," Dover sneered when he said *grandfather's*. "My boss resides in this doldrum; the sword is his prize possession. It is his constant reminder that he has unfinished business."

Maxwell jumped at the Manip, but his hands were tied behind him, so Dover easily slammed him back into his chair. "You don't even come close to the Protector abilities of your grandfather," whispered Dover. "But Norris believes pain inflicted on those your enemy loves is far more severe than on your enemy alone. He always enjoys spilling Justice blood."

Dover turned to Trumble and commanded, "I'm going upstairs to rest. Keep your eyes on him and don't talk. Don't leave him for a second." Dover went upstairs, scowling. Trumble dropped down into a chair and said nothing.

Dover obviously thinks he's in charge, thought Maxwell. *Maybe I can use Trumble's dissatisfaction with the command hierarchy to my advantage.*

32

Not as Planned

Moments before, the Protectors were flying full speed toward the entrance of the doldrum. They were within ten feet of the entrance when it simply disappeared. All three Protectors came to a stop where the doldrum had been. Jack ran to the imprint the doldrum had left in the grass, looking for clues where the building may have gone.

"He's gone," said Eden, out of breath. Her hands were still tied in front with the lava line. Gem had given her the sword, which she could still swing remarkably well, even though she was still bound.

"I can't believe they got away!" exclaimed Jack. "We were so close." Jack scanned the forest edge. "Uh-oh," said Jack, looking off into the distance. Both Eden and Gem looked up.

"What is it?" said Eden.

"It's the cavalry," replied Gem as they watched Adele coming out of the sky with approximately ten to fifteen Protectors and angels. Many of her acquaintances were larger in build, and may have had an advantage against the Manips. Jack and Gem knew they were in trouble. They were undeniably second-guessing their decision to listen to Maxwell. Adele was not smiling when she walked up to the three Protectors.

"What happened?" she demanded.

33

Desert of Despair

Back in the doldrum, Trumble sat silently in his chair, as he had been ordered to do. Maxwell kept seeing lifeless faces walking by the window outside. Every few moments, one of the bodies would run their hands over the window, as a blind person might do if feeling for something he was trying to identify. Their faces would pass by the window, staring into space, seeing nothing.

"They creep me out every time I come here," said Trumble without thinking.

"Who are they?" asked Maxwell, surprised by Trumble's comment. He wanted to keep him talking. Trumble glanced at the stairs to make sure Dover wasn't in hearing distance.

"If you purposely live your earthly life taking advantage of others who are weaker or less fortunate than yourself, you come here. This includes bullies, child abusers, and those who take advantage of the elderly or handicapped, just to name a few. They truly only care about themselves and feel no guilt or remorse for those they hurt," whispered Trumble, still glancing at the stairs. "We Manips are exempt, of course. I'm rather glad about that. But after all, we are the standouts." Trumble smirked and stood up to walk to the window.

"Have you ever been out there?" asked Maxwell, using his head to point toward the window.

"Yes," replied Trumble, "for just a moment. They make all new Manips come here. If we mess up as a Manip, they threaten to send us here for a stay." He didn't elaborate about his experience but continued his description, "It's hot out there, and no one can see. Part of the punishment is everyone loses their sight while they are cast into the desert. To the occupants, it's dark, hot, and dusty. You can tell when the new ones arrive. They haven't learned to listen, so they are constantly running into each other. They wail and scream for someone to help them. But no one ever does. They don't even consider helping each other. Why would they?" Trumble laughed under his breath. "We call them the 'Wanderers.' It's scary out there, even for a Manip. We can't hear their screams in the doldrum, but every once in a while, one of them will find the doorknob and open the—"

Just as Trumble said this, the very thing he was describing happened. The door swung open, and the most terrifying noise Maxwell had ever heard rang in his ears. Trumble turned away from the window, shoved the body back through the door, and slammed it shut. Dover ran down the steps.

"Shove a table in front of the door!" ordered Dover. Trumble pulled a table from under the window and shoved it across the doorway. "You have to keep the Wanderers out, Trumble! We don't want to deal with one of those inside," said a distressed Dover as he ran both of his hands through what little hair he had left. "Our location will change in another twenty minutes or so, but we are behind schedule because of the hasty exit from earlier."

Dover stood still, contemplating his next move. After a moment, he seemed to come alive and produced a creepy smile for Maxwell to see. "I've already contacted Norris," he said, threateningly. "He's meeting us at our next landing, and I told him we had a tremendous surprise waiting for him. He's going to be shocked when he sees you. He would never expect us to reel you in on our own."

Maxwell kept quiet, as did Trumble. Neither wanted to do or say anything to cause Dover to change his fragile mood.

34

Not as Planned Cont'd

dele stood still as Jack tried to explain what had happened. He took the blame, saying the idea was his to make a move an hour earlier than the plan they discussed with her so they could try to free Eden. Gem spoke up saying that was not true. *She* had been the one to come up with the plan, and it was just like Jack to say it was his idea. Adele interrupted both of them in the middle of their argument.

"You are all to blame!" she said harshly. "All of you, except Eden," she continued, somewhat more calmly. "And, the truth be told, if Maxwell is anything like his grandfather, it was probably his idea." Adele paused to consider her words. "I can see none of you are going to give me the accurate version. What your behavior has amounted to, however, is the Manips have who they've wanted all along. You played right into their plan."

Jack and Gem lowered their heads. Eden did the same, not wanting to stand apart from her friends. She knew they had risked their lives to save hers. "May God help Maxwell. He's the only one who can now," said Adele in a defeated tone.

35

Back Inside the Doldrum

Maxwell hacked out a loud, dry cough. Trumble looked at him. Dover had returned to his quarters upstairs after the excitement with the beings from the desert. Maxwell waited a couple of minutes and hacked again. "Cut it out!" said Trumble sternly but in a hushed tone so as not to disturb Dover again.

"I need a drink," said Maxwell. "I think some of that orange dust made it inside and it's choking me."

"It's nearly time for the doldrum to move," replied Trumble. "You can wait."

Maxwell knew he had to act now. He knew his only chance of escape would come when they were changing locations, hopefully back to earthly dimensions. He knew he didn't want to escape out into this forsaken place.

Maxwell let out a series of loud coughs as if his death from choking was happening this moment. Trumble panicked, unsure what he should do. He didn't want the Justice heir injured when Dover returned. "Oh, all right, you weakling," said Trumble. "But drink it fast." Trumble went over to the sink, filled a large glass nearly to the rim, and returned to Maxwell with the water.

"You need to release my hands," said Maxwell in a manner of instruction as he stood up. Trumble sat down the glass of water and went to release Maxwell's lava line, then stopped.

"I don't think so, pea brain," said Trumble, feeling proud of himself for discovering Maxwell's plan.

Just then, the doldrum trembled. Maxwell knew they were changing locations. The doldrum shook with more force. With no time to think, just to try some form of disruption, he stumbled backwards into the surrounding furniture. He hit the glass filled with water, drenching his arms, which were still tied behind his back. The lava line disappeared as soon as the water covered his binding. Maxwell's restraints were gone.

Maxwell tried to hide his surprise at being released, but Trumble knew something was amiss. He noticed the spilled water on the floor, so he moved toward Maxwell to investigate. Maxwell jumped out of his reach and grabbed the mind ball out of his pouch.

Trumble drew his sword as he watched Maxwell throw the ball toward his grandfather's sword, which hung out of everyone's reach above the fireplace. He could not allow the Justice heir to retrieve his grandfather's sword. Trumble knew he would have to kill him. Dover would be mad but not as mad as Norris if his Protector sword were gone. The mind ball left Maxwell's hands at the same moment Trumble lunged forward with his sword. Maxwell didn't have time to dodge the blade because his concentration was focused on aiming for his grandfather's sword.

Trumble's blade pierced straight through Maxwell's stomach area and out the back. Trumble pulled back the blade. Puzzled, he looked at a still-standing Maxwell. He reacted with no pain, no blood, nothing. Maxwell, stunned and waiting, remembered the necklace. His hand instantly went up to feel for the shield pendant, which was almost back upright to the latch. He knew his protected time had almost expired. His grandfather's sword came tumbling off the hooks.

Maxwell shoved a stunned Trumble off balance, and he fell to the floor. Trumble was still in disbelief that Maxwell remained unaffected after being pierced through his middle. Maxwell grabbed his grandfather's sword, which was much heavier than he expected. Trumble struggled to all fours, trying to stand up as Maxwell turned his grandfather's sword to the flat side and whacked Trumble on top of the head. It knocked him out cold due to the weight.

As Trumble hit the ground, the doldrum landed at its new location. Maxwell heard Dover start down the stairs. He ducked behind the first chair he found but knew immediately that this would never do.

Trumble, sprawled on the floor, was in plain view, and anyone who has played hide-and-seek knows there couldn't be a poorer hiding place than behind a chair.

Maxwell looked out the window to see the doldrum landing back on Earth. The terrain looked similar to the forest close to Golden Acres, although the location seemed different. He had to get out of the doldrum *now* before Norris arrived.

By this time, Dover was down the stairs, looking at Trumble on the floor. He knew something had gone terribly wrong while he was out of the room. Maxwell peered over the chair, then stood up. He still held his grandfather's sword. Dover drew his weapon. With their swords raised toward each other, the Manip and Protector circled one another.

"I saved you for Norris, but you have forced my hand," said Dover in his usual growling snarl. "Prepare to die!" With his last sentence, he charged Maxwell.

Maxwell raised his grandfather's sword to block Dover's swing. It took all his strength to absorb the blow. The swords rang out when the steel clashed together. Dover swung his sword in a series: left then right, then left again. Back and forth, Maxwell returned every strike with a counterblow. The more he swung his grandfather's sword, the lighter and more maneuverable it became. Maxwell was backing Dover up and almost had him against the wall when he heard a noise behind him. Trumble heaved himself up on one knee, rubbing his head. Maxwell could see he was still dazed, but time was running out.

Maxwell noticed a door behind Dover and knew this door led outside. Adele had explained that doldrums have two doors: one out and one in. Because the creature from the desert had entered through the opposite door, he knew this door led to his freedom. He just needed to get around Dover.

Dover noticed both the pause in Maxwell's attack and his eyes darting about. He decided to be more aggressive and make his kill before his prey escaped. He ran toward Maxwell and used his weight to shove him backwards. Maxwell slid back without tripping and kept his sword up in front of his body. Their swords clanked. Both held their swords firm, crossed in the middle, pushing with all their might.

Maxwell noticed Dover sweating profusely when his face moved close to his grandfather's sword. He remembered the effect of Protectors' swords on the Manips. He had an idea. Dover's eyes darted toward the window.

"My commander just landed in the front yard," hissed Dover, still sweating. "I may allow you to live so I can watch him destroy you in the most painful of ways."

Without even pausing to react, Maxwell tipped the side of the blade on his grandfather's sword against Dover's face. Dover howled in agony as he released his grip on his own sword and instantly grabbed Maxwell's to push it away. With this move, Dover did shove the blade off his face, but it began searing his hands. In the confusion, Maxwell let go of his grandfather's sword, which is not something he wanted to do, but he in no way wanted to help Dover remove the blade from his smoldering hands. Maxwell used both hands and one leg to topple Dover, who landed on top of the sword from which he could not let go. Again, Dover screamed in pain.

Maxwell darted for the door in the back of the doldrum. He turned the doorknob. It clicked open. Trumble was standing by this point, but he had trouble balancing himself. As Maxwell closed the back door on his way out, the front door of the doldrum opened. Maxwell extended his wings and shot straight up in the air, looking for cloud cover so as not to be seen by anyone inside the doldrum. He knew Golden Acres lay just east of the Continental Divide, which stretched out before him.

36

When Norris Arrived

orris walked into the doldrum and couldn't believe the sight before him. Trumble stood there wobbling and holding his bleeding head. Dover was still facedown and screaming for someone to help, yet Trumble remained motionless, unable to assist him. Norris walked over to Dover to find out the reason for all the yelling. He saw his prize sword sticking out from beneath Dover, which immediately infuriated him. He quickly flipped Dover over and kicked the sword out of his still-clutching hands.

"I couldn't l-l-l-let g-g-go of it," stammered Dover.

"What are you doing with my trophy off the wall?" questioned Norris, still furious. "You know *no one touches the sword!* I swear, if both of you weren't half-dead already, I would make sure you wished you were dead."

Norris walked around the room, inspecting the damage. The room was a mess. "Now, what was so urgent that I had to come to the doldrum immediately? I left a meeting with Recco and Spear because you said it was urgent. Those snakes are probably plotting against me as we speak," mumbled Norris, not meaning to say that last part out loud.

Dover and Trumble had not answered Norris's question. The two Manips looked at each other, each waiting on the other to speak.

This is a good time to mention an interesting bit of information concerning Manips, which the Protectors are not aware of. Manips cannot lie to those in authority over them. This is ironic since most of their human lives are spent lying to whomever will listen. In this stage of their existence, lying to their superiors was not an option for Dover and Trumble. Both Manips knew they had to answer. The only question that remained was, who would go first?

Trumble spoke up first, either from stupidity or from the earlier hit on the head. Most definitely, it didn't stem from being the bigger man or wanting to protect his fellow Manip. "We believed we had apprehended the grandson of your greatest foe, Alexander Justice," said Trumble, beginning to cry.

"You had *who*?" replied Norris calmly, getting very close to Trumble's face. "Stop your blubbering!" he screamed. Trumble tried to hold his breath to help him stop.

"His name is Maxwell O'Malley," Dover spoke this time. "He is the grandson of Justice. We wanted to surprise you, but things didn't work out as we planned."

"Let me get this straight," replied Norris, his face turning red. "You had him here in the doldrum?" No one spoke, but both Manips nodded their heads yes.

"But he is not here now?" continued Norris. His tone was still calm, but he was now the color of crimson. Both Manips nodded their heads no.

"He has escaped?" The Manips nodded yes. "From a doldrum, where no Protector has ever escaped?" said Norris. Both Manips nodded yes as an eerie silence descended. Norris's face was so red now, it looked as if his head would explode.

The two Manips impulsively moved closer together. Perhaps if they closed ranks and took the hit as one, they could survive the onslaught. Within seconds, Norris exploded into a fury. What happened next is still a blur to Dover and Trumble. What they can recall involves pain, darkness, screaming, and regaining consciousness back in the Desert of Despair, with no doldrum to protect them.

The sound of a particularly horrific wail woke both Manips. They instantly covered their ears with their hands, but then they realized where Norris had sent them. Wanderers surrounded them, with more coming in their direction. The two Manips, locked arm in arm, ran straight through the Wanderers' bodies, like a running back in a football game heading for the end zone. With the strength of two, they were able to bust through the crowd.

When they had gained some distance from the Wanderers, their eyesight began to fail; they could barely see the stones and boulders scattered across barren, orange sand. The Manips ducked behind large boulders for a rest, but unbeknownst to them, the Wanderers could smell the newcomers in their different location. The Manips had no idea the hopelessness of their situation.

Within minutes of hiding, they were discovered by the Wanderers, who wailed and cried for the newcomers to give them relief. No one, not even a calloused Manip, could take this sound for long without going mad. The Manips would run away from the sound of wailing and crying, tripping over stones or running into boulders. No rest or relief could be had as the scene repeated itself over and over. Death would be welcomed here, but it was not an option.

37

Wings of Return

$\mathcal{A}$s Maxwell approached the Rockies, he came upon the same location where the exchange had previously taken place. He saw two groups of individuals in the middle of a clearing below. As he flew out of the clouds, he recognized one of the groups as his three Protector friends and Adele.

Eden, Gem, and Jack had been standing there for over an hour with Adele. Just when they were sure she had neared the end of her verbal lashing, she would drop another, "If only you had listened," or, "Maxwell wouldn't be in this mess if only." Though this reprimand was meant mainly for Jack and Gem, Eden knew if it had been one of the other Protectors who had been taken, she would've been right in the middle of the rescue attempt with her friends. The Protectors felt terrible. They knew there was more than likely a chance Maxwell was already dead or worse than dead. When the Manips are involved, worse than dead is a real possibility.

Adele continued to walk back and forth between the group of rescuers who accompanied her to this location and the three Protectors. Eden, Gem, and Jack assumed they were discussing a rescue plan, but they had no idea for sure because Adele wasn't talking in front of them. She would walk over to the rescuers, return to the Protectors with more questions about Maxwell's abduction, and then circle back to the rescuers again.

Adele was standing with the three Protectors when Maxwell emerged out of cloud cover. Jack saw him first. His only reaction was a grin as wide as his face. He elbowed Gem, which caused Eden to glance over as Jack nodded in Maxwell's direction and smiles appeared on all their faces. Adele had her back to Maxwell's approach, so she saw nothing except the smiles on the Protectors' faces. She stopped her questioning.

"I would like to know," questioned Adele, irritated, "what on earth do you have to smile about?" No one answered. Jack just pointed in Maxwell's direction, still smiling. Adele turned just as Maxwell landed. All her anger evaporated as she threw her arms around Maxwell and hugged him tightly. "I didn't know how I was going to tell your grandfather I had lost you!" exclaimed Adele.

"Well, now you won't have to," replied Maxwell happily. Jack, Eden, and Gem all circled around Maxwell, talking at the same time. Adele returned to the group of rescuers, throwing her hands up in the air.

"How on earth did you escape?" asked Jack enthusiastically

"Where are Dover and Trumble?" asked Eden.

"What did the doldrum look like on the inside?" asked Gem.

"Did you use the items in your pouch?" asked Jack, without waiting for an answer to his previous question. This reminded Maxwell about his necklace. He reached up to feel the pendant, but it was gone. It had already returned itself to the sanctuary.

"Did they tie you with the lava line, too?" asked Eden, who had been freed from her binding by Adele.

"Here," said Gem, "I still have your sword." She pulled the weapon out of her belt and handed the hilt to Maxwell.

"I'll answer everyone's questions in just a minute," said Maxwell. "Do you think we could all get out of sight so I can relax for a bit? I've been flying full throttle since I escaped, and I would like to sit down without worrying we'll be attacked." Everyone agreed they should move to more cover.

"When I left the doldrum, Norris was coming through the door. I don't think he followed me, but I would feel safer if we were back at Golden Acres or at least under shelter." Adele said goodbye to her team of rescuers and returned to the Protectors.

"Oh, no you don't," replied Adele, overhearing Maxwell's last statement. "No more Golden Acres for any of you. You have completed your assignment. William Carter is exposed for what he truly is. The lot of you are heading back to Everwell."

"How do we get back?" asked Jack.

"Normally, you would have been instructed on your means of return when you gave your last report to Amanda," instructed Adele. "Nearly all of our rookie Protectors return from their first assignment via Retrievers."

"Who are Retrievers?" asked Eden.

"They are our fastest angels," replied Adele. "They are so quick, they can break the dimension barrier without assistance. You and I need a portal to send us back and forth, but Retrievers do not. Everwell has instructed me to return all of you through the sanctuary due to the high risk of abduction. Thousands of Manips could be looking for you by now. We just don't know the threat level at this time."

"Great. We get to see the sanctuary," said Eden. "Maxwell told us how amazing it was, but we all want to see it with our own eyes."

"I thought we might return from inside your apartment, similar to

Wings of Return | 263

the way you left earlier," added Gem. "Or even from the outside clearing at Golden Acres, the area where we arrived."

"It isn't possible for the four of you to return to Everwell through my portal," replied Adele. "But that information is for you to learn during your next training. Most of your future assignments will have you return by way of the sanctuary, so we are ending this assignment according to future protocol. Everwell normally waits until your second or third assignment before returning Protectors through the sanctuary. You four are fortunate enough to have a former Protector who can personally instruct you on your return." She winked at the group. "Okay, Protectors, follow me." Adele flew up into the air followed by Gem, Eden, Jack, and finally Maxwell, who knew exactly where they were going and wanted to make sure none of his friends lost their way.

As Maxwell followed Adele and the other Protectors, his mind kept returning to his island home. He couldn't wait to see his grandfather and get a first-hand account of his adventures from WWII. Maxwell would be able to update his grandfather with more detail on Norris and his Manips.

Adele gently landed on the wooden porch of the sanctuary, with the Protectors following close behind. She turned the aged brass doorknob, and the door opened effortlessly.

"That reminds me," said Maxwell. "You never told me how to open the front door of the sanctuary." The other three Protectors looked at Maxwell, puzzled.

"It was locked when I tried to turn the doorknob last time," replied Maxwell to their stares. All the Protectors looked at Adele, waiting for an answer.

"After you return to Everwell by means of the sanctuary," began Adele, "the door will never be locked for you again. Once you pass through the Wings of Return, you will have access to all sanctuaries and all statues scattered around the planet."

Maxwell's expression looked more confused than before. "You answered my locked door question, but now I have three more questions."

Adele paused in the doorway and looked at Maxwell, waiting for him to finish. "What is a 'Wings of Return'? How many portals are there on earth?" Maxwell counted down fingers one and two. "And what do statues have to do with any of this?" Maxwell concluded by counting down his third finger.

"Would you just follow me?" said Adele. "You will find out all of this soon enough. Everything will be covered in your next training. You four will most likely be the only Protectors in the second session who have traveled by Wings of Return." She paused a moment, thinking, then smiled. "I bet the trainers will use you to demonstrate for the group." This created more anxiety for the Protectors. From past experiences, they knew demonstrating for the class was not a comforting thought.

The four Protectors followed Adele into the sanctuary with Maxwell in the back of the line. She held the door open as everyone filed through then shut the door behind them. Immediately, Maxwell hurried over to the wall cabinet and opened the doors. Woodrow was there, just as he had left him as Maxwell picked him up. Woodrow opened his eyes and smiled, looking at everyone.

"Woodrow, my friend," Maxwell greeted him as he held up Woodrow for his friends to see.

"Maxwell, you have returned in one piece from your adventures!" answered Woodrow. Jack, Eden, and Gem looked at each other with wonderment as Woodrow conversed with Maxwell. Woodrow looked toward Maxwell's acquaintances. "So, these are your fellow Protectors?"

"Yes, these are my friends and fellow Protectors," affirmed Maxwell.

"Wonderful! I can tell you are all a clever and capable team," said Woodrow as he turned his attention back to Maxwell. "I trust the sanctuary items served you well?"

"They did, indeed," replied Maxwell. "I wouldn't be here with you now without them." Maxwell smiled at Woodrow.

"Be sure to return the items to their original location," said Woodrow. "It will be helpful to the next Protector who needs assistance if I do not have to search for them." Maxwell rolled his eyes.

"I see you haven't changed since our last visit," replied Maxwell, "Still bossy and nagging the Protectors." Maxwell returned the items he was carrying to their original locations as best as he could remember. Woodrow wasn't listening. His concentration centered on whether Maxwell put the items where they belonged.

"Good, good," said Woodrow as he observed Maxwell returning the items. "All safe and sound. Good to have you back." Maxwell could have sworn Woodrow spoke to the items and not to him.

"Time to get all of you back to Everwell. Everyone, upstairs," Adele said, leading the way. Gem, Eden, and Jack turned to follow her as Maxwell returned Woodrow to the shelf and closed the cabinet.

Once upstairs, they passed several open rooms as they followed Adele. Maxwell noticed the room of books Woodrow had spoken about earlier. They also passed another room with several beds that resembled a hospital room. None of the surrounding equipment looked recognizable to the Protectors. They were walking so quickly, the Protectors didn't have time to glance in all the rooms.

Adele walked into a circular room containing four statues. The statues were of four angels, all made of white marble with faint swirls of gray. They were positioned at equal distances around the room, facing the center. The angels were dressed in armor, which can only be described as gladiator style, with a sword at their waist and a shield in one hand. The statues stood nearly eight feet tall and their extended wings made them seem even taller. The Protectors looked at the craftsmanship of the statues with awe. "It looks like Michelangelo carved these," whispered Eden to Gem. Gem nodded in agreement.

Adele walked to the center of the room. Near the spot where she stood were four circles on the floor, approximately twenty-four inches in diameter. The circles sparkled like diamonds. Everyone took notice that Adele was careful not to touch the circles with her feet.

"Now, Protectors," Adele began her instruction, "when each of you step on the transport rings—the four circles in front, behind, and on both sides of me—the corresponding statue located behind the ring will begin the Wings of Return." The four Protectors looked at each other, still with no clue what she was talking about. Adele noticed their confusion.

"Don't be alarmed," continued Adele. "Transporting through the Wings of Return emits a feeling very similar to when you first arrived at Everwell from the earthly dimension. The difference is you won't feel dazed when you arrive at your destination. We only added that feature on your first trip to lessen the shock. You will, however, still have the same feeling of comfort and security you experienced on your first trip. Our Protectors always experience this when they return to Everwell.

"I don't want one of you stepping on the rings while the others watch. I want all of you to step together and go together. No harm will befall you; plus, I have other matters to attend to. You don't need me to stand here, holding your hand as you return one at a time. You are not toddlers, now, are you?" Adele reminded Maxwell of his grandfather when she spoke. She had a strong, commanding manner, just like him.

"No, of course not"; "Definitely not"; "We're fine," the Protectors answered in unison. They were actually relieved to be going back at the same time. This way, no one had to go first, and no one had to go last. Whatever happened, they would be together.

Adele walked over to Maxwell. She took from around her neck a golden necklace that had a pendant with an angel who had four wings. "Give this to your grandfather," said Adele. "I've been keeping it for him for some time now. It's time he had it back."

"What is it?" Maxwell asked.

"Your grandfather knows," answered Adele. "I'm going to put it around your neck for safe keeping until you get home." She slipped it over his head and stepped back to her previous position.

All four Protectors stood frozen, waiting on Adele's command. She looked at them. "What are you waiting for?" She clapped her hands twice. "Chop. Chop. Go stand beside your rings." The Protectors jumped into motion and hurried around to the different rings.

"Wait for my signal," instructed Adele. "Then, everyone will step into their ring at the same time. When you get back to Everwell, Finnae will be waiting for you in the transport room. I have alerted them to your arrival. Ready, Protectors?"

"Ready!" they all repeated.

"Begin," said Adele. The four Protectors reacted as if they had used the Wings of Return many times before. They calmly stepped inside the sparkling rings, which lit up instantly. Each of them looked around the room at the other three. They were all still there. They didn't have long to stare because, the next moment, the large marble statues kneeled down on one knee without crumbling. As they were lowering down, the statues also rotated around with their backs and faced the Protectors. While kneeling and rotating, they were also sliding to the center of the room, drawing closer to each corresponding Protector, as if pulled by a conveyor.

The Protectors were no longer looking about the room waiting for something to happen. Everyone watched the backward-facing statue sliding right for them. They remained firm, standing in their rings as they stared into an ever-approaching set of giant marble outstretched wings. They leaned back, waiting for impact. Some even closed their eyes (I won't mention who).

"Don't step out of your ring!" instructed Adele. "Steady, steady," she repeated slowly.

This reminded Gem of caring for her horses back home. When they were nervous, she would steady them. Her calm, reassuring voice would settle the horses just as Adele's voice reassured the Protectors. They trusted Adele completely and knew they were safe in her care.

Gem saw the large wings lowering down around her. She glanced over to Jack, who was on her right, just in time to see his statue's wings closing around him, with her statue's wings only a second behind.

With the wings completely enclosing her, everything went pitch black. Gem kept her eyes open because, oddly enough, it made her more relaxed to watch what was happening. She noticed the statue wings were no longer hard marble but now were soft as down feathers. The wings never stopped moving around her, even though she felt motionless. Gem suddenly felt a twinge of anxiety. She felt certain she had not moved. *What if her Wings of Return had failed? What if the wings opened and she still stood in the sanctuary? Would Adele still be there?* Doubts flooded her mind. *What if?*

Gem's Wings of Return opened. She had arrived in one of the transport rooms at Everwell. Eden and Jack were already clear of their wings, and Maxwell's were just beginning to open. Gem felt a little ashamed she had lost her confidence so quickly. She made a mental note to do better next time. Hopefully, no one had noticed.

Eden spotted Gem's expression of relief as her Wings of Return opened. She had always been a perceptive sort of child. She never let on when she picked up on things because most people could be defensive when they were out of sorts. As soon as Maxwell cleared his wings, the four grouped together in excitement.

"Wasn't that great?" exclaimed Maxwell.

"I never felt myself move," added Jack.

"I love the Wings of Return," said Eden. "I wish we could travel that way on Earth. Can you imagine?"

"Very cool," said Gem calmly. She overcompensated in covering up her short-lived fear during her return. Eden smiled at her, put her arm around Gem's shoulder, and gave a quick, one-armed hug. Gem felt fortunate to have a friend like Eden.

Finnae was waiting on them, just as Adele had said. "Protectors, you will need to go to debriefing next door. Let's have the guys meet with Amanda, and the other team, the girls, will meet with Tillie. They will want to hear every detail of your assignment. They will compare your debriefing with your daily reports, which will help them in deciding your next assignment. If they need any details cleared up, they will ask you tonight before dinner. The goal is for the Protectors to be as thorough as possible on their daily reports to Everwell as it helps with their instructions back to you on how to handle your assignment. We are trying to get away from the Protectors making all the decisions of action during their assignment, especially those new to protecting. An experienced leader or group will help you make better choices."

"Not always," whispered Jack to Maxwell.

"There goes our next assignment," replied Maxwell.

"After debriefing," continued Finnae, ignoring the boys' whispering, "which can take minutes or hours, you will dine with us for one more dinner before returning to your earthly homes. Finnae walked over to the four Protectors. We are glad to have all of you with us fighting the evil that abounds." He shook hands with each one of them. "Debriefing is across the hall," he reminded them.

The Protectors left the transport room and went across the hall, just as Finnae had instructed. When they opened the closed door and walked in, only a couple of other Protectors were inside. Obviously, not every team finished their assignments at the same time, which made sense.

Each team met with their designated leader to go over every detail of the assignment. Eden and Gem felt they covered the material rather quickly. What had taken several days to unfold was covered in less than an hour.

Maxwell took a little longer on his debrief, due to his experiences in the doldrum. After the girls and Jack were finished, they waited for Maxwell in the hallway. Josiah walked up and saw the three Protectors waiting. "Run along Eden, Gem, and Jack," instructed Josiah. "Maxwell will join you soon."

Maxwell walked out the debriefing door and overheard Josiah. Jack looked at Maxwell, not wanting to leave him to perhaps take a punishment alone. Maxwell gave him an "it's fine" nod, which Jack acknowledged.

"Well, girls, it looks like you will have my company all to yourselves," bragged Jack as he stood between the girls and put his elbows out, one for each of them to grab. They both smacked his elbows out of the way and giggled as they walked past him, leaving him standing alone. "Wait up!" called Jack, running after them. Maxwell laughed at his three friends and their antics.

"Follow me to my office," instructed Josiah. "I will not keep you long from your friends." Maxwell followed Josiah through halls, around corners, and up a GUST. Finally, Josiah took him down a long hallway, which Maxwell assumed was the location of all the trainers' offices. He passed several doorways, outside of which hung a gold plaque with a name etched in emerald. Maxwell only recognized a couple of the names in passing, two of which were Deborah and Rachel. Underneath their name was etched their position at Everwell.

When they reached Josiah's office, his nameplate read, "Josiah, First Assistant." Maxwell knew this title meant he was next in command after Raphael, and he felt he understood the order of things here a little better with the passing of each day. Deep inside, he wondered if you could ever understand it all.

A peculiarity Maxwell immediately noticed was the absence of doors on the offices, but you couldn't see inside the entrances. The door opening was covered with a sparkling mist. Some openings glittered green, some red, and some, like Josiah's, a silvery black.

Josiah stopped in front of his entrance and spoke to another trainer, whom Maxwell didn't recognize. Maxwell waited a moment, then decided to try to feel for the doorknob. He maneuvered slowly around Josiah and pushed his hand into the sparkling mist. His hand clunked against a solid object. The mist looked pliable, but it was as solid as steel. Josiah looked over at Maxwell and stopped talking when he heard the clunk. He excused himself from his acquaintance.

"Let me enter first," said Josiah, moving Maxwell to the side, out of his way. Josiah disappeared into the mist. As soon as Josiah could no longer be seen, the silver black mist turned emerald green like many of the other doorways they had walked past earlier. The green mist matched the emerald color on the nameplates outside their offices.

Maxwell put his hands out in front of him, like someone in a dark haunted house, as he walked into the green mist. He could no longer see Josiah, nor could he see inside the office. Walking head-on into that steel barrier he had felt earlier was not something Maxwell wanted to do. As he stepped forward into the mist with his arms outstretched, he felt nothing. The barrier had disappeared. Maxwell kept his hands out in front of him until he cleared the mist into Josiah's office. Once inside, so as not to look ridiculous, he quickly dropped his hands back to his side.

Instead of resembling an office back on Earth, it looked as though they had stepped outside into a tropical paradise. Josiah had tropical plants everywhere, with no defined walls. Instead of carpeting, bright green moss covered the floor with flat stepping-stones lying about. His desk was a large piece of granitite that Maxwell assumed had been hollowed out. How else could Josiah sit behind it and put his legs underneath? Behind the desk were many sticks and straw woven together to form shelves, which held scrolls and rolled-up parchment. Everything looked as if it belonged in this natural setting. No pictures were hanging on walls, only plants that gave edges to the room. Openings were spaced periodically around the room from which small waterfalls were trickling. Maxwell saw some birds playing in the trees and flying from one side of the room to the other. No ceiling was visible, just open sky. He assumed the birds were able to fly in and out as they pleased.

"This office is amazing!" exclaimed Maxwell, still taking it all in. His eyes followed Josiah over to the doorway they had just entered. On the wall beside the entranceway was a keypad with three colored buttons. The buttons were silver/black, green, and red. Josiah pushed the red button. Immediately, the doorway, which had been glittering emerald green, turned to glistening red.

"This will let anyone outside my office know I am here but do not wish to be disturbed," said Josiah. "I guess you have figured out, green is a go to enter, and black means no one is in." Maxwell shook his head in agreement as if he had known about the colors all along.

"Thank you for the compliment on my office," continued Josiah, smiling. "Everyone is free to decorate their offices as they wish. Any time I am not working, I enjoy spending time in a tropical region of your planet. So, I brought a replica of that part of your world here. It is most relaxing."

Josiah made his way back around to his desk. "Have a seat, Maxwell." He motioned for Maxwell to sit on one of the chairs fashioned from driftwood, which was positioned in front of his desk. Josiah took his seat behind the granite.

"I'm sure you have many questions, Maxwell, and in time, all of them will be answered. I know you are now aware of much more of your family's history here. Rachel and Deborah felt I should have told you everything when you first arrived. They had a special friendship with your grandfather and worked closely with him during his assignments in the Second World War.

"I struggled with my decision to withhold information from you. But I felt strongly that you should get your bearings in our world first. Who would want to follow in the footsteps of someone like your grand-father from the beginning of training? I felt you needed to come into training with no expectations, to simply have time to become the best you could be. This was imperative to your success as a Protector. You have proven that you have it within you to be a successful Protector, which I knew you would do all along."

Maxwell understood more of the reason for the secrecy. Josiah wanted him to succeed or fail based on his own merits—not because of his family heritage. "We chose the more dangerous option, but it benefitted you in the long run." Josiah's words interrupted Maxwell's thoughts.

"A real threat out there wants to see your grandfather's legacy dead," continued Josiah. "We all felt Adele could protect you and your team, which she did and could've done better if the three of you had not tried a rescue on your own. We are fortunate that Dover and Trumble—not Norris himself—grabbed you. You most definitely would not be standing here today if Norris had been your captor." Josiah's voice trailed off to a whisper.

Maxwell decided it was best to remain silent and not try to explain his reasoning for the rescue. They were fortunate not to be in any greater trouble for their deception. Josiah paused for an unusually long time before he spoke again.

"And, who knew the brewing trouble at Golden Acres was so severe with Mr. Carter?" asked Josiah, not expecting an answer. "Adele alerted us of the possible threat, but she is highly skilled at defusing problems, so we left the situation in her capable control. She did have her hands full with the four of you, though." Josiah mumbled that last bit under his breath, saying it to himself before he continued. "All of you did an outstanding job exposing William Carter for what he truly is before any of the citizens were harmed. We knew the four of you would make a great team."

Josiah stood up and declared, "I believe that is enough information for this rotation. I will talk to you more next time if there is a need." He then clapped his hands together in a manner to hurry Maxwell along.

Maxwell stood up. Josiah answered many of the secrecy questions but not nearly enough concerning the situation between his grandfather and Norris; maybe, when he returned home, his grandfather could fill in some of the holes.

"Your friends are waiting for you at dinner. After your meal, you will return to your rooms to change into your Earth clothes and head to the transport room for your trip home." Josiah put his hand on Maxwell's shoulder and walked him to the door. He pushed the green button and the doorway returned to a green glow. "We are glad to have you back safely, Maxwell." He squeezed Maxwell's shoulder. "The information you gave us on the doldrum is some of the most valuable intelligence we've ever been able to attain. We are very fortunate to have you with us."

Maxwell turned and put out his arm to shake hands with Josiah. "Thank you for inviting me to be a Protector, Josiah," said Maxwell sincerely.

"Oh, no, I have nothing to do with the selection process," corrected Josiah. "You were chosen based on your reactions to situations on Earth."

Maxwell wondered about what he had just been told but figured it must wait for another time. He wanted no more of asking questions and hearing vague answers. Maxwell walked through the green, glitter-like smoke and out the doorway. He was in a rush to see his friends. Josiah did not join him.

38

Back Home

Maxwell arrived at the dinner table to find his friends consuming their food at full throttle. "Thanks for waiting for me," laughed Maxwell.

"We planned on waiting," replied Jack, looking up at Maxwell but continuing to chew his food, "but we forgot how good the food smelled. Sit down and join us, or I might have to eat yours, too."

"I don't think so," said Maxwell, sitting down. His meal instantly lowered from above and landed directly in front of him. Before him lay a delicious meal: the warmest bread, the coolest drink, and the gooiest dessert. What a wonderful feeling every time you sat down to eat, knowing it would be the best you had ever eaten up to that point. Maxwell wasn't sure if the meals were really that tasty or if his taste buds were now keener to the flavors. Probably both. The reason really didn't matter. It was delicious, and that's all he needed to know.

He no sooner began eating than the girls leaned over to find out the purpose of Josiah's meeting with him. Jack was interested in his story as well, but his mouth was too full to talk. Maxwell filled them in on the description of Josiah's amazing office, the weird doorways, and of course, the conversation between them. Maxwell continued eating during his retelling, which took longer due to his chewing between sentences. Eden and Gem tried to be patient since they had already finished their meal. Jack didn't care how long Maxwell took because it gave him an excuse to eat a little more.

As the four were returning to their rooms after dinner, the girls were discussing Maxwell's conversation with Josiah. "It makes perfect sense they would keep that information from him," said Eden to Gem. "I wouldn't want to know if I had a super-Protector grandmother—especially not at first. Josiah made the right choice." They arrived at their respective doors.

"We'll meet you girls back here in ten minutes," said Maxwell. The girls went into their room, and the boys went into theirs. Jack immediately grabbed his Earth clothes and went to change. Maxwell turned on his behold-a-scope while he was waiting.

He zeroed in on downtown Main Street and noticed it was snowing. All the tourists had left, but he did see several snowmobiles parked downtown, so people were out and about. He noticed a young couple running zigzags down the street, throwing snowballs at each other, enjoying themselves. Maxwell laughed as he thought about the fun they were having. He saw Brad Conley, his brother's best friend, helping his parents get groceries at Doud's Mercantile. He couldn't wait to get home.

Jack came out of the bathroom dressed in his skateboard garb: hoodie, board pants, sneakers, and a hat. "I never realized how much I missed my old clothes," he said. "No matter how comfortable our stuff is here, it can't compare to my cool rags from home."

Maxwell flipped off his behold-a-scope as he walked past Jack, high-fiving him in passing to silently signify his agreement to his last statement. After he changed, they opened their door to meet the girls. They, too, had their door open and were nearly ready. When everyone had all their belongings, they made their way to the transport room to head home. Finnae was still there.

"Do you ever take time off?" asked Jack. "You are always here."

"Take time off from what?" replied Finnae.

"From work," said Jack, "from the transport room."

"The transport room is not work," corrected Finnae. "I love being here. When I'm not transporting, I'm developing new means of movement. We need to strive to be one step ahead of the Manips at all times and it's my responsibility to get you where you are going safely."

"Okay, okay. Forget I said anything," replied Jack.

"Well, just so you know, it makes us feel confident to know you are always here and will be able to bring us back to Everwell when the time comes," added Eden, giving him a big hug. The others agreed. Finnae blushed with the praise.

"I have been notified the four of you will be returning to your respective earthly homes today," said Finnae.

"Yes," answered Gem. "Will we be traveling by the Wings of Return?"

"Gracious, no," answered Finnae. "You will be returning to the earthly dimension by Light Tunnel."

"I'm afraid to ask, but here goes," said Gem. "Is it the same as when people on Earth almost die and see a tunnel and a light?" Gem had a worried look on her face.

"Yes, actually, it is, but in reverse," answered Finnae. "They see where they are and walk into a light, yet they cannot see until they pass through. You will be walking out of the light, into a tunnel that will draw you to your other half currently on Earth. You simply keep walking until you are standing directly on them. You will instantly combine with your physical body again. Simple and painless." Finnae noticed Gem still wore a concerned expression.

"You need not worry when traveling by Light Tunnel. You see where you are going when returning to Earth. There are times when we may use the Light Tunnel to return you to us and you will not be able to see because of the light. You have nothing to fear because you know what waits in the light, the transport room of Everwell. Traveling via Light Tunnel after death is somewhat different in that you don't go to Everwell." The four Protectors were absorbing every word spoken by Finnae.

"Okay, Protectors, time to move along," instructed Finnae. "I will send each of you home one at a time. Ladies first." Finnae looked at the chart on his podium. "Gem, let's get you back to West Virginia. Finnae walked to his control panel and hurriedly moved his hands around. The Protector's view was partially obstructed, so they couldn't see what he had done. A large hologram of a rotating Earth in full color, glowing from the inside, appeared in the center of the room. Everyone looked up as the hologram floated directly in front of them.

It reminded Maxwell of the amazing picture he saw in a textbook of an astronaut's view of the Earth from space, only larger and in more detail. You could see the assortment of mountain ranges, deserts, the Nile River, and his beloved Great Lakes. Maxwell wondered just how much detail the globe could show. How close could they get?

"This is an exact replica of your planet," said Finnae. "We call it the Celestial Locator. It is continuously updated and so precise, it shows every bug in your yard, every rock, pebble, and sand speck on the beach if you zoom in close enough and, of course, the movement of every human on Earth. This model is used solely for transportation purposes, but this same technology is used in other departments for protection assignments."

Finnae stopped the rotating globe when he saw North America. He used the screens positioned in front of him to magnify the globe. The

North American continent appeared on screens hung above the Protectors, so they could watch Finnae's selections as he zoomed in closer until you could only see the United States and then closer still until he had West Virginia in his sight. Majestic mountains, covered with a thick growth of trees on steep slopes came into view, with deer grazing in an open area, close to a nearby stream. Finnae followed the Kanawha River, looking for Charleston through the valley until the golden dome of the state capitol came into his view in the distance. He magnified Lovell Farms and saw Gem's other half walking out of the house with her two sisters, Candice and Tabitha.

"Gem, walk through the Light Tunnel at the left of the room," instructed Finnae, pointing to a large tube, big enough for a car to pass though, covered by a dark drape and leading out of the room.

Finnae continued to instruct Gem: "The tunnel is light on this end and gets darker as you get closer to Earth. It will look like the tunnel is getting smaller, but that is just the darkness closing in around you. Remember, it's nothing to fear. At the other end of the tunnel, your other half will be very near. Step into your body, and you will be back home. Your sisters are there, but they will not be able to see you." Finnae noticed the three girls on Earth walking toward the barn. "Better hurry, Gem, in case they are going to ride horses. If that is the case, it could be a tricky maneuver for me to get you close. We will monitor your progress from here."

Gem walked through the shroud blocking the light. For a moment, her eyes were blinded due to the brightness. She kept walking forward, and in a moment, the light was behind her. While making her way back home, she could see nothing outside the tunnel. It felt as if the light carried her forward at a much faster speed than her legs could possibly go. She could tell her end destination was coming quickly. As quick as a thought, she saw her other self and jumped back into her body.

"Eden, you're next," Finnae spoke hurriedly. He ran through the same maneuvers, only more quickly this time. Jack went after Eden, but at an even faster pace. The three remaining Protectors decided Gem had pulled the worst straw having to go first, but in hindsight, at least she could take her time going through the process; in contrast, they felt shoved through without pause.

"We're finally working our way north, Maxwell." This was Finnae's explanation for why he went last. It was all about the geography. During Jack's return, Maxwell made his way over to the control panel where Finnae stood. Finnae didn't object to Maxwell watching.

"Don't touch anything," instructed Finnae. Maxwell stood perfectly still. He saw no buttons, levers, or switches, only horizontal and vertical beams of light all over the control panel. Some beams were short, some long, and all were different colors. One light curved into a circle shape and was surrounded by a clear covering that kept the light beam contained. Maxwell wondered how this was done, but he dared not talk for fear of Finnae making him move.

Finnae ran his hands through the light beams and the globe would respond by turning. No lights were labeled. *Finnae just knows how to get all of us home*, thought Maxwell. He watched in silence as Finnae touched the numerous beams of light.

"Your turn," said Finnae, looking at Maxwell. "Mackinac Island, Michigan?" he looked at Maxwell for confirmation, but he knew it was unnecessary. Maxwell shook his head yes in agreement and then ran over to the drape covering the tunnel. Maxwell looked back for one last look at the transport room. He waved goodbye to Finnae, who was already zooming the Celestial Locator in on a little island located at the top of Michigan on Lake Huron. Maxwell ran through the covering into the blinding light.

Like the others, he passed the light in seconds. He knew he was running faster than what was humanly possible, and he, too, felt carried by the light. Up ahead, he could see his other half brushing a horse in his grandfather's stables. Almost instantly, he was there in the stables holding a brush. He didn't even remember stepping into his body. Perhaps Finnae threw him back in.

To take a minute and let his mind get its bearing, he stopped brushing the horse standing in front of him, who, in response, turned to see why he had stopped. It was Ole Henry, the calm, elderly horse Maxwell loved. He wasn't much of a workhorse, but he seemed to enjoy pulling the small buggies for tourists who wanted to drive themselves around the island. Henry's drawback when out with the tourists amounted to him wanting to stop pulling the buggy to eat grass along the way. He would stop at every opportunity—sometimes eight to ten times per run. When the tourists rent the buggies by the hour, this could be a problem. Maxwell's grandfather didn't mind if Henry's buggy came trotting in late. He knew it was due to his horse's dining habits, so he never charged the customers any extra fees. His grandfather loved Henry and would never think of getting rid of him. He wasn't a beast of burden; he was a companion his grandfather could count on and one who had been with him through many tough years.

Maxwell gave Henry a big hug. He put his face in Henry's soft mane. It felt good to be home. "I never knew you cared so much for Ole Henry," said his grandfather. Maxwell nearly jumped out of his skin. He turned around to see his grandfather standing in the barn doorway with a bucket of oats.

"Neither did I," replied Maxwell. He turned back around to face Henry and continued brushing. He wondered how long his grandfather had been standing there. Had he seen him come back and reenter his body? Finnae said they would not be seen, but what about being seen by a former Protector? Adele had been able to see the Manips as well as the Protectors. Maybe he could see as well.

Maxwell's grandfather didn't move. He just stood there, staring at Maxwell brushing Henry. Maxwell glanced back at his grandfather. He looked different to him; bigger, stronger, taller. Maxwell knew these were crazy thoughts, but the knowledge about his grandfather's past was affecting his memory of him. Maxwell glanced back again, still no movement.

In a few minutes, Maxwell finished brushing Henry. He walked around the front of the horse to refill Henry's drinking water. His grandfather began walking toward him slowly. Maxwell knew he needed to talk to his grandfather about what he had just experienced, but he didn't know where to begin.

His grandfather filled Henry's trough with the oats he had carried into the stables. Maxwell could feel his grandfather's stare, but he dared not look at him. The silence between them became almost awkward. Alexander refilled his bucket of oats, then came back again. He stopped walking toward Maxwell and Henry about halfway between them and the stable door. He just stood there again, as if he was deciding what to say. Maxwell was in front of Henry now, scratching his head while he ate.

"They called you to be a Protector, didn't they?" asked his grandfather, breaking the silence. Maxwell looked up at his grandfather but didn't speak. He slowly shook his head in agreement. Alexander dropped the bucket of oats and ran to his grandson. He hugged Maxwell and held him tight. Maxwell returned the embrace but was no match for his grandfather's tight hold.

Maxwell felt safer here than he had felt his entire life, especially since his brother's death. He had felt strangely uneasy since that tragic day. But today, he had no worries with his grandfather close by. There were no Manips, no trainers, and no other dimensions to think about, just his grandfather, himself, and Ole Henry. He never wanted his grandfather to let him go.

"I never wanted this for you, Maxwell!" his grandfather exclaimed, looking him square in the eyes. "It's too dangerous. You've got to give it up. You've got to quit." His grandfather was insistent and firm.

"But I love it!" replied Maxwell. "You didn't quit and look what a difference you made. We would be living in a very different world today if you hadn't become a Protector. I want to make a contribution as well."

"That's all the more reason why you must resign," his grandfather cut him off. "The beings I fought will stop at nothing to hurt me by killing you!" Alexander stared hard into his grandson's eyes without blinking. "I couldn't live with myself if I lost you."

Again, he hugged Maxwell tightly. Maxwell said nothing. He just continued to hold his grandfather as his mind raced. His reaction had been a surprise. Why would his grandfather be so protective, especially when he had once been a Protector? He would talk to him later about his assignment because he didn't want to argue. Maxwell was just glad to finally be home.

He helped his grandfather get Henry's bedding ready for the night and finished the chores for the other horses in the barn. "Let's get you home," said Alexander to his grandson. He put his arm around Maxwell's shoulder and gave him a squeeze. They both walked to the barn door and paused as they watched the gently falling snow in the moonlight.

About the Author

L isa Pence has a Master's Degree in Adult Education and is the author of *An Illness Observed with Reluctant Eyes*. Lisa, and her husband, reside in Charleston, WV with their two dogs, Rosie (Golden Retriever) and Penny (Cavachon) and two stray cats (Lulu and Winnie) who they have adopted.

CPSIA information can be obtained
at www.ICGtesting.com
Printed in the USA
LVHW111815030820
662267LV00008B/1338